In Loving Memory
"Mauney"
Best friend, sister, right hand gal, guardian angel, buckle bunny!
May you stretch your wings and fly, may your innocence never leave you.
May you always know how much of an impact you made in my life!!
Thank you for the memories Buckle Bunny!!
Love Always
Deer Chick

"A friend is someone who knows the song in your heart, and can sing it back to you when you have forgotten the words"- Anonymous
Thanks for always knowing the words to my songs!

This novel is also dedicated to all the people in this world who believe that dreams really can come true. This novel is for all those people fearlessly chasing impossible dreams, those who are overcoming high hurdles and obstacles along their journey. Not only is this for them it is for the people who have a large amount of self- doubt and have a hard time believing. What I hope this novel teaches you is to believe immensely in all the possibilities. This world is yours for the taking and this novel is for you!

Carol –

Thank you for supporting my writing! I hope you enjoy a travel through Skyler Kay Pendleton's life! Take care + God bless,

Skyler

Skyler's heart raced as she entered the long entry way into the American Airline center. She had lived in Texas for two years now, and this was her first time out of Abilene. It was an adventure she was glad to be taking however. Her whole life had revolved around her dream of working for the BRA, the Bull Riding Association. One of the topnotch bull riding circuits in North America, known to have the rankest bulls, the toughest cowboys, and a chance for instant fame and fortune for some. She had dreamed of fixing rodeo cowboys with her mentor and all time favorite doctor: Tate Feldman. The tall doctor had been working for the BRA ever since the beginning. His dark brown eyes determined to diagnosis every injury at the lowest possible cost to the cowboys. He was a cowboy himself and knew that these guys had to ride to make the pay…which could be seldom if an injury popped up. Skyler met him for the first time when she was seven years old. Her father was riding at a rinky dink rodeo in Billings. She saw doctor Feldman massage her father's sore neck and ice his aching knees. He had been around the business she knew that for a fact. It was a fact that Skyler loved.

It was that very fact that got Skyler the internship for the summer. Dr. Tate Feldman had challenged all the colleges in Texas to compete in an internship program. Skyler tried everything she could to win the opportunity of a lifetime. The day the acceptance letter came in her grandfather's mailbox, she laughed; she cried: she called her mom.

"Great job hunnie" her Mom said, ever the encourager.

"Mom, I know this is weird, but do you think Loren is proud of me."

"Well of course she is Sky. She always wanted you to chase your dreams. You know Loren Sky, she sure loved those cowboys."

They both chuckled, as they reminisced about Loren, who had been Skyler's best friend for twelve years. A major instigator of trouble, and the biggest buckle bunny Skyler had ever met in her life.

"So, Sky, you going to take it?" I think you should. Your grandpa didn't let you go all the way to Texas to be a ranch hand you know."

Skyler laughed, all her and Loren dreamed about was living on her grandfather's ranch and helping him with the daily chores, as any ranch hand would. Skyler told her mom goodbye, hung up the phone and planned for an adventure that would last three whole months.

Those three months of preparation had brought her to Dallas, her first shot to prove to

Tate that she deserved a spot on his staff. Her heart began to beat out of her chest as she found a door and opened it. She quickly realized that it wasn't the Sports Medicine room.

"Oh my Gosh, I am so sorry" Skyler said with a shock in her voice.

"No It's okay, you must be new here" The stranger replied ever so calmly.

"Yeah, I sure am. I'm lookin' for the Sports Medicine Room. Do you know perhaps where I can find it?" She said trying to keep composer. As her eyes scanned up his tall lanky body, she could tell he was in great physical condition. She couldn't help but want to laugh at the fact that he wore money sign boxers. His blue eyes met hers when he began to give her directions.

"Down the hall and to the left" and before the mystery cowboy could say any more she was off to the sports medicine room this time.

As she walked in, she saw a button up with her name on it. She couldn't believe a moment like this was occurring as she changed. As she finished buttoning it up her shirt and looked at the ceiling and started talking to her friend like old times.
"Hey Lor, are you listenin'? Of courses you are, you hear everything I say. Well Loren I'm finally here, it took six years but gosh Loren it

couldn't feel any better. Don't even think about me asking Jace for an autograph it's not happening buckle bunny. Hey Loren by the way…He was really cute do you agree? I know I shouldn't have scanned him like a piece of meat, I couldn't contain my eyes, by the way Loren do you mind watchin' out for me kid? Thanks! "

    She wore the shirt with pride. As she spun around and looked at herself in the mirror, Dr. Feldman walked in. "Hey! So you must be Skyler, I have heard a lot about you from the professors at Abilene, they say you have strong potential. Plus they say all your presentations pertain to rodeo, so I guess that proves to me you have the passion for it."

    "I sure do sir. My father was a bull rider, my grandfather, even his father. Bull riding and rodeo has been engraved into my blood, not to mention it's kind of a safe haven. I find comfort in three things in life: Christ, family, and rodeo."

    "Well Skyler, sounds like you're pretty grounded. I'm sure you will be proving me right in my assumptions about you. Get settled in, a few guys may come in before the event starts for taping, and then you can do the supply checklist. A good staff member should know how to keep track of supplies, since we get charged a pretty penny for it."

"I understand sir. Will I get to tape some of the riders that come in?"

"Of course, I'm getting a little to old for tapin' up limbs if you ask me."

Skyler giggled, she loved Dr. Feldman's zest for life.

"Oh and by the way Skyler, just call me Tate."

"Well Tate, call me Sky."

"Alright, Sky, well you need to get your station ready, who knows how many cowboys will need your help tonight."

She immediately took out tape: shrink-wrap, a tape shark, and all other instruments she would need for the taping process. She was hoping that she could show the staff all the tricky techniques she had learned, but twenty minutes before show time and no bull rider had shown up. Until the door swung open, and her eyes met his once again.

"Hey can you tape my wrist?"

"Sure can, come over here and take a seat." She said politely.

"She couldn't believe it, it was the guy who directed her down to the room. The guy she had gazed at for a long time. She couldn't look him in the eyes; instead she focused on her tape job.

"So you kind of ran away real fast earlier, I guess you are really into your work." He replied.

"Yeah, I'm an intern, it's not like I've done this before, only in a classroom." Skyler mentioned in a defensive tone.

"Hey chill. I'm not attackin' you. We all do stupid things our rookie seasons, believe me. I once walked in on a hot shots press conference, can you say embarrassing." He looked at her sympathetically.

"I'm sure it was, and I'm sorry again, but I was so hyped up on adrenaline. I was day dreamin' that my best friend was standin' next to me, and the next thing I know there you were." Skyler stated.

"Well, I'm sorry that can't be an exciting adventure. I'm Kale by the way."

"I guess it kind of was, but I'm still not used to all of this. I'm sure I'll learn in time, I have the best teacher in the world. It's nice to meet you Kale."

"You too, it's my pleasure. Dr. Feldman is an amazin' doctor." Kale's eyes lit up like a light bulb with excitement.

"He sure is. I remember the first time I saw him tapin' my dad's ankle in Billings. I knew then that this is what I was supposed to do." Her voice sounded distant as if she was reliving that moment again.

"Billings? That sure is a long way from here. What brings you all the way to Texas?" Kale asked in a wondrous tone.

"Graduate school. Texas programs are renowned. Montana well...we haven't caught the fever yet."

Kale chuckled, "So you care to tell me your name Montana?"

"Ah, you don't need to know, really, it's nothing special. Plus, I'm here for three months, please call me ma'am."

"So, ma'am, is it true your name is Skyler, you hail from the Big Sky Country, and that you have the most beautiful hazel eyes in the world."

"Yes on the first two, most people call me Sky though. About those hazel eyes, I guess it's somethin' positive that my Mom gave me."

Again Kale left out a small chuckle. "Well Sky, I hope to see you around soon, hopefully not tonight though."

"Yeah stay safe, I don't want to carry you out of that arena tonight." She said sarcastically.

"Don't worry you won't have to. I'm a Texas native by the way so if you need anything, rookie, ask." He said with his crooked smile.

Skyler couldn't believe the feeling she got from even glancing at him. Of course his eyes were the prettiest blue green she had ever seen, his brown hair was buzzed underneath his cowboy hat, and it was something about the way he talked that brought a smile to her face. He had a smile that brightened up his face, like the sun brightens the day. His laugh was a low baritone, but could bring a smile to anyone's face. He had the beginning of what Skyler was looking for. Although, she couldn't fall for him, this summer was for work. She didn't want it to get complicated by a sweet talking native who happened to steal her heart in one fowl swoop.

Dr. Feldman walked in the room and found Skyler's head resting against the small metal desk.

"Tired? Too many ice bags you've had to make?" He said sarcastically which was out of character for him.

"Not tired; more like mind boggled. I figured I would be wrappin', and helpin' you make decisions, and yet I'm stuck being secretary of all the items in this small room. It holds an awful lot of supplies. Not exactly what I pictured my first job with the BRA to be." Skyler said with a little attitude behind it.

"Sky, I know you understand this world works on a hierarchy. You are under my real staff, basically why you are called an intern? Sky, I promise you this…it's not goin' to be this way the entire summer. Sometimes we will be busy and you will be doing some many things at once. Other times, we will be dead…counting supplies will become a fun task. Don't worry Skyler; we have plenty of time to put that passion to the test." Dr. Tate Feldman retorted.

"Sorry, I seriously didn't mean to come off ungrateful. It's…It's I wanted this to be a summer of adventure. I guess to also be a summer of research for my dissertation on concussions. This wasn't part of the plan, but hey you gotta roll with the punches." Skyler shrugged her shoulders and smiled.

"You are writin' a dissertation on concussions?" Dr. Feldman smiled.

"Sure am, most fascinating thing around, I can't believe all the different treatment methods. A universal system sure is needed, but they are tricky to diagnosis so why not be tricky to treat."

"Well gosh darn Skyler. I think you have been readin' my mind. What are your views on the rodeo helmet?"

"Smartest thing since the invention of the vest; would be better however, if they made it mandatory." Skyler could sense the thrill of excitement from Dr. Feldman, if only she had told him all this stuff earlier she thought.

"What are your views on the concussion policy?" Tate questioned knowing that she would have the correct answer.

"I believe that right now each case needs to be taken step by step individually. One day however, I hope we can fast track diagnosis by making treatment different for the various types of concussions."

"So Skyler, you sure have a strong stand on the issue. I sure hope you get to see a little bit of the applied treatment. I'm sure that you spice up a dissertation. Believe me Sky, things will be slow, then fast. It's the cycle of a rodeo doctor's life."

"I know, and thank you so much again Tate, I don't know what I would do without this opportunity. Really, thank you." Skyler said in a grateful way.

Skyler heard nothing behind her other then the whoosh of the metal door. She decided it was probably smart to head back to the hotel, so that she could be ready for the twist and turns that tomorrow might bring. The hotel made her feel at home, the bed was so comfortable, the sheets felt warm around her, and, of course, snuggling with her teddy bear always made any new situation a little easier.

Staring into his brown eyes, she remembered the day she got him. Loren had given him to her the same weekend as one of the biggest rodeos in Billings. It seemed as if he was a perfect addition to the macaroni and cheese and little cowboy figurine. Something about his fluffy, soft fur made her feel at ease.

It helped also that Loren had one. It made the ties of their friendship stronger.

As she drifted off to sleep she remembered the night Loren was there and gave her all the neat presents.

"So you like him Sky, I thought he was so cute for you. Plus now we each have one, since we love to cuddle you know."

"We sure are Loren. Of course I like him, it's more like love him, he makes me feel so much like a little kid. That's something we will always be Lor; we will always be like little kids."

"Yeah and if I could Sky I would fly away with Peter Pan."

"Loren, seriously, what is so cool about Peter Pan? He never grew up. He regretted it in the end, when he couldn't be with Wendy."

"Sky, think about it though. No one has ever been able to stay young forever. Sky to be eighteen forever, you could do so much." Loren looked at Skyler with her big blue eyes and smiled.

"Yeah, but Lor, I wouldn't pick eighteen. You are still not a legal adult."

"True, but we need to go to bed cowgirl, we got a big day ahead of us tomorrow."

"We sure do, turn and face the wall, you little Buckle Bunny. I'll see your bright and smilin' face in the mornin'." Skyler teased.

A screaming match outside her room brought Skyler out of her memory of Loren. She figured it was a bull rider and his wife. Maybe the wife had caught him with other women, or maybe it was about financial stability. She didn't know for sure. All she knew was she wanted one good night of sleep so that she could be a valuable part of the team. So she rolled over, like she had done before on many occasions, and closed her eyes.

The morning sun rose swiftly through her window pane. The sunlight accented the room and brought Skyler back to the feelings of what Loren must experience everyday in heaven. She rustled with the sheets for a few minutes before getting up and climbing into the shower. The warm water washed over her like a warm Tibetan flood. She couldn't help but try and find pleasure in the last droplets of water coming out of the showerhead. She quickly got out and got ready to explore Dallas. She had five hours before the event, and she was going to use every moment to her advantage, even if that advantage was shopping.

Skyler took in the sights and sounds of Dallas, all the fast paced automobiles on the interstate, the smell of BBQ being made, and, of course, the sound of bellowing cattle. She had never imagined herself loving a big city, but this city had so much of the same small town feel as Abilene.

    Skyler couldn't help but wonder what tonight would bring for her. She figured that she would be counting supplies again, or maybe a bull would run over a cowboy. So her real showing to Dr. Feldman would happen. She took a cab back to the hotel, hoping to relax a little before heading back to the American Airlines Center.

Kale

    After last night's poor performance Kale couldn't have been any more frustrated. He had been doing well, until that one moment, one strange yet amazing moment. He hadn't seen a girl like her before. She seemed so perfect, her smile, her innocence, her undying passion, all seemed like a new adventure to him. He couldn't shake her memory for the life of him. Even while he showered it brought him back to vivid images of her. Her hazel eyes, like fire raging inside of him. Her short petite frame, prefect for him to wrap his arms around, she had an amazing smile, and when her cheeks got red from embarrassment it showed Kale that just like him…she was new to a situation like this. He remembered her defensive nature, but who wouldn't be defensive around a guy she doesn't even know. Her fond adoration of Dr. Feldman made Kale see her true calling really had been to work on the BRA. Who was his father? He wondered, he knew of the northern cowboys, one being Ben Pendleton his hero. Skyler had a God fearing presence about her that captivated him. He loved repeating his name, the way it rolled off his tongue so sweetly like a honey suckle in the summer breeze. He knew that Skyler had to be the most beautiful girl that God put on this planet, but was this girl for him, he wondered as her heard the door open and his roommate walked in.

    Brayden Carter was a true cowboy; he had grown up in the hills of North Carolina. It was had for some people to see why his average height made him a prefect candidate to ride bulls. His frame was also well built, and his dark hair sometimes curled out of the bottom of his hat. Bull riding fans alike, loved to compare him to the late, great Lane Frost. Brayden didn't care though, he was riding not only because he loved it, but because his wife Dakota had fallen in love with the sweet talking North Carolinian at a summer rodeo in

Greensboro. He had become Kale's traveling buddy because Kale had no one else, and Brayden and Dakota were his friends. He liked hanging with Brayden, but knew that once Brayden heard about Skyler, that he would get razzed for a lifetime.

"What are you doing in their pretty boy? Putting on make up for the cameras you know all the girls love that."

"No, I'm buttoning up my shirt. I'll be out in a few minutes."

"You do know the event starts in about an hour, we have to be there in forty five minutes."

"Yes, chill Brayden. Go call your wife or something."

"Kale it ain't funny. Kota is mad I didn't bring her like always."

"I'm sorry, Bray. Sometimes you just go a little over board."

"It's what you do when you're married, Kale, but you won't know until you get there. Who's Skyler, by the way? Some buckle bunny who bought you a round at the bar last night?"

"No, Skyler wasn't at the bar last night, she works for Tate. She is real nice. She taped my wrist."

"Oh, maybe that's why you fell off last night."

"No, she did an amazing job. I don't even think it hurts anymore."

"That's called lust, man. Nothing good is goin' to come from it. She'll leave like any buckle bunny does."

"Thanks Brayden. I don't need a father. Go call your wife. Seriously I have to finish gettin' ready."

Kale was relieved when he heard Brayden on the phone with Dakota. Why was it so hard for him to tell Brayden about Skyler? Maybe because he didn't know how to figure Skyler out himself, but he knew she was more than a buckle bunny. He knew Skyler was a real person in a sea of fakes, but he couldn't confirm his feelings until she gave him a chance to do so. He wanted Skyler to give him a chance more than anything after last night. The way her hair fell in front of her eyes and she blew it away to continue working. The way her shy voice could send electricity up his spine. She was different that was for sure, but a difference he couldn't figure out by a single meeting. He looked at his cell phone for the time and hit Brayden with a pair of his socks.

"Hey dude, what was that for" Brayden crooned while giving Kale a methodical glare.

"You and your mushy love story; Do you have to say goodbye four times?" Kale glared back as he replied.

"Yes, and again Kale you won't understand until you're married. So, after your childish action I assume you are ready to hit the arena." Brayden murmured.

"Sure am, goin' to prove to Texas why I'm one of there Home State Cowboys."

"Yeah, as long as you stay up on your rope, you don't think of random women, and you focus. Then you'll get the job done for Texas." Brayden said as stern as any coach would give his star pupil pointers.

"Thanks coach, really I needed all of that pep talk. Now I'm goin' to win. It will be because of you." Kale's sarcastic nature resonated through the truck.

"Kale I just want you to succeed, like you want to. So don't get all sarcastic with me, Texas, or I'll have to kick you sissy ass."

"Did you forget, Carolina, I can box: and I'll knock you out. You won't even see it comin'."

"Right, right. Drive! Maybe you will get to see Skyler." Brayden teased, topping it off with his crooked Carolina smile.

"Knock it off Brayden. Seriously Skyler is nothin' but a girl."

"She must be some girl then, cowboy, cause you sure are starry eyed."

"Could we quit talkin' 'bout this?" Kale's face started to appear red. He wasn't ashamed of his new found crush; he didn't want the whole tour to know. With Brayden knowing it was only a matter of time before everyone knew.

"No, for once...I get to tease you. Besides its kind of fun being on the other end of the cross fire" Brayden balled up his fist and hit Kale.

Kale returned Brayden's hit, as they pulled into the parking garage of the arena.

Skyler

She walked into the Sports medicine room, ready for the night's events to start. She couldn't help but wonder if she would see Kale again. Skyler wanted to become his friend. He seemed like an awfully nice guy to her. He didn't care she had walked into him, and he was easy on the eyes. She didn't think it would work out that way though. When she became friends with a guy, it normally ended up in falling for him. She let her hopeless romantic side take over, and only imagined the kind of guy Kale was.

Twenty minutes before the event and with no bull riders in sigh, Skyler went to counting supplies. It wasn't until she was half way done with the ace wraps when a cowboy stumbled through the door.

"Can a help you?" Skyler retorted a little surprised to see him.

"Yeah, can you tape my wrist?" He asked politely.

"Sure can, come take a seat over here." Skyler patted on the small table, and turned away to gather taping supplied.

"So what's your name?" Brayden said.

"Sky Pendleton, and yours?" She asked looking at him with wonder.

"Brayden Carter, it's nice to meet you Sky." Brayden cocked his eyebrow and smiled.

"You too." Skyler knew her response sounded too rhetorical but it was all she could think of.

"I don't see a ring on your finger." Brayden came right out and said with no fear.

"No, but I see one on yours. Congratulations, I'm sure she is a lucky girl."

"Yeah, she is, but I'm sure whoever snags you will be pretty lucky too." He replied.

"Thanks, although I'm sure I would be one big complication for them. Who knows, maybe one day there will be someone. I guess I gotta find him."

"Ever think he may be a bull rider?" Brayden knew the answer before it even came out of his mouth.

"Always have. My father was a bull rider. There is something about you guys that draws a girl near. It could be the hats, boots perhaps, but I love the addiction to danger." Skyler bit her lip to try and control her mouth from running wild, even though she knew it had probably ran too far.

Brayden laughed "My wife always says it's the wranglers."

"She's right ya'll do look good in them wranglers. Drives any cowgirl crazy, we hate to see ya'll go but we sure love to watch you leave." Skyler's cheeks appeared red. Why in the world did she let herself go to far? She should have shut up way before the comment, but something about Brayden Carter made her laugh. He wasn't shy, he was blunt, and something Skyler had always wanted to be.

"Don't be embarrassed. Thanks. You did a great job tapin' my wrist. Take care Sky." He said in a soft reassuring tone.

"Thank you, good luck tonight Brayden, I'm rootin' for ya." Skyler mentioned as she turned back around to finish counting supplies.

The sound of the door slammed, and Skyler knew Brayden was going to find his place along the cowboys. Skyler couldn't believe she had talked to Brayden the way she had. She was raised to be courteous, and restrained when it came to interacting with a married man, although Skyler knew her mouth could always find a way of getting her into trouble. She started to sweep the floor as she mumbled to Loren.

"Loren, Can you believe me sometimes? Tellin' a married man such things you know is so inappropriate for a lady. Who am I kiddin' Loren I ain't no lady. Sure Loren Brayden is an attractive guy; the point is however that he is married. I have to go off on tangents about why girls fall for cowboys and rave for their clothing choice. Hey Loren, quit laughin' I hear you buckle bunny. You know you would have done the same in my shoes, well should I say boots. So Loren, what am I doin' with this Kale thing? Also should I apologize to Brayden for being so out of line with him? What are you sayin' Loren?

She didn't even see Dr. Feldman walk in with a rider around his arms. The guy stood at 5 foot 8, was a little stocky in the arms, and she could tell her was a foreigner. She could see his compatriots walk in along side Dr. Feldman, speaking in their native tongue. It was too late however for Skyler to take back the things she said out loud.

"Who's Loren?" Dr. Feldman asked with a keen sense of curiosity.

"My best friend, it's a long story really. You need help?" Skyler bit her lip, hoping Dr. Feldman wouldn't question her anymore.

"Yeah, can you get the scissor? We need to cut the bottom of his jeans and check his ankle."

Skyler didn't respond, she went and grabbed the scissors. She then went to fetch an ice bag to help combat any swelling.

Dr. Feldman stepped aside, and gave Skyler a nod, she was utterly nervous. What was she to do, now? She took a huge deep breath and started to cut the bottom of the rider's jeans. Once cut Skyler started to assess the riders injured ankle. She soon taped the ice bag to his acute ankle sprain and smiled at Dr. Tate when she was all done.

"Great job Sky. I have never had an intern who took such control over the situation. You must have been preparing for this." He mentioned with a smile.

"Actually sir I just reacted, I didn't even know what to do. I took a deep breath and my mind moved away to let my hands do all the thinkin'. I used my gut the whole time. I guess that sounds bad but I couldn't really think straight. I was using what I learned in college sir." She said a little bit prideful then before, but with a hint of modesty.

"Congratulations Sky. You had your first big test, to let you know you passed with flyin' colors."

"I did? You mean it? I passed with flyin' colors?" Her voice raised an octave in excitement.

"Sure did. That ain't a lie so the next event would you like to man the arena with me. I am sure you are tired of this tiny room." Dr. Tate Feldman smiled a genuine smile.

"It would be an honor to man the arena with you, Tate. Thanks so much for the opportunity. I don't know where I would be without it." Skyler smiled back, knowing it was true. Without this internship, her dreams of even being employed by the BRA full time would still be a small dim light in the back of her mind.

"No problem Sky. Keep this cowboy company will ya? Call me if the swellin' doesn't go down or you need my help with somethin'."

"Will do, although I think I have it all under control."

Skyler smile grew. For the first time in her life, she felt like she had helped someone. A feeling she had been dreaming of feeling ever since starting graduate school. Skyler felt amazing on the inside and out, but also was antsy in anticipating the next event on the tour.

Kale

Pulling on his helmet, he couldn't help but want to mount his championship round bull. He knew if he could score in the high eighties he would clinch the title and move from third overall to first. It was a hard task, but a task he knew he had to complete. He slowly lowered himself on top of a bull named Noise Control. The little roan Brahma was stocky. He had been on the tour for two years now, and had a reputation for being a spinner and taking the guys into the well. Most riders hated him for his bad attitude in the chutes, and the loud bellow he released after he would buck off a rider. Kale didn't care about his reputation; he only cared about covering him. He could keep hearing Brayden repeating stick to the basics in his head. So before he nodded, he scooted up close to his rope. A sudden hush fell upon the Dallas crowd. Kale's heart suddenly felt as if it was jumping out of his chest. The feel of the steel chute leaving his hand felt smooth along his palm, smooth as ocean sand. The smoothness was so replaced by the grit of the arena dirt. He couldn't let Texas down. He couldn't let himself down. As the bull whipped right he could only think of Skyler and thought how she must be watching him right now. How much of an idiot he would look if he didn't cover this bull. This bull was in his prime, a strong bucker with a bad attitude. He could whip around faster than a cowboy could reply with a counter action. The dirt slung around them, as if a haze rolling in on the horizon. Kale could feel his grip loosening and all he wanted to hear was the eight-second buzzer.

The eight -second buzzer rang in the nick of time. Kale untied what was left in his hand of his rope. He ran to the side of the arena, knelt down and prayed.

"Dear Lord, Thank you so much for that ounce of strength out there. I owe ya one. Thanks for the safety of the bullfighters and me. Amen."

He then went over and threw a couple of jabs at the rodeo clown. A tradition he had started when he first entered onto the tour. He waited anxiously in the alleyway to see his score. Everyone could see the disappointment on his face. He fell a quarter of a point shy from the lead. He couldn't believe it. He had the home arena advantage, and yet he blew his chance.

The walk back to the locker room seemed long to him. He found the bench his bag was resting on and sat down. He didn't know what to say. What if Skyler was watching? He knows she was, and he knew…that ride wouldn't impress her any day. Kale looked down at the ground and saw Brayden's signature black and blue boots walk his way.

"Tough break dude, I think judge three had to have been blind, definitely too low of a riders score." Brayden looked at Kale as if he could cheer him up like normal. Normally, Kale would blow off some steam, sit silent and when Brayden cracked a joke the disappointment would leave. It wasn't that way this time.

"I was out of shape. I deserved the score I got." Kale said with a stern look of contentious. He wasn't going to make it easy for Brayden to cheer him up this time. It wasn't about how Brayden felt. It was about how he felt, and he felt like crap. He knew Brayden wouldn't stop with the talking, so he looked at him to proceed with the disagreement.

"No, you weren't only for like a millisecond. That doesn't constitute the low markings. I wanted to tell you I talked to Skyler before the event; she seems like a pretty amazing girl. Although, it creeps me out that she kind of reminds me of Dakota. She agreed with her that Wranglers is what makes girls fall in love with cowboys." Smiling as he waited for Kale to rebel back.

"You didn't know that? Brayden you must have been livin' under a rock then. All cowboys know that Wrangler butts drive cowgirls' nuts."

They both laughed. Brayden knew he could crack Kale. Kale was kind of surprised for the spout of laughter. He was still pissed. This was his first chance to prove to Skyler he was a somebody on this tour, it was his chance to prove to himself that he was a somebody; not just an anybody.

"Thanks Brayden you sure know how to cheer a guy up when he is down."

"Again Kale, it's something you won't know until you're married. You don't only have yourself to worry about cheering up, it's kind of fun actually. I always love seein' a smile on Kota's face."

Kale rolled his eyes. At times Brayden's overt mushiness drove him crazy. "I'm sure it's better than seein' tears rollin' down her face that's for damn sure."

"Sure is, I don't know what is more heartbreaking, not riding a money bull or not seeing a smile on your wives face. I think I would say the later, but don't tell the guys." Brayden face turned kind of red. He was tough, and knew the guys couldn't tell him otherwise. However, he also knew that he could be more romantic then most. Brayden looked back at Kale sitting on the bench. Kale was shaking his head contemplating his next statement.

"Brayden, you are a sissy. That's why you're on this tour man. We are takin' you from boyhood to manhood." Kale smirked as if he had an evil plan brewing.

"Whatever Kale seriously, I'm more of a man then you are. You can't even come across Sports Medicine girl. She ain't scary man; actually she's nice and easy on the eyes."

"Yeah I know, I know about everythin' you're sayin'. I was the one who told you about her anyways. She's a great girl; don't get me wrong. Brayden, I don't see myself as her type. She is in graduate school; I didn't finish an undergraduate career. Plus, I suck at ridin' bulls. Though, I love it so much, she probably needs a man who can support her. Well maybe not support her I forgot she is about to be a doctor."

"Quit pitying yourself Kale. She is a Pendleton. She loves cowboys. She is from Montana. She loves wide-open country. She is smart; you need a smart woman sometimes. What it boils down to Weston is the fact that you're scared?"

"I'm not scared. How do you know she is a Pendleton? Do you mean Ben is her dad? One more reason I can't talk to her. I ain't half the rider her father was, if she is a Pendleton." A panic look graced his face. His dream girl could be his hero's daughter. Not only that, he couldn't imagine Ben Pendleton letting a guy like him get with her.

"Well, I know 'cause she told me. I don't think she is the lyin' type now Weston. You said it yourself she was different than other girls. She didn't seem to come off to me like those kind of girls. So what if she is Ben Pendleton's daughter. She doesn't act all high and mighty." Brayden laid his thoughts on to Kale gently. "You should go talk to her seriously."

"After autograph signin'; I'll ask her to go out for a drink. I am sure some gal wants to have my name on her official souvenir of the BRA." Kale knew he was allowing himself time to chicken out if need be.

"Seriously Kale, don't flatter yourself them fans are out there for a small piece of North Carolina." Brayden put on his cocky attitude and smiled.

"Sorry to burst both your bubbles, those fans are out there for none other than me." Jace Montgomery interrupted as he walked into the locker room. Jace had street credentials. He was a great bull rider; it was in his gene pool. He also had the tall body, the six pack abs, and the shit face grin that dragged even the nearest single lady in. He was Brayden's friend until Kale came along, but at times the three of them could be found taking small town USA by storm. Kale knew that both Brayden and Jace were great riders, and he admired being accepted among their elite in crowd, but sometimes Jace's abrupt entrances made Kale a little irritated.

"Damn Jace, you sure have a big head. I guess you have to in order to fit those ears on it." Brayden smiled. Poking fun at Jace was what he lived for. He had been the first cowboy from North Carolina to come on tour after the famous Jarred Durham, who happened to be his mentor through the years.

"Yeah, well, what can I say? If the buckle fits, then why in the hell not wear it."

They guys walked out of the locker and down the alleyway. The lights of the arena dimmed like stars in the sky. The fans had swarmed like bees around the first three or so rows of the arena. Each of them smiling and screaming a different cowboy's name, trying to congratulate them on yet another weekend of great rides. Others wanted to make memorable moments though still others were lookin' for a little more than an autograph to take home. As Kale picked up poster after poster, he tried to formulate exactly the right words to say to Sports Medicine girl. He knew however by the time the last fan left. She would be gone, back to wherever she had come from. His talk with her would have to wait until the next weekend.

A fan yelled at Kale as he rounded the backside of the arena.

"Hey Kale, you did amazin'. Too bad you couldn't have won it though. You sure do make us here in Texas proud."

"Thank you, I appreciate it." He murmured in that same soothing southern drawl of his, but autograph after autograph all he could think about was what he would say to her when he saw Skyler again. He didn't know why bull ridin' suddenly took the backseat to the girl workin' sports medicine. He knew somethin' was up; it had been a long time since anyone had stolen his heart like this. He couldn't believe Skyler had done it with a simple smile, her kindness, and her passionate eyes. What if he seriously wasn't the man for her? He thought to himself. What if she happened to be Ben Pendleton's daughter? Would he be able to live up to her standards? Standards he didn't even know that she had. After, stopping by the locker room to pick up his bag he decided to mosey on down to the Sports Medicine room. He could tell the light was off, and when he tugged at the door it didn't budge. She was on her way back home, not worrying about the entire incident that had gone on. While he pondered the next move that needed to be made, he didn't want to lose a chance to talk with her. What eased his mind was he knew he would have an opportunity next weekend. He shuffled his boots against the hot, dusty pavement. He got into the parking garage and found Brayden sitting in the drivers' seat. For the first time in six months, neither cowboy cracked a joke to one another. Instead they drove back to the hotel in silence.

Skyler

The ride back to Abilene seemed peaceful. The night sky sparkled much like it did before Loren died. After that fateful night however the stars shined a little bit brighter to Skyler. Loren had always loved anything doin' with stars, from the sky to clothes. An obsession Skyler once shared before she turned her attention from the night sky to the arena dirt. She knew there was no place for her in outer space and alien life forms never did peak her interest. She didn't mind leaving the mysteries of the night sky to Loren. The stars luminosity attracted Skyler in to a memory she held so dear in her heart. *Loren and she were sleeping outside. Both girls excitement was oozing through their veins. It was the first time Skyler was taking Loren to meet her grandfather down in Abilene. Skyler knew Loren would fall in love with the place just like she had done, but she was also excited for Loren and her to be able to explore the possibility of owning his ranch someday. She could still smell the crispness of the night, the cool breeze and she could hear the laughter. She knew Loren would catch the same fever she did. The Texas fever she called it. Skyler could still feel the wood from the old tree house. It hadn't been the most architectural sound tree house, but it was something they were proud of. Like many times Loren came over to spend the night, the girls would be up for hours talking about some of the most random things. Though, the night's conversations turned to the stars.*

"So Skyler, What do you think of the stars? Loren bubbly personality turned serious when questioning her best friend.

"Beautiful scattered dots a great navigational tool back in the day. My grandpa Jesse always told me about how the cowboys on the long round ups and cattle drives used to use them to guide themselves home." Skyler mentioned ever the treasure chest of historical knowledge.

"Skyler, more than cowboys used them you know. You and cowboys Sky...I just don't understand. They are addicted to danger, sure horses are pretty and they are talented guys. What's so great about cowboys Skyler?" Loren questioned as if she knew she was about to unleash a monster in Skyler's answer.

"Just wait. My Grandpa is livin' proof that cowboys are honest men. The addiction to danger is kind of sexy Loren. Who else would speed quickly on a domesticated animal of the wild and rescue a girl in need. Plus, the jeans, hat, chaps, spurs look real good on 'em. It's hard for me to explain it to you until you get to Texas. Grandpa tells me they grow the finest cowboys in the south."

Loren laughed as the fog started rolling in. "Sure hate how the fog is ruinin' the night sky."

"Sure is, in Abilene we won't have this problem. I promise." Skyler's face was sincere and Loren knew it.

"Sky, I am kind of getting' tired. We have a long day tomorrow cowgirl. You're drivin' the long haul, so you better get to bed."

Both girls turned to face opposite sides of the tree house.

The lights off a truck traveling behind her as well as the country song squealing on the radio brought Skyler out of the memory of that fateful night that turned Loren from dancer to buckle bunny. The song had been her and Loren's their final summer together. From the beat to the harmonics and even the attitude behind the lyrics gave the girls something to relate to.

"We sure are a different breed ain't we Buckle Bunny." She said as she tilted her head towards the sky. "Just to let you know although I'm sure you already know. Jace won! I'm proud of him Loren. It was one of your dreams to see him succeed and now he is fulfilling that for you. Don't even think about it Loren. I do not like Kale….maybe just a tad. I need a complicated free summer Lor; one without complications, one with a bit of adventure and a lot of places to escape. Plus, you know what would happen. I would fall hard Lor and be left in the dust once this is all said in done. Please Loren, tell me that I can stop thinkin' about that pretty smile. That Texas drawl, that tall lanky body, and who could forget them gorgeous eyes. Please Loren, I'm beggin' you to keep me strong buckle bunny. Don't let this turn out like a damn country song…my life is always that way. A non-complicated, educational summer that's all I ask for."

    She had no clue why she was pleading with Loren. She knew deep down inside Loren knew exactly what she wanted. She did want to get to know Kale. She wanted to know the mystery behind the mask. She thought about all the possibilities of who Kale was and what he stood for. Although, her shield was telling her to leave the idea of Kale behind as it left her more puzzled and searching for answers. She wanted her career with the BRA there was no question, but what made her think she couldn't have Kale as well. She contemplated getting both but her mind told her having both would be messy. Her life dream of working on tour with Tate could not be overshadowed by the sweet talking Texas native. He made her defenseless and speechless. He made her question everything she ever wanted. He made her wonder where life was taking her. It brought Skyler into self- doubt. What would Kale want with a girl like her anyways? She was stubborn, she had a hard time letting people in, she was more into getting her dream job than falling in love, and she was a northern cowgirl trying to make a name for herself down south.

    She also knew Kale could have any women he would ever want at the drop of a hat. The long gravel driveway of her grandfather's ranch abruptly appeared. As her muddy Ford F-150 barreled up the drive the only thought when the headlights hit the classic red barn was to go in and check on her horse JB. She slowed down and turned off the headlights. She could see that the barn door was cracked and knew she could quietly sneak in and take a peek at him sleeping. As she climbed out the truck she threw her bags against the barn and snuck inside. The small overhead lights were dimmed. Though just enough light gleamed down so that Skyler wouldn't trip over anything. She knew after the roundup she would need to clean out the barn. Shovels and wheel barrels lay up against the stall doors. She finally reached the end of the twenty-stall horse barn and caught her first glimpse of her sleeping prince.

JB was a five- year- old Paint gelding. He had classic markings, with dark sorrel socks on his hind legs. His mane was cut so that it would grow out evenly again and his tail had been braided to insure that it wouldn't bother him while they did chores. JB had been a going away present from Loren and everyday while Sky worked with him, she felt as if Loren was still right there by her side. It had been hard losing her, but it was something about JB that made the grieving process a little easier. Skyler didn't know why but she felt at peace with the loss of Loren whenever JB was around. As she slowly turned to leave the barn, JB awoke. She couldn't help but smile although she felt bad for waking him.

"Go back to sleep, you have a roundup in the mornin' boy. You have to be well rested. I am sure Gunner won't be able to do most of those cuts tomorrow. It will be all you boy." She kissed his forehead and gently stroked his mane. "You are the only boy for me ain't you hunnie." JB softly nickered into Sky's ear. The sound of him neighing sent butterflies to Sky's heart. JB had stolen her heart long ago. Exactly, as Loren had predicted when she took Sky out to the ranch to pick him up. Looking into his dark eyes Skyler could see the girl she had been years ago. She also saw the shy enigmatic girl she had become. After kissing him one more time she proceeded to leave the barn.

"Lay down JB. I will see you in the mornin'. Go ahead boy, Go on." She swiveled around on her boots and the soft clank from her heels echoed throughout the barn. Her bags lay lifeless against the pane of the doorway. She picked both of them up. It took her a moment before she could move in towards the house. She didn't want to wake grandpa. She walked loudly and knew that if she tripped over the coffee table or any other piece of furniture he would be up in a flash. In the stillness of the night she took a glance at the old farm horse. It had a clear mix of French Antebellum and Gothic architecture. The divisions in the roof made the house seem whimsical as well as haunted. As she reached the back door she noticed the chipping in the rich cherry red that once coated it. She slowly opened the back door and closed it softly behind her. As she lugged her bags through the cluttered space she lifted her leg over the ottoman that had been pushed up against the wall.

"Ah ha. I caught you. Go check on your horse before you come in to see your own grandfather." The old man's face showed a look of disappointment. "What kind of granddaughter are you? You don't love me anymore?"

"Of course I do Grandpa. I just needed a little JB time is all." Sky replied a little more defensive than normal.

"I understand. You thought I was sleepin'. I couldn't sleep a wink, thinkin' that you were drivin' home late tonight." His face slowly turned from disappointed to slightly concerned.

"Well I'm sorry to worry you Grandpa. You should really be goin' to bed. You know that you can't run a roundup on five hours of sleep. You aren't in your prime anymore." She said smiling.

"Not in my PRIME ANYMORE! Well I will so you who is in their prime." He responded as he walked towards the bedroom door.

She watched as he opened the door. She hadn't intended on making him mad but sometimes her sarcasm got the best of her. She continued the trek to her bedroom. The climb to her room felt shorter than normal. However, as she opened her room a feeling of abandonment came over her. She couldn't pinpoint it's location but hoped the feeling would subside. She dropped her bags near her closet doors. As she made her way to her bed she couldn't help but think of Kale. What was he doing at that exact moment? Was he getting ready to go to bed too? She spread her arms and fell back upon her bed. She took off her boots and threw them against the bottom of her bay window. She slowly motivated herself under the covers and laid her head down. Before too long she had fallen asleep.

Kale

His house seemed empty as he walked into the front entryway. There was no stirring from anywhere. He expected his dog Cooper to round the corner any minute but Cooper was nowhere in sight. Kale laid his duffle bag by the newly delivered couch. He looked around at the empty room full of boxes that needed to be unpacked. He then turned to the staircase and took the short climb to his bedroom. When he opened the door he spotted Cooper lying in bed. He knew Cooper had no intention on scooting over. Kale didn't mind; however he adored Cooper. Thought most nights when he finally ended up in bed he wished a woman would be in Cooper's place. He ran his hand down Cooper's back gently. Before he could make many strokes Cooper had fallen fast asleep. The Australian Sheppard was out like a light and snoring a tad. Kale didn't mind, the snoring counteracted his busy mind at work. He didn't know why he wanted someone to replace Cooper. He had been his companion for so long. Though he remembered he didn't buy this ranch for him and ol' Coop to grow old on. He bought this ranch to start a family. He wanted to revamp this old farmhouse into something for all to relish. For some reason all those thoughts also encompassed Skyler. Skyler seemed at least at second glance to be the kind of girl that would soak in something like his beat up ranch. The kitchen was huge a feature he barely used but wished could be someday. The front porch was a wrap around and he knew that late nights and the view could be a sight for her eyes.

He couldn't believe as he fumbled with the pillows that one moment could drive him absolutely crazy. Something about Skyler stayed glued in his mind. Like an expensive French painting no one wanted to touch because of its cost. To Kale she had the same beautiful mystery that the Mona Lisa possessed. Who was Skyler? What was she made of? He hoped though he could overcome the initial beauty and enchantment. He wanted nothing to hold him back from getting to know her. He wanted to be her friend and if more ensued than fine by him. He also wanted his parents to like her, although he couldn't see why they wouldn't. She wasn't the stereotypical girl he brought home for them to inspect and prod. She had a sense of being on a ranch before. A since of country heart and soul, looking for money and fame seemed far from his mind about who she was.

He pulled Cooper close in order to snuggle. The newly assembled ranch was far cry from productive. Although to Kale, Cooper was a great asset to him. He minded and helped in his own way with chores. He also was Kale's friend who didn't talk back and didn't tease him about who he was or what he was doing with his life. He glanced over Cooper's long body to see a small stack of packaging boxes. Between cattle, Cooper, and bull riding events Kale struggled to unpack. The small stack was a mere reflection of the long hours he spent ranching, practicing for the next event, and traveling from event to event. He knew life was chaos, but it seemed normal to Kale. Sometimes he wished for more hours in a single day or to freeze a point in time to make it last longer. Kale knew that was never possible. He knew that he needed to find time to unpack soon. Before his friends believed he didn't want them to see his place. His head slowly found the perfect spot on the pillow. His eyes became heavy and his mind quit its wondering. His arms rested comfortably around Cooper. The warmth from his canine made it easier for Kale to continue his plummet into a deep sleep.

As the light peaked in through the blinds he couldn't help but roll over and try to fall back asleep. Though the attempt didn't last long before Cooper started to softly nudge him, when the nudging failed he resorted to his specialty: licking.

"Stop that Cooper. Stop that." Kale demanded softly pushing Cooper away.

"Hunnie, if you don't get up I can't fix you breakfast." Softly rang out from a slightly familiar voice, a voice of a beautiful stranger.

He looked up and saw no one. Why was his mind playing tricks with him again? Why was it that Cooper felt something, some urge to like him. Did he imagine someone was there too? He rolled out of bed a bit confused. Cooper trailed him closely behind as they walked down the stairs. Cooper made his way to the sliding glass door a cue Kale knew all to well. He stumbled to the kitchen and put a pot of coffee on before opening the door and letting Cooper out.

"Stay out of trouble boy." He dictated as he patted the top of Coopers' head.

As Cooper ran toward the pasture, Kale wondered why he would even hear a voice. Sure he felt lonely and wanted to share his home with someone. To drown out the desperation he turned on the radio. The radio barreled out the sounds of a George Strait song. He poured himself a cup of coffee and paced around the kitchen. He had so much to do before heading to Greensboro. He always had too much to do. He placed the worn out mug on the counter and ran upstairs to change.

Walking down the steps two at a time his list of to-dos spiraled around in his mind. Feed the livestock, check on the new arrivals, and make sure Cooper stays out of trouble. All these things resonated as he opened the sliding glass door.

The coffee quickly settled in and he could see Cooper in the corral with Cash. Cash was Kale's trusty Quarter horse. He could never remember exactly when Cash became a part of his life but he knew every moment that contained Cash in it was special. Kale only hoped Cash wouldn't hurt Cooper. Cooper was a sly dog and could be feisty at times. Sometimes he knew Cash hated all the barking and other days Cash paid no attention to the dog chasing him. Kale knew Cooper loved to provoke all the larger animals. It made him feel as if he was big too.

    Kale felt the morning pass by slowly. He was pleased in the presentation of the new cattle. They were all beefing up at a good pace like he wanted. The horses showed no sign that they cared about the world around them. Cooper, on the other hand was fishing for mischief and like many times before, Kale decided to take him on a walk through the woods.

    The first time he took a glimpse of the land he imagined what he would see. He imagined deer grazing, turkey gobbling, and birds soaring high up in the trees. He envisioned Cooper and his crazy antics. He imagined a big happy family. Turning twenty three had thrown things into perpetual motion for him. He yearned for a wife, a yard full of kids, and something to be proud of. He wanted a fairy tale ending to the chaotic life he had led thus far. He found himself the odd-man-out in the locker room. Many were thirsting for a cold beer and a one night stand but not Kale. Others had girlfriends, fiancés, and wives. Either you were in one or looking for one, Kale hated being in the later group. He was ready to be committed to the women of his dreams.

The wind blew throughout the pecan trees. In his mind the strangers' voice rang once again.

"Kale, I love you. Come on; come on over here darlin'."

He couldn't believe his mind continued to play tricks with him. He knew no one else was in the woods, especially any women. Most of the women he chose to date were petrified by the tiniest bug. As his past relationships unraveled before him he realized how different Skyler was. Those differences seemed so important to him. She wasn't like the girls in his past. She worked hard, smiled harder, and found self gratitude in accomplishing her dreams. There was no doubt in his mind that she was raised with the up most respect for people. Her presentence seemed too emanated next to him as he thought about her. He had no trouble picturing her on his ranch. He knew she would take excellent care of the livestock, fall in love with crazy Cooper. He also knew Cooper would fall in love with her adorable smile and love filled eyes.

His world seemed cruel. Bringing Skyler into it so she could disappear from it in three months time; three months was all he had to make a solid connection. Hoping that connection would lead her back to him in due time. He knew he would have to muster up the courage and take the initiative to start a friendship with her. His wondering mind kept pace with his legs as he made it back to the edge of the house.

He needed to mow and Cooper wasn't far behind him. He felt a rush of energy surge in his heart. He only hoped the energy would be sustained until he made it to Greensboro and saw Skyler again.

Skyler

She couldn't help but feel back in control of things as she mounted JB. Ever since the first summer her grandfather taught her how to rope cattle the power she felt in the saddle had been unmatched. Not evening acing one of her test matched the feeling. The power she felt in the saddle was the power she wished she mastered in medicine. She wanted to be confident like Dr. Feldman. To make the right decisions for her patients, knowing there was no other option or route she could take. Right now she felt defenseless around Dr. Feldman and his staff. If she messed up it didn't look bad on only herself, but her institution. She loved the ranch though because she could get away from the bureaucracy of it all. She could escape classes and have fun. Even though the work was meticulous at times she loved ranching but in her heart she knew medicine was a perfect fit.

    She didn't know why both medicine and ranching fascinated her. The complex challenges both possessed her to think outside the realm of concrete thinking and use a more objective style. The ranch had a lot to offer Sky as well as the classrooms at Texas Tech Health science institute. The ranch brought her freedom while the classes gave her structure. She had fallen in love with the ranch and wanted to be able to live a similar life to the one her grandfather led. The wide open spaces drew her in like a warm blanket. It wasn't long before Gunner had closed the gap between himself and JB.

    "So we didn't get to talk much last night." Her grandfather mustarded up the phrase slowly, "is the internship all it' cracked up to be?"

    "No, but Grandpa, life isn't everything it's cracked up to be. I dreamed Loren and I would someday own this ranch. Look where Loren is now Grandpa."

The last phrase left a sting in his heart. He wanted to take away the pain his granddaughter tried so hard to hide. He wanted to be able to make her realize that things were starting to look up for her. Though the pain she harbored mimicked the same pain he once harbored himself.

Skyler could see the resurgence of pain in her grandfathers' heart when she looked into his dark brown eyes. She knew he was recalling the exact moment the doctors told him that his wife of
Forty five years wasn't going to make it through the night. Skyler had vivid images of her grandmother, but her grandfather had never led on that he was hurting. She knew it was part of the lifestyle; a cowboys lifestyle. However, his undying strength gave Skyler an abundance of hope. Sometimes she needed a little piece of his hope to keep moving on.

"Sky, I know I didn't let you or your mother see me cry after your grandmother passed, but one thing I regretted every summer that you came down here after that was the fact I never told you much about her. She was an amazing woman, Skyler, much like you. There wasn't a task on this ranch she wouldn't do. There was nothin' she couldn't do if she put her mind to it."

Skyler felt privileged to be her grandfathers' outlet. She always thought highly of him. That was one reason that graduate school in Texas appealed so much to her. The other appeal came in the form of having the family traditions passed down to her. Her grandfather had passed it down to her mother although Sky's mom rarely used them. She knew that she would have to learn from her grandfather as well. In order to preserve the great legacy her family once relished in. She also knew he wouldn't always be around to teach her. She wanted him to teach her everything he knew about the Wild West. He had done an amazing job thus far but she only hoped the learning didn't stop here. She loved to soak up his stories about round ups and cattle drives. About pickup trucks and ancient rodeo arenas, she loved her grandfather but at times his stubbornness got annoying.

"Sky, you're avoidin' somethin'. I can see it in those fiery eyes of yours. When you're fine, they sparkle like the finest diamonds. When you're avoidin' somethin', they cloud up like a Texas rain shower. Your pupils almost seem as if clouds are rollin' in as we speak." He was concerned for his granddaughter. She was his responsibility and if something was wrong he wanted to know.

"Nothin' Grandpa, thinkin' about this comin' weekend in Greensboro. It's goin' to be weird without my truck." She knew she had lied through her teeth but hoped it was a good enough answer to get him off her back.

"Skyler Kay Pendleton, don't you lie to me. This ain't about your truck or the cattle, so what is it? Did you decide the rodeo circuit wasn't your callin' after all?" His face gave off a stern contrast to how his heart felt. He couldn't play nice with Skyler. She would easily walk over that. He had to keep pressing her until the truth came out.

"No Grandpa, more like I found out it's exactly where I belong and want to be. Exactly! However, I feel somethin' may ruin my perfect opportunity." She had a look of concern even though her voice never quivered.

"Elaborate. I was never good at readin' minds. You think I would have inherited that trait as many times I had to guess what was on your grandmothers' mind. Skyler, I can't help you unless you tell me. Is it a boy?"

"No! How could you get a foolish idea like that?" Skyler knew her grandfather had broken through the barrier. There was no getting out of talking about Kale now.

"What's he like? Is he a bull rider? What's his name? Is he goin' to take care of my granddaughter?" The questions just kept spilling from his mouth.

"Grandpa, I barely know him. His name is Kale, and of course he is a bull rider." Skyler's voice rang with a tinge of anger.

Her grandfather turned Gunner around and headed for the barn. Skyler couldn't believe she had raised her voice at her grandfather. She had never tried to disrespect him before, but she didn't want to talk about Kale. He was a patient and that's all he should have been to her. Her mind crossed the line with all the replay of what happened in Dallas. She couldn't take the haunting memories though they weren't nightmares. They were full of blissful moments. Although, the lack of moments also gave her lack of evidence on whom Kale was as a person. All she knew was he wore money sign boxers; he needed his wrist tape so he must have bad wrists, and he was a Texas native. To Skyler that was not enough to base a sound relationship on. Though, something in her heart told her a relationship could be made. It also told her that Kale would steal it a million times over.

She dismounted JB and started to give him a good rub down. Her grandpa walked inside smiling at her as the door closed behind him. She couldn't imagine Kale with her grandfather or her father. What would happen when they met, if they ever met? All the crazy stories grandpa would have about Skyler's first time around the ranch, but it didn't matter to her, because like she had heard from her mom many times before "if someone truly loves you, they will love you for who you are."

    Skyler's ears echoed with her mother's quote. If Kale really was the guy she made him out to be he would love her for what and who she was.

    After putting JB into the barn, she couldn't help but run inside to relax for a bit. However, her mind told her she should cook grandpa an amazing dinner. So as soon as she walked in through the sliding glass door she headed for the kitchen. To Sky, between the acreage and the kitchen, Abilene seemed so much like a paradise. Her grandfather had designed the kitchen by himself. From the high ceilings, to the granite counter tops.

    She searched every nook and cranny for her cookbook. She had inherited it from her grandmother and it contained only the best recipes inside, as well as the most cherished ones. Like her great-grandma's egg noodles, her great- grandfathers rib recipe and the one she enjoyed most of all; her grandma's Chicken Supreme. She knew it was her grandfathers' favorite. It had instantly become hers all those summers ago. She also knew it was Loren's. The look on her face after her first dinner in Abilene gave Sky the relief of how strong their friendship truly was. A small teardrop hit the corner of the page.

She held the worn out and crinkled page as she memorized the recipe in her head. She shut the cookbook softly and went to retrieve the ingredient from the refrigerator.

"Sky, what smells so good?" Her grandpa asked smiling.

"You'll see. Go rest; sit down, somethin'…anythin'. Dinner will be ready here in a second." She replied softly pushing him out of the kitchen.

"Why are you cookin' dinner? Skyler, what did I tell you about that. You are the guest." He sternly mentioned to her.

"Grandpa, this isn't like summer visits anymore. I live here; I breathe the Texas air, Grandpa…I'm no longer a guest. This is as much my home as Billings is. I couldn't and wouldn't change that for the world." She reminded her grandfather with a smile.

He wrapped his arms around his granddaughter. He didn't have the right words to say so he held her close, hoping the moment would last a while. Skyler broke the embrace so she could set the table.

"So, Skyler, this boy you talked about, tell me more about him. I'm not tryin' to push your buttons, but you know I ain't goin' to let your average Joe come and take my granddaughter away."

"He isn't. Grandpa, you have nothin' to worry about, don't fret." She said placing his plate of chicken, smashed potatoes and corn in front of him.

"This looks amazin' Sky thanks. Though I doubt you know those are the exact words your momma used. She told me your father was the man of her dreams. She told me not to worry. The next thing I know she is getting' taken off to Montana." His voice had a tone of disappointment.

"Thanks Grandpa. It's nothin' like grandmas but I tried. Again, you have nothin' to worry about Grandpa. I am goin' to be in Texas forever." She retorted between bites and potato and corn.

"You say that now, but things will change. Don't get me wrong. I want you here forever, but Sky; you haven't even had the chance to experience life. That's why I thank God everyday for this internship of yours."

"You mean you like that I'm not here? You like that I'm miles and miles away from you at all times?" Her voice seemed heartbroken. She idolized her grandfather for his strength but his lack of compassion seemed to be one thing Skyler disliked about him.

"That part no, but Sky, what I'm tryin' to say is, you have a mindset that fits rodeo: bull riding in particular. You work prefect in that setting, always will, but others can't look at a situation with such a high level of cognitive ability. Sky, I always teased your momma about your smarts, and how you must not have been related to us. Skyler, those brains someone may not find sexy right now, but, hunnie, when the right guy comes along, that will be one of the sexiest things to him."

Skyler smiled. Trying not to show her grandfather that his last statement creeped her out. She couldn't help but laugh. Her grandfather had a way to cheer her up. It definitely made up for way the round up had ended. She picked up her plate and took it to the sink.

"Sky, leave the dishes."

"No Grandpa, I cooked, I can clean too. You should go watch the *Grand Ol' Opry*. You love watching that you know. I can clean up I promise." She smiled as her grandpa gave in. He stood up and passed her the plate. She finished the dishes in time to catch the end of Randy Travis singing. She only hoped the rest of the evening would be filled with more civil conversation between the two of them. Maybe, she would have the guts to beg for a puppy again. She didn't know how the night would end, but slowly situated herself on the couch to watch *Lonesome Dove* with her grandfather.

Kale

He couldn't help but wonder how Greensboro would go. He knew he was leaving Texas earlier than normal, so he could hang out with Jace, Brayden and Brayden's wife, Dakota. He couldn't wait to be back in the Tar Heel state. The year before he had won second place, his first second place finish in the series. He also didn't mind the fact that Dakota would be around. Maybe he could ask her how to approach Skyler. He knew that he needed help in the ladies department, and that Dakota was just the girl to set him straight.

Cooper came running into the room about the time Kale laid on the bed. Cooper was an amazing dog, but sometimes he wanted more than his dog to welcome him home. He turned on the TV. It soon lit up with photos and videos of Ben Pendleton. His smiling face, the cowboy hat turned down to the ground, and a girl, a little girl in his arms. As a traveling buddy started to talk about Ben he heard the name that had been resonating in his ears all day: Skyler. It was true, Brayden wasn't joking with him. He was falling in love with a legends daughter, and not just any legend: his hero.

He looked at Cooper and could only imagine what Sky would say walking in the door of his place. Cooper rounding the corner with the same speed as a barrel horse has running home after a solid run. He would run to her for attention. His paws landing perfectly on her thighs, he could see it all now. Sky laughing, himself smiling, and Cooper, well he was always happy no matter what happened. He could hear Sky say "You have a nice place here, and your dog is cute." He also could hear her angelic voice speak to him. "Kale, can we be together forever."

"Yes." He replied, until he realized again there was no one in the house other than Cooper. What was it about Skyler? She had him wrapped around her little finger; and she didn't even know it yet. He got up from the bed and started packing his bag for Greensboro.

Skyler

She was woken up by the sound of the house phone.

"Hello." She replied with a yawn.

"Hey Skyler, its Dad," rang the voice on the other end of the line.

"Hey Dad. How's the ranch?"

"It's fine. Your mother says she can still see you running around. Sometimes I do too."

"Awe, I'm glad I provoke memories at least. I'm also glad I get to spend time with Grandpa." Her voice got high like a little kid as she spoke.

"How's your grandpa Jesse doing anyways? Oh, Mom told me about your internship, how's that going squirt." He questioned hoping to get a truthful response.

"Good, I get to be on national TV this weekend. Grandpa still thinks he is a young gun on the rodeo circuit. It worries me how much he pushes himself, but that's Grandpa Jesse for ya." She rolled her eyes knowing he couldn't see her gesture of disrespect.

"Sure is hunnie, and TV. That may cause some problems for me. I'll have to be fending off the boys you went to school with. They will be knocking on my door asking for your hand in marriage." He knew she was frustrated with him but he wanted nothing more but to continue the conversation with his daughter. It had been a long time since he had heard her voice. After the revealing of a rumor he had tried to cover years earlier. He knew her being around some of the bull rider may stiffen her struggle with him. He didn't like knowing his daughter went from viewing him as a hero to now seeing him as a cheater. He hadn't cheated but he couldn't get all the "hard evidence" out of her mind. So, he tried his best to show his daughter he was telling her the truth all along.

"You are insane Dad, but I guess that's why I love you." She knew it sounded sarcastic but hoped he didn't take it that way. She did love him; she just didn't love his judgment all the time.

"Your Mom said my insanity is what led her into a whirlwind romance with me. I don't ever think your Grandpa like that much."

"It wasn't that, it was the fact you guys were too busy to have a proper wedding. Mom didn't even get to wear Grandma's gown. Ya'll were in Vegas and the next phone call they got was from Mom sayin' she was married and movin' to Montana." Skyler sounded like a teenage smart-aleck trying to prove her point.

"You know this how?" He couldn't wait to hear his daughter's response.

"Grandpa told me the other day on the round up. He wanted to walk Mom down the aisle is all? It's like a father's rite of passage or something." She knew she had the affirmative hand in the conversation.

"Well, I'm sorry Sky that I hurt your grandfather. You're going to learn from my mistake. No Shotgun Wedding!" He knew she was probably tired of listening but had to prove his actions somehow.

"You can't have a wedding without being in love." He could hear the defiance in her voice.

"Well what happened to that one kid, the tall one. Goodness Sky the one going to school for equine medicine." He wondered. They had seemed so in love and the young gentleman seemed ready to welcome Skyler into his family.

"Chase! Chase Harper! Dad we broke it off a year and a half ago." She couldn't believe he even thought of Chase. Sure he had been a nice guy and all but under his conservative outer shell he had nothing else really to offer her.

"How come you never told your mother and me?" He was a little pissed at this point. Sure he knew his daughter had led the past few years under silent radar but she should have told him about this.

" 'Cause you all adored him, I didn't want to let you guys down. So I figured in due time you would know we weren't together and it wouldn't matter at that point." She sincerely meant every word she uttered to him.

"Hunnie, what did I tell you when you were a little girl?" His fatherly instincts kicked in.

"Find the guy who treats you right and makes you happy." She recited as if a robot was spitting out important information.

"Exactly Sky, we love you kiddo you know that. Nothing you do makes us feel let down. Quit thinking like that. You're a Pendleton. You're destined for greatness kiddo." He hoped his pep talk would convey to her how he truly felt. He hoped it would help her to finally bury the hatchet.

"Love you, too. Tell Mom I said hello. If you need me this weekend call my cell phone; I'll be in North Carolina." She had the closest thing to a real conversation with her dad. She couldn't believe that he had been resilient and stuck with the conversation. Normally, she heard the phone slam. Something was going to change between the two of them and she couldn't put her finger on it.

"Have fun sweetie. I can't wait to hear of your great adventure."

"I will. I'll do somethin' to make the story interestin'." She was pulling his leg now.

"Skyler Kay Pendleton, don't go getting your self in trouble." He was serious. He didn't want her to ruin any chances she had of chasing her dreams.

"I won't, don't worry. Go on now; go do what you have to do. I have taken up enough of the daylight already." Her wise cracking ways seemed to find a way into the conversation.

Skyler hung up the phone. It seemed that being away caused a little tension between them. She enjoyed the phone conversations but she felt like they were pulling her back into their orbit. Not ready to let her go but trying to push her away at the same time. One thing Grandpa wouldn't dare to do to her. She ran downstairs, but didn't see grandpa sitting on the couch. Normally, this time he was watching hunting shows on *Versus*.

    She opened the front door to go outside and saw him working with Gunner. There was something about her grandpa that mesmerized her. Partly, it was the way he could handle a horse the rest was that he didn't care about the world outside the ranch. He would rather be isolated and happy, than famous and depressed.

    "So I still ain't in my primes eh?" He was razzing her for that comment.

    "Grandpa, I didn't mean it that way. You're amazing. More than amazing actually, I want you to take care of yourself. Those bones of yours ain't nearly as strong as they once were. Bull ridin' helped deplete their strength. Fractures make your bones weaker and more susceptible to breakin' again." She hated to pull out her library of knowledge but sometimes it was all he listened too.

    "Sky, I'm not one of your case studies okay. Yes, I realize I need to be careful, I always am. This ranch is all I have, all I ever wanted, you know that as well as the rest of them Sky."

"Yeah, I know. Mom used to tell me about the day you moved into this house. How beautiful the place looked. Before too long, it was a workin' cowboy ranch. Boomin' with all the sights and sounds: oozing with the energy of the rodeo circuit: a hop, skip, and a jump away from true paradise." Her eyes glazed over as if imaging the words as she spoke them. Her grandfather smiled. It was something about Sky's illustrious explanation from her mother's point of view that made him feel good inside.

"What Grandpa? Are you okay?" her concerned voice echoed through the wind.

"I'm fine sweetie, so, what do you see when you look out the back windows." His voice trailed off.

"I see green pastures, animals who love this place. A land drenched in tradition. A place of solitude, but a solitude that brings relaxation: I see birds fly high in the sky. I see a world so foreign to many in this day and age."

"So, it had taken this long for me to get through your thick little head."

"No, every summer Mom said it was time to come visit you, I would get excited. Even if Billings retains a western feel at times, it's nothin' like this. I remember when I started bringin' Loren. How fun it was to run through the wildflowers out by the creek. How spinnin' in those empty corn fields seemed to be a release from this world, almost like butterflies soaring through prairieland. Everything here holds a piece of me: every tree, every animal. They capture me inside. It's captivity like no other. It's hard to explain, Grandpa. You know the ranch and the graduate program is the reason I came to Texas. Who knows what would have happened if I had chosen to stay in Billings." She seemed concerned as if her explanation wouldn't be up to par. She wanted him to understand how important the ranch was to her as well.

"You sure wouldn't be workin' for the BRA right now. You wouldn't be thinking about the boy you're always thinkin' about." He knew the last one would peak her interest. It did surprise her that he pulled out Kale. He didn't even know him nor did she. Though he did find a way to be on her mind; she knew in a few short days she would see his blue eyes and crooked smile again.

Kale

After getting off the plane in Greensboro, he had an hour drive to Randleman. He was excited to get to see

Brayden. He knew that he also was about to have one of the best meals in his life. He loved coming to North Carolina or any weekend that Dakota happened to be around. She treated him like a brother and to him she was a little sister. At the same time he sometimes wondered how she and Brayden ended up together. She was sweet as could be: she couldn't and wouldn't hurt a fly unless necessary. She also, had a great head on her shoulder; which he knew at times was a stark contrast from Brayden.

    The drive to Randleman seemed long. However, pulling into the driveway he could see the pale yellow house. The white shutters contrasted the traditional red barn and the long stables wrapped around behind that. He could see the make shift arena was empty and in the back two hundred and fifty acres he could see a few of the cattle grazing. He saw the metal sign announcing to him that he was at the Carter ranch. He could smell something delicious coming out of the kitchen windows. He honked the horn and out came Dakota. Dakota was a tall blonde with sea blue eyes. Her smile lit up her face and her hospitality was sweeter than honey on a biscuit. She had her hair tied back and a head band pushing back her bangs. He couldn't help but be excited to spend the weekend at the Carters' place.

"Look at you." She retorted in the same North Carolina mixed accent. She opened the door for him and he jumped out and hugged her.

"Yeah well, look at you, gorgeous as always."

Dakota hit him. She knew if he wasn't being serious that he deserved every hit he would get from her. "Come on Kale; don't try to butter me up. You know your presence here does just that." She sprinkled the last phrase with a drop of sarcasm.

They both walked inside. Dakota took Kale upstairs to show him where he would be staying for the weekend.

"Hope it's clean. I told Brayden to clean it a couple days ago. You know him, always finds something else to tinker with or do." Her comment seemed as if she and Brayden were in a little argument. Kale couldn't figure out, but he didn't care. If the room was dirty it would remind him of home.

"Don't we always find a way to get out of work? It looks fine to me. Besides, you don't need to treat me like some kind of royal guest." He smiled as if hiding his some master plan.

"I do too Kale, now stop that. Brayden went to the store and hopefully following the list I gave him. I am going to make you a North Carolina special tonight?"

"Oh. I'm so excited!" He knew Dakota would smell his bull shit from a mile away. She gently took another swing at him.

"What is up with your sarcasm, you have never been this way before. I am getting a little concerned."

"It's called spending time with you husband on the road." The matter of fact statement seemed to fill the room.

"I can believe that. Take off your boots, make yourself at home. Get comfortable."

"I will do that. Dakota, thanks for letting me stay here to save a little money. I owe ya one." He was grateful to have friends like she and Brayden.

Kale watched as Dakota left. He quickly changed his shirt and took his boots off. He threw them near his bag and took off down the stairs to the kitchen.

"Need anythin'?" Dakota knew the look on his face was searching for answers. If she could be of service than she might as well try her luck.

"Yes, actually, I do." He had no doubt that Dakota had some sense to where the conversation was going.

"What?" She was getting a little ticked. Most of the time Kale would come out and spill to her. She knew now that he was spending too much time with Brayden.

"Advice mainly, it's about a girl." He hoped she didn't through this out of proportion. It wasn't serious and he wasn't going to marry her right away. Knowing Dakota however and looking into her eyes he could tell he had sent her into a small tail spin.

"Kale Joseph Weston it better not be some gosh damn buckle bunny again." She lost count of how many buckle bunnies Kale had been with. How many girls were digging their claws into his hard exterior in order to soften up the interior? She was only looking out for him. She hated seeing him getting used.

"Dakota it isn't. I promise you that. She works, well more like interns for Tate. She is short but you know me its fine. Her hazel eyes, boy they could burn a hole through any mans heart. Her smile: I don't even have words in my vocabulary to describe it."

She could see small specks of drool coming from the corner of his mouth. She knew he had been bite by the love bug. "Sounds like she had you wrapped around her little finger." She glanced at him preparing for one of Kale's answers that told her differently.

"You could say that. Although, Dakota her last name is Pendleton." His insecurity reflected in his voice as he pronounced Sky's last name slower than the rest of the phrase.

"You mean like Ben Pendleton, one of the greatest cowboys to come out of the great state of Montana?" Her voice became quite exuberant and she thought about all the questions she could ask Kale's girl about her father.

"Yeah, I think that's her dad. I saw a special on him on a sports channel. A picture flashed on the screen and his old traveling partner talked about him and a little girl. He said something like 'other than God, his wife, and Skyler, nothin' else mattered.'"

"Hun, there are people who have the same name. Look at Brayden. There is another Brayden Carter. I think he sings or something and sometimes I wished I married that one." She was trying to lighten Kale's heart. She couldn't tell if her method was working on him.

"Dakota, what would Brayden say if he heard you say that?"

"He would say well I should have married Reese Witherspoon. He still has a huge crush on her." She knew Brayden would never have a chance with Reese so it didn't really matter to her who he had a celebrity crush on.

"Highly doubt it but you think what you want. It's none of my business." Kale rolled his eyes. He knew Dakota was tryin' to get him to smile. She wasn't helping much. Although, getting to talk about Skyler lifted a ton off his chest.

"So this girl; what she got that others don't?" It was time to grill him now. He had let him slip by with simple answers but now the hard questions surfaced.

"She's smart." His mind drew a blank. He once had a list in his head of all the differences and the first one that came back was her intelligence.

"Well at least you found one who uses her brain." Dakota meant what she said. Most of the girls who found a way to get to Kale were ditzy. They knew nothing about his occupation and only wanted money out of him. She couldn't relate to them which is one thing she wanted. She wanted Kale to be able to find her someone who could gossip with her about their boys.

"Yeah, yeah; you're no help. I'm going to go out back and take a look on that bull of yours Outlaw." His voice trailed as he cracked open the door.

"Kale, don't get yourself hurt out there." She wasn't lying. Outlaw could be unpredictable at times. She didn't need Kale getting hurt before the event. If he did, she knew she wouldn't hear the end of it.

"I won't. I promise. Yell at me when the man of the house makes his grand appearance."

They laughed. It had been a long time since it was him and Dakota. He met Dakota one summer at church camp. She was the only one he could talk bull riding with. The only one who seemed to understand? It didn't matter to him though; the day she called him and told him she met this guy was one of his proudest moments. She was excited and rightfully so. He was one of the best bull riders around North Carolina. He was a little cocky but his sense of humor made up for it. Then when Kale finally joined the circuit; Brayden did his best to take him under his wing. After that it seemed as if his relationship with Dakota had strengthened. He saw her as a little sister although she was only two years younger. She didn't have any siblings and he took pride in being her big brother in a weird sort of way.

    The sun starting to set, but he was on the lookout for Outlaw. Brayden and Dakota had won him in a poker tournament. He had also brought buckles to their small ranch. Dakota was working towards her stock contracting dream. He was a good start. The only problem was he could be mean. Most guys wouldn't dare practice on Dakota's pin because of him. He wanted fame and fortune. He also wanted to eliminate any guy who thought he would easily surpass him. He adored Outlaw. His coloring and pedigree rang true to most American bucking bulls. Kale also loved Outlaw because Dakota's other bull Hectic Handful didn't want anything to do with him. He couldn't blame him though. All the toughest bulls shook in fear when he was around them. At least he thought as much.

He heard someone scream from the porch. "What are you doing out here sissy boy? Didn't you know he eats cowboys for breakfast?" Brayden hollered so Kale could hear him loud and clear.

"So I've heard. I had to see it for myself. He sure hasn't made a move on me yet." Kale couldn't help but strive to be like Brayden. His crazy antics always made a situation easier, though he also was jealous of Brayden.

"So cowboy, what you think? The last time you were here it was a little run down looking. Now it's like new again or as close to new as it can get." Brayden spoke with pride. He wanted Kale to love his place as well. He helped do some of the work a year and a half ago. He wanted Kale to see that he could provide for Dakota.

"Sure is, you guys did a wonderful job on the place. Can't say the same for the bulls though; what did you do quit feeding them?" He knew Brayden would have an amazing comeback.

"Excuse me, I don't think your bulls buck at challenger tour events no do they. Plus, that one over there; he is Kota's ticket to the big leagues." Brayden knew what he was saying was true. Hectic Handful was showing his true colors. He knew Cade the livestock director for the BRA was looking at putting him on tour as a re-ride option.

"Why'd she name him Hectic Handful? Was it a nice way of telling you something?"

"Sure Kale. That's exactly what it was." Brayden couldn't help but unveil his mastery of sarcasm. "I think she always like the name. So when she found the perfect bull she used it. The name couldn't suit him any better."

"Nice to know, so I hear she is cooking me a North Carolina specialty. I sure hope it's good." Kale stomach rumbled as he spoke.

"Ah, you know man. It sure will be. Everything is better here in North Carolina."

"Brayden I think you ripped off a commercial. I heard that line before. However, it was for a different state." Kale knew that Brayden could be lame but reciting a commercial that was really lame."

"So what if I did? They weren't using it." Brayden scoffed.

They both walked into the house, Brayden took Kale around to every room. He made sure to point out the exact things they had changed. It seemed like forever to Kale since he had seen Brayden. This felt unusual to Kale but that feeling reminded him how much he depended on Brayden.

"So Weston, what are your plans for getting Skyler?" At times Brayden could be precocious. He wanted what was best for Kale.

"I don't have a plan, why would I? If she is goin' to fall in love with me she will, I can't force her to love me. Besides, who knows if she is stayin' in Texas?" He knew he needed to work on his bull shitting.

"You won't know unless you ask." Brayden shook his head. It was simple as that, though to Kale nothing was simple unless it was to the point and out on the table.

"I know but I'm sure since I'm sleepin' here and she is sleepin' at the hotel there won't be much interaction." Kale knew Brayden wouldn't believe him.

"Kale, you could miss out on a lifetime of happiness. I'm sure the next guy who walks into the sports medicine room will try his luck with her. Kale she ain't ugly. It's not like people ain't going to try and get her attention. While she will be out with this Mr. other guy character you will be formulating the perfect moment. While possibly the perfect moment has passed you right by. Kale dude... I don't know what moment you're waiting for because right now everything is a perfect moment. Go after her man, balls to the wall." Brayden hoped his illustration would be painted clearly in Kale's mind.

Kale knew Brayden was right; though his father also told him not to press a woman about the subject of love, not until the woman possessed a sense of readiness. He knew deep down inside Sky wasn't ready to be with him, but that didn't stop his heart from longing for her.

At dinner, Dakota could tell Kale was distant. She had no idea what was so different about this girl. What made her any better than the last? It frustrated Dakota sometimes how Kale leaped before he looked. He always saw a future with these girls and to her none of them deserved him. So, she finally got the courage to ask Kale again about Skyler.

"Kale, this Skyler girl, what does she have that other girls you dated didn't?"

"She has a sense of direction. Her dream career is not a house wife. She smiles, and the world seems to pause for a moment. Her eyes, they could incinerate a house if she looked at it hard enough. She holds herself with high esteem."

"Are you sure that's not a delusion inside your head? Are you sure the last name isn't making you fall in love with her?" Dakota was anxious for Kale to respond.

"I didn't even know her last name. I wasn't even sure if Brayden was telling me the truth until I saw that show. I don't think her last name makes her who she is."

"But she is a Pendleton. It makes a world of difference. It would be like people who marry the Cash's they marry on to Johnny and June. Maybe that's why their marriages don't last. I'm not saying you would be the kind of person to do that. Kale…I'm really concerned you're diving in over your head again."

"Thanks Dakota, really; were not even dating and if we were, marriage would be far from our minds."

"By ours you mean yours and hers. Kale you have been in the marriage mindset now for a year. One after the other the women break your heart because she wasn't wife material. Sometimes I don't even think you give the girls a chance because you're so ready to tie yourself down." Dakota didn't falter as she dug into Kale about how he had been acting.

"Not true, it didn't work because we weren't compatible." He shuffled around his green beans on his plate as he spoke.

Brayden interrupted "Kale, Kota has a point. You have been searching this whole continent for the girl of your dreams. Man, sometimes you have to find something close to that dream and let it grow."

"Okay guys, I understand, and I ain't saying that either. So maybe I love the idea of Skyler. Somethin' inside me however tells me its more than Skyler's smile, there is somethin' more supposed to happen there." Kale had reached his breaking point. He was tired of talking about her and getting ridiculed.

"We understand Kale,: they said in unison.

The rest of dinner drifted to talk about the bulls, the land, and of course, there was always the topic of dessert.

Skyler

Skyler landed in Greensboro. She couldn't believe how big the airport was. She went to get her bags and glanced over to see Matt Leeton. Matt was one of the elite riders on tour back in his earlier days. Matt stood at five foot eight inches tall and had a body that screamed athlete. Matt's brownish- black hair was buzzed and his blue eyes were eyeing the floor. Matt was known for his enigmatic nature although friends and family seemed to see another side of Matt. Matt had been one of Skyler's heroes. He had won the world championship and world finals in the same year. His record still stood in stone on the series. It was also Matt's undying devotion to Christ that made Skyler admire him. He used the bible as a road map. He surrounded himself by those who would spiritual help him. Matt's smile made many star struck and in awe of things. To Skyler he was one of her many employees. He could any moment need her assistance. Though of all the riders Matt was starting to become one of Skyler's close friends and she didn't mind that.

"Hey! How are you doin'?" Matt asked catching a glimpse of Skyler from the corner of his eyes.

"Doin' good, how's the thumb? Oh how rude how are you?" She still had trouble communicating to him.

"Still there, it tingles at times. It happens you know accidents; tryin' to make the best of it. I'm doin' great the Lord has been there for me a lot lately." Matt smiled.

"Come in the room Tomorrow night. We'll see what we can do for that tingling. It may need to be stabilized better than that brace you have on it. I think I have somethin' that may help."

"Will do; Sky, thanks for all the attention. It's a measly dislocation, and you are treating like royalty."

"You're royalty, even if you don't see it cowboy. See, I think that lady right over there wants your autograph." Skyler pointed in the distance to a short lady with long brown hair.

Matt laughed, "Sky, that's my mom."

Inside Skyler felt like a huge dork. She knew she had to pay it off. "Well still, you probably should go. You guys seem busy and I need to go check into the hotel." She thought her excuse would make up for her idiocy.

"See you tomorrow, Sky." Matt waved as his voice echoed from the high ceilings of the airport.

She felt like a dunce. There she was talking to her favorite riders and she goofed up. To her Matt was royalty. He had some sort of finesse about him that drew people near. To Skyler, Matt had raw talent that only a bull rider can be born with. Her Dad on the other hand had to learn the things Matt could easily sense once he mounted a bull.

She checked her watch and saw the same yellow bag go around the luggage carousel. She went to the service counter. The line was long and she could only imagine the kind of service that she would get. When it was finally her turn she walked up to the attendant and mentioned that her luggage hadn't shown up. The lady took down Skyler's name and cell phone number. It had been on an adjacent flight to LA.

Skyler checked her carry on for her wallet. She had six hours before she could check into the hotel, she could go shopping She exited the airport and went to the car rental place. She smiled as the man at the register gave her keys to a brand new Ford F-150 King Ranch.

"I have never seen a woman's eyes light up as much as yours when I handed them over a key." The man who appeared to be in his late fifties explained to Skyler.

"Well sir, you gave me keys to my dream vehicle. Grandpa won't buy me one. He says 'a girl shouldn't have that much power under the hood.' "

"Your grandpa sure is old school but most are. Be careful don't let the power get to your head."

"I won't," she said as she finished signing all the paperwork.

She climbed into the driver's side of the black King ranch. She couldn't believe how amazing this truck was compared to her beat up Ranger at home. She took her sunglass out of her purse, put them on, and went to finding the nearest shopping mall in Greensboro.

The drive seemed relatively short when she spotted a strip mall with a few western stores in it. She took the left exit and followed it around to the bigger of the western wear stores. The store was conveniently named Rodeo. She couldn't help but laugh. Her whole laugh had revolved around the sport. It was now the sport that consumed her. She couldn't imagine a better career then the one she was living for a short time. She got out and maneuvered her way to the women's section. She couldn't believe all of the amazing shirts they had for sale. She found one in all her favorite colors. She also rummaged through the jeans to find her size. She made her way to the dressing room, when off in the distance she saw someone who looked familiar. She couldn't remember why the girl appeared to be someone she knew.

She took off her shirt and put on a blue button up. She had a hunch that she picked blue because it was the color of Loren's eyes.

"What do you think Loren? Does it scream professional? Or does it scream I'm a cowgirl addicted to shopping. I thought professional too, so this is definitely a yes."

She couldn't help but smile as she left the dressing room. She thought she had found everything, until out of the corner of her eye she found a sundress hanging on the wall. As she went to try and get it, she couldn't reach it. She knew her short stature would prevent her from easily finding her size.

"Need some help?" A voice behind her rang.

It frightened her at first but after the initial shock she responded.

"Yes, I do. Aren't you….Jace Montgomery's girlfriend?" Skyler felt bad asking but at times she could stick her nose into business and this was one of those times.

"Sure am. How did you know?" She was a little weirded out by the fact she recognized her.

"I work for the BRA, as an Intern. My name is Sky. He talks about you an awful lot to Tate while he is getting his knees iced." Skyler felt a tad more awkward telling her this information.

"Nice to meet you Sky, I'm Shannon. I also guess that's a good thing." She finished sorting through the sizes. "Here you go. It will look great with the boots you have on."

"Thanks. I appreciate all your help Shannon. Maybe I'll see you around this weekend."

"You sure will." Shannon mumbled to her as she walked to check someone else out.

Skyler couldn't see a problem with her, other than the usual buckle bunny ways. She had to try the sundress on. Her mind started drifting to how Kale would react to her in it, she slipped on the green and yellow faded sundress that ruffled at the bottom, and instantly fell in love with it. She quickly changed back and went to pay.

"So did you find everything alright?" Shannon asked in a retail fashion.

"Yeah, I sure did, probably found too much." Skyler laid the pile of clothes on the counter.

"So you say you work for the BRA, I'm guessin' with Tate. Do you know what Jace does all the time?" Her eyebrows rose hoping Skyler could give her any reformation on Jace's whereabouts.

"No, I'm sorry. I use see him and the other cowboys before or after an event. I haven't gone to an after party yet. Most the time I stay in my hotel room." Skyler knew it was typical of girls to worry about their guys whereabouts. It however concerned her how Shannon had a tight leash on Jace.

"Oh I see, I was just wondering. He seems a little distant lately I don't know why. I thought maybe it was another girl." Shannon voice wavered as if she was about to cry.

"I highly doubt that, you are gorgeous. He would be stupid to leave you." Skyler wasn't lying but she also wasn't telling the whole truth.

"Well thank you that was very nice of you. Your total comes to 250.00 dollars."

Skyler took out her checkbook and started to write her check.

"Cute checks, you only imagine all the checks I see, but yours are so cute."

"Thanks, I actually got them custom made. The horse in the background is JB. It was a picture of my Grandpa's ranch last fall. My first Texas fall more beautiful then I could have imagined." Skyler smiled as she remembered taking the picture from the back porch.

"That's awesome. Jace wants to get land in Texas. I don't think I could though, my whole life is in North Carolina." Her smile turned down on her face as she spoke to Skyler.

"That and his best friend, his mentor and his family are here, I don't think you have much to worry about. He wouldn't make a change like that without consulting them first. I don't believe you have anything to worry about." Skyler had a knack for assuring people things would be better than they possibly were. She however couldn't use her talents on herself. Who often times was a pessimist in an optimistic body.

"Well thanks Skyler. You give good advice."

"I should be thanking you for all the great help. I guess we will see each other later." Skyler wasn't exactly thrilled but she had a way with words that didn't let Shannon sense her lack of sincerity.

An uneasy feeling swept over Skyler as she exited the store. She felt sorry for Jace. Loren had told her everything she would ever need to know about the North Carolinian. At times Loren played off the fact that she liked Jace. More often than none Skyler picked up on Loren's senses. Skyler had no clue why but she always believed that Jace and Loren would have made an amazing couple. Loren had the best brains and the athletic ability to match. She had the greatest sense of humor. She was also a troublemaker, exactly the kind of troublemaker Jace Montgomery was. Though she knew Jace would pull Loren into the party scene she had no doubt that Loren would have brought Jace front and center with his religious insecurities.

Skyler's heart couldn't help but ping from the heartbreaking thoughts of

Jace never getting to spend his life with Loren. If Loren was still on Earth would Jace even be dating Loren? Would Loren be the girlfriend Jace dreamed of? She knew Loren would be, but how would Loren's life have changed because of the tall handsome bull rider from Mooresville, North Carolina? She knew those were questions that would never be answered, but she couldn't help but imagine the answers. Loren would have been so happy to have Jace in her life and Jace; well he would have adored Loren. About Loren's life changing of course it would. They wouldn't be less than fifteen miles away anymore. She could hear Loren's Montana accent transform into the infamous North Carolina drawl in her ear.

"So Loren, Jace's girlfriend is kind of nice. I guess if you like buckle bunnies. She is a little too demanding for me. I guess if he is happy then we are happy. Also, Loren, I can't help from laughin' as I'm thinkin' 'bout you with a North Carolina accent. I can only imagine the phone calls. As I'm sure you know they lost my luggage, has to be the first time in ten airplane trips. I had my cute black dress in it. I was goin' to wear it to an after party, but Loren I got that gorgeous sundress. I think it looks pretty amazin' so I could possibly wear that. I better pay attention to the road. This city ain't like where were from and that's for sure." She silenced herself with the radio station. The sounds of Dolly Parton whaled out as the pretty little blonde sang Jolene.

Greensboro was bustling much like Dallas. However, to Skyler Greensboro lacked the same appeal. It was too fast paced for her. She turned the corner and entered the hotel parking lot. She quickly found a place to park. She scrounged around the shopping bags and her carry on, she then headed inside. Her jaws dropped when she saw the long entryway. She had never stayed in hotels this fancy before. She couldn't believe hotels let cowboys in places like these. Most of Skyler's life staying in a hotel was a privilege. The family RV suited her father fine. They would stay out on the rodeo grounds away from the chaos that each city held. She walked up to the service desk to finalize her stay. With keys in hand she walked up the three flights of stairs to her room. She gently set the shopping bags near the dresser and threw herself on the bed. She rolled over on her belly to reach into her carry on. She moved things around and around until she found her teddy bear. Her eyes became heavy as she fell asleep almost instantly.

Kale

The sun shined brightly through the oval window. Kale didn't want to get up. He wasn't ready for his battle against a one ton beast. What he wanted more than anything was another hour, maybe two, of sleep. A day of relaxation and a night of excitement, he knew that this night could and would be exciting, he however couldn't imagine to what degree. He heard pans clanking in the kitchen. He knew with no doubt in his mind it was Dakota. He rolled over and put a pillow over his head but the cling-clank of the pans persisted. At this point he knew there would be no way he would fall back asleep, and no way was he going to lie in bed and look at the ceiling. Rolling out of bed, his feet hitting the cold wooden floor of the loft; he loved what Dakota and Brayden did with the place. On the other hand he didn't imagine how cold it was.

He walked down to the kitchen and saw Dakota over the toaster sticking a bagel in.

"Need some coffee cowboy?" Dakota couldn't help but yawn as she spoke.

"Sure do miss. How much I owe you?" Kale loved to pull her leg at times.

"Nothing, I know you ain't got any money, unless you win some this weekend. Then, half your winnings for new stock I can always use new bulls."

"Hell no. Doesn't your husband give you enough bull allowance for rebuilding up the herd?" Kale was firm. If he won anything this weekend it was going straight to savings.

"My husband, you mean the man asleep right now. The bull money comes from my own job dear. Gosh, I can't believe the things Brayden tells you." Dakota shook her head in disbelief.

"He tells me all the time how much he loves you." Kale figured he should spill a little to her.

"That's good at least!" Dakota exclaimed as she passed Kale a cup of coffee and sat down. They sat in silence. The questions he had about Skyler had been answered last night by Dakota. He didn't think Kota approved of Sky. She didn't even know Skyler. Although, he knew what his heart was telling him. His heart was telling him that she was something worth trying for; but how was he going to try when he had no plan. He wasn't going to give up. He glanced up at Dakota and couldn't help but laugh. Her hair was messy and she came across as if she had a rough night.

"What is so funny....come on and explain it to me cowboy?" She knew something was up.

"Nothin'... I don't remember the last time I saw your hair messy, because at church camp you were all so done up."

"Kale, its eight in the morning, I haven't even gotten around cowboy. I need a little bit of a jolt before I can do things these days." She smiled. She was glad they could still be close after the disagreement last night.

"Need any help with the cattle? I'd be glad to help. It's the least I can do for you guys." Kale didn't know if begging would work but he figured if it was his only option he would get on his knees.

"No, here in a few hours we have to pack up Hectic Handful. Cade said if there was a re-ride then he was in. I need to make sure he is familiar with the arena, so in case the re-ride comes, he can prove to Cade that he is worthy of more than a re-ride option." Dakota's tone changed when she was in competition mode. She knew her bulls could blow the next stock contractors out of the water. Although, Cade hadn't been easy to impress these last few events; Dakota felt Cade was trying to see if she was tough enough. She was more than tough enough and she was ready to show the world that she could conquer the bull riding world with one bull, one bull that would be legendary.

"Dakota, you know what I admire about you?" Kale figured he should help boost her confidence a little.

"What?" Her curiosity was sparked.

"You're smart about your bulls and you believe in their potential. I think my problem is I'm looking for the next legend, but I guess legends are no born, they are made." Kale placed the coffee mug on the table.

"Well, not true. Some legends are born, but the majority of legends are made. Shouldn't you be stretching, maybe box a little bit to get yourself all pumped up before tonight's competition." Normally he was bouncing around the place now. Either running up steps or trying to be the next Muhammad Ali.

"I only do those twenty minutes before my ride." He knew it use to be different but now he made it a pre-ride routine.

They both turned as they heard Brayden walk down the steps.

"Need some coffee, hunnie." Dakota said with a smile.

"Sure do, babe. What are you doing down here so early? Trying to fraternize with my wife, are you?" Brayden questioned Kale.

"I sure am. She makes better conversation then you. Plus you were sleepin'. What was I suppose to do your chores?"

"Would have been nice of you then I would have had time to relax."

Dakota glared at him, she knew he was lying through his teeth. He was always relaxing, using sore muscles as an excuse.

"Baby, don't stare at me that way." Brayden retorted to Dakota who was standing near the sink.

"I can stare however I want you big baby." Dakota started cleaning the dishes.

Kale couldn't believe they were having a disagreement in front of him. Normally, they made those issues less private to those around them. He had a feeling they were play fighting and that all would be well in a few hours.

"So Kale, you predict your score for tonight?" Brayden was trying to put subtle pressure on him.

"Brayden, seriously your makin' me guess. I think it's a no score, you have seen my last few attempts." Kale didn't like his lack of confidence but his riding was suffering.

"Remember bull riding is a game of chance. Guess." Brayden wasn't going to allow him to back out.

"An 88.00 flat, I'll be damn lucky to get that."

"Let's make a small wager. Get an 88.00 flat and I owe you three hundred dollars. You get more than an 88.00 than you owe me three hundred." Brayden knew Kale loved to gamble. Not that he was addicted to it but he loved to prove people wrong.

"Deal this will be too easy." Kale's ego kicked into overdrive.

They both shook hands as Dakota shook her head.

"Sometimes, you both are extremely stupid." She had no problem telling them how dumb they were.

"Why's that," they said in agreement with one another.

" 'Cause three hundred dollars is nothing in bull riding land, we all know this, plus, if Kale gets over an 88, more than likely he will win the round. Three hundred dollars isn't even half the pay out." Her eyes rolled in reflection of how ignorant they were being.

"Yeah, well hunnie, I don't want to take him for all he is worth. Then Skyler will have to be the breadwinner." Brayden arrogantly suggested.

Dakota chimed in; "Well isn't that the way with us?"

"Not all the time." Brayden felt his manhood slipping.

"Not all the time but most." Dakota was assertive with putting Brayden in his place.

Kale became engulfed in the conversation again, "It's a fact. When you marry a bull rider, you don't marry him for his excessive wealth. Most the time he has it spent before he even makes it."

"Oh my gosh! You do have some brains in that thick head of yours." Dakota loved to joke around with Kale. He knew some decisions he had made were stupid.

They all exploded into laughter. It was like old times. Exactly like old times. Kota took Kale's coffee mug and laid it in the sink.

"So boys, what are your game plans?"

"Well, Kale and I can load up Hectic Handful for you, while you get ready for the event tonight. You need to look impressive if Cade is going to keep you as more than a re-ride option. Plus, you have things to do once we get there, so this will be one less hassle for you." Brayden was sucking up to his wife.

"Don't injury him, either one of you, or I will injure you." She shouted with conviction, "and I mean it."

Brayden knew she was under a lot of stress from her parents. They believed marrying Brayden was the biggest mistake Kota made. She took care of him more than he took care of her. He didn't know how to change that. He didn't want a nine to five desk job. He wanted to rodeo, and that's exactly what he did. Brayden leaned over and Kissed Kota before she ran upstairs.

Kale reached over and hit Brayden on the arm. "So you ready for this? I heard this bull was a handful."

"Kale, have you ever been told you're a dork, because you are. You always will be."

"It's better than being a sissy, that's for sure." Kale pushed in the chair he was sitting in.

"I ain't a sissy. I can show you that I ain't a sissy." Brayden shoved the chair under the table and went to put Kale in a headlock.

"How do you think you're going to get out of this one boxing boy? Is it too much for you to handle Kale?" Brayden taunted.

Kale balled up his fist up and lunged it at Brayden's abdomen. Brayden gasped for air before telling Kale exactly how bad it hurt. "Dang you Kale, that freaking hurt."

"I proved a point. So are you gonna cry about it, or are we gonna go load up Hectic Handful for your wife. You can't let this be another broken promise cowboy." Kale knew the buttons that would drive Brayden crazy. He liked to press them from time to time.

"Kale, sometimes you make me mad. I kind of hope you get him as a re-ride and he stomps you into the dirt." Brayden didn't want to see Kale hurt but he also didn't want him to beat him.

"Same here! Although, I'll get away faster than you would; I'm naturally quicker than you." At times their bickering came off as two immature teenagers. There competitive nature perplexed others however. They acted like two brothers, they also fought like siblings.

Skyler

She felt the urge to go on a run. So she put on her tennis shoes, shorts, and an oversize shirt. Her hair got thrown into a messy bun. The temperature outside the hotel was perfect. Eighty five degrees with a lot of sun; so she decided to take a detour through the park; the park was full of trees, people with their oversized dogs, and kids playing on the playground. Sky couldn't imagine living the life they did. If the only part of nature they had was a square plot of land with a man made pond. She figured she would go insane. As the rounded the picnic tables she saw Matt Leeton and Walker Pratt. Walker stood six feet two inches tall. He could be spotted with Matt about one hundred percent of the time. He was the complete opposite of Matt. People loved him for his extroverted personality. Walker was always a man with a gag. He had black hair and brown eyes. His smile was nostalgic and his faith matched only by Matt's.

It was not hard to realize why he and Matt got along. They both were at the same stage in their lives. Walker was Matt's support system and vice versa. They were two best friends sweeping the continent one city at a time. As Skyler approached him the freakiness began.

"What are you two doing so far from the hotel?" Skyler hadn't seen the guys outside the arena or sports medicine room; other than the one time running into Matt at the airport but other than that they seemed like phantoms to her.

'Same thing you are doin'; stretching our legs before we have to lower ourselves into a steel death trap." They both said simultaneously.

"You two spend way to much time together. That was utterly freaky." Skyler knew it wasn't too uncommon for best friends to know what the other one was thinking. Loren and she could do the exact same thing, but in the case of Walker and Matt it seemed bizarre.

"Can't you and your best friend do that?" Matt wondered.

"We could, boy we could, but she isn't here anymore. I don't have many friends except for grandpa." She still found the strength to smile.

"Sorry Sky," Matt muttered sympathetically. "I didn't know." He looked identical to a deer in the headlights. He had no clue if he had offended her but hoped with all his heart he hadn't.

"I know you didn't know. Its okay, it's been almost five years. I have learned to adapt. That and my long distance calls to heaven every day can't be cheap."

They both laughed, "Skyler I'm sure it's free. Remember God died for us. So our salvation is free." Walker had a way with words when it came to religion.

"Yeah, salvation is free. I don't think however that includes a twenty-four-hour-a-day long distance phone call. Who knows, God may start chargin' me for holdin' up his phone line."

They were amused by Skyler's explanation of things.

"Want to run back to the hotel with us?" They both motioned extending the invitation to her.

"Sure, you have to remember I'm shorter than both of you, so keep your strides short. If I get lost you guys will be screwed tonight." She emphasized the screwed part. She loved her job and knew the cowboys would be shit out of luck if they couldn't have wrists taped, braces put on, and a little pain management. The three of them took off in the direction of the hotel.

Kale

Showing up at the arena made his nerves jump threw his skin. He wanted a strong showing. He didn't want to let his family down. He didn't want to let his fans down. He helped Dakota and Brayden unload Hectic Handful. He hadn't noticed how muscular he was compared to his pen mats. Rapid Revolver and Twisted Texas were the typical American Brahma bull. They where massive weight wise, but their weight is what gave them the maximum power to buck off even the top cowboys. Their sire was the legendary Yellin' Jasper and much like their father before them, they had a reputation for elimination, high marked rides, and a cocky exit from the arena. They came from Harley and Donaldson. A father- son team who had claimed the top tours prize of stock contractors of the year twice already. Kale saw Mr. Donaldson approach from the corner of his eye.

"Hey, Kale." Mr. Donaldson had known Kale for a long time. Kale use to ride their practice pin when he was younger.

'Howdy, Mr. Donaldson. You have some amazin' stock here. Rapid revolver is sure to help some guy put up a high marked ride this evening."

"It's your luck then Kale, you've drawn him tonight." He muttered with a tinge of excitement.

Kale smiled at Mr. Donaldson a man who stood five feet 5 inches tall. His short cropped hair hiding under a cowboy hat: sporting his leather contractor jacket from the finals, and his finest black snake skin boots. His crooked smile reflected back to Kale. Kale was petrified and he couldn't help but want to vomit.

"Good Luck Kale, don't stare at your competition too long. He's smart enough to psych out his opponents." Mr. Donaldson chuckled.

"I'm sure he can, he has a boxer's mindset I can see it in his enormous eyes." Kale retorted, swallowing the big lump in his throat.

"Sure does, whatever you mean by that. I'll see you in a bit. I'm goin' to check back at home with the wife. See how the rest of the stock is doin'."

"Alright, hope everythin' is goin' we'll tell your wife I said Hi." Kale again smiled.

As Mr. Donaldson exited the holding pens all Kale wanted to do was run to the bathroom. He didn't want Dakota to see him as a wimp.

"What's wrong Kale?" He appeared pale which worried Dakota.

"For the first time in my life, I'm lettin' a draw effect me. Holy Cow! I can't ride Rapid Revolver, the last guy who rode him well...you know he got his face smashed. I can't even recall the last few rides on him sense then." His palms were sweating, and the lump in his throat seemed to be growing bigger by the minute.

"Kale, chill, you can ride anything you put your mind to. Remember everything your Dad taught you. You ruled this arena last year. It ain't going to be any different this year. You better go catch up to the rest of the guys. Plus, who knows if mystery girl is somewhere around here. Kale, I'm rooting for you Bud." Dakota wanted him to be at ease. She believed he could ride anything he put his mind too. She wanted him to believe that as well. Dakota went in to give Kale a hug. He smiled at her as he walked down the hallway to the locker room.

"What took you so long to get in here Kale?" Brayden asked a little surprised at Kale's late entry into the locker room.

"A little moment I had to get taken care of it all." Kale didn't want to tell Brayden he had a mental breakdown. The least he needed was Brayden picking on him.

"You went and saw Skyler?" Brayden was shocked.

"No, I didn't. It's fine though, I have bigger fish to fry." Kale paced the locker room before he went to his bag and pulled out his rope to start brushing off the old resin.

"What do you mean?" Brayden curiosity got the best of him.

"I mean Rapid Revolver." He could feel the ridicule coming.

Brayden shook his head at Kale. He was being such a baby about it. If he was so scared of Rapid Revolver than why didn't Kale quit right then.

"Kale, really dude: go out there and cowboy up!"

Skyler

She finished unpacking her bag when Matt walked in.

"Hey Skyler, Someone told me you had a miracle cure for dislocated thumbs." He was trying to make her smile.

"Not a cure a solution. Come over here and take a seat." She patted the nearest bench.

She gently pulled Matt's thumb back into place and put a brace over it.

"I'm goin' to wrap it around a few more times to stabilize it. You ain't hurtin' are you?" She could only imagine the pain he was in from his small cringes.

"I'm fine Sky. I trust you. You ain't gotta tell me what your doin'." Matt did trust her. She knew what she was doing.

Skyler stayed calm as she heard the door open. It was Dr. Feldman. She finished taping around Matt's brace.

"Geez, Skyler, miracle worker not even jokin'. I can actually kind of bend my thumb."

"Yeah don't bend it to much you don't want to jolt the bone more than it needs to be. It was the technique it wasn't me." She couldn't help but cock a smile.

"Sky, don't be so modest. You'll make a great assistant one day." He added the last part to stir thoughts in Dr. Feldman's mind.

"Thank, cowboy. You better run, they're about to announce everyone soon. If you ain't out there it may be kinda funny when they say your name and you don't walk out. It could also be embarassin'." She knew she would laugh but she couldn't imagine what it would be like being Matt.

"Thanks again, Sky."

She watched as Matt left the room.

"Well Skyler, you told Matt he would be late, but you my intern are about to be late yourself." Tate liked to tease her.

She didn't mind Tate's teasing. She also couldn't believe she would be standing behind the chutes with Tate making sure all was well in the arena. She was going to be submerged in her dream tenfold. The one she and Loren would giggle about until all hours of the night. Loren always wanted Sky's dreams to come true. As she recalled Loren she felt her heart ache. She knew Loren was rejoicing with her but she wanted Loren to be there. To scream with her, to be able to go to the after party with her; she knew she was there, but only in her mind and heart.

As the round got underway, Skyler's nerves inched from the tips of her toes to the top of her head. She had never been face to face with danger. Sure when her father was a rider she saw it from the stands but from the seats you couldn't feel the sense of apprehension from the riders. It was a feeling foreign to Skyler. She saw bull riders as fearless but in those short moments; she remembered that they were human too.

Nothing medically important went down in the first half of the round. Skyler took in the sights and sounds; the roar of the crowd, the bright lights, the barrel mans crazy antics, and of course all the hustle and bustle of bull riders, and stock contractors. Sky felt in her element, nothing else in the world felt so safe. Matt walked up smiling.

"What cowboy? What you grinnin' for?" Sky was confused.

"Nothin', looked like you needed to be knocked back into reality, you were getting' pretty cross-eyed. I'm grinnin' because my thumb doesn't even hurt. Where did you learn that technique?"

"From graduate school, I had to use it on a few of the freshman on the football team. Tacklin' wrong can cause a lot of problems; a thumb dislocation is one of them." Skyler felt a little nerdy as she rambled on.

"Wow, didn't know you treated all sports." He could tell by the look in her eyes she didn't want to treat all sports she wanted to treat bull riders.

"Yeah, but rodeo is definitely my favorite. That and baseball."

Matt knew why so he wasn't going to ask. "What are you doin' tonight? Walker and I were goin' to the after party for a bit. We were wonderin' if you wanted to come along and talk, dance maybe." Matt wanted to get to the bottom of Skyler keeping herself bottled up inside.

"I feel like you guy's little sister. It's like your tryin' to protect me from the big, bad bull riders. I ain't 18 anymore Matt. I know who is wrong to hang out with and who is okay." Skyler seriously felt seventeen again and like she had to check in with her older brother.

She loved Matt and Walker's concern but she was a big girl and she got a little offensive.

"Someone had to protect you, so we stepped up to the plate." Matt laughed. He hadn't laughed in front of Skyler, but the look on her face told him a different story.

"Thanks. I appreciate it, but I'll probably go back to the hotel, watch a mushy love story on television, cry myself to sleep, and do it all over again tomorrow." She could tell Matt was becoming bored with the conversation.

"Skyler, you're such a girl."

'Well, if it wasn't obvious enough, I'm glad you figured it out cowboy." She waved as Matt walked away holding his head in shame. She had won this round with him.

Matt walked away in disbelief. He had never found someone to match his wits before Skyler. Sometimes he thought there was no way to push her off the top of her game.

Skyler couldn't help but share her head. What was Matt so concerned about? That she would fall in love with one of his competitors, lose all sight of herself and fall into the forbidden love triangle of a cowboy, the love of their life, and a one night stand.

The second half began and Skyler was ecstatic for the action to continue. She saw B.J. Jones ride Raging Thunder for an 86.25. It wasn't soon after B.J.'s ride that his friend, Tommy Blakely, was out of the chute. The ride only lasted a few seconds, as the crowd gasped at the sight of the bulls' hind leg coming down on Tommy's ankle. Skyler jumped from her place behind the chutes and went running down the stairs. It seemed to happen so fast, her boot slide off the third step, and there she was in a freefall. It was all a blur but she could feel a set of arms belonging to a cowboy wrap around her. Pulling her close to him and to safety; as the blurry vision subsided she was face to face with Kale. He had caught her.

"Funny how we always seem to meet this way," Kale thought he was being nice by poking fun at the situation.

"Yeah, it really is Kale, but I have to help Tate. Tommy's hurt, I got to go." The words couldn't have flown out of her mouth any quicker. She left Kale's arms in a trail of dust.

She felt bad for not saying thank you. He wasn't her top priority right then. It was Tommy, and that was who she was going to focus on. She saw as Tate and Blake carried Tommy to the table in the room. For the first time in her life, treatment seemed to be out of her reach. Everyone was barking orders out and here she was trying to decipher them. It didn't take long for them to diagnose his ankle was broken and he had to be send off to the hospital to get x-rays and for them to set it for him.

"Skyler, I can't throw anything at you that you can't handle." Tate's excitement was flowing out of him.

"I'm sure you could sir, but the name of the game here is to find the problem, fix it, and if you can't then send them off to someone who can. That's the game plan I play by, sir." Skyler felt like she had said too much but hoped that Tate could see through her complicated explanation.

"True but most things are stable until a later date. He just needed immediate care beyond out controls. After the round is over I'm going to go check on him. Would you like to go on a follow up visit?" Tate phrased questions so simply it seemed. Of course she wanted to go. This was her first big case since she had started the tour.

"I would love too. I know he is in the best hands right now, so I won't worry much about him." She was lying threw her teeth but she knew worrying was a sign of weakness.

"Yeah, you never worry in this line of work. Worrying is being untrusting of the rest of the doctors in the field. This field works because we all trust each other's judgments." Tate's stern explanation made it clear to Skyler why she had fallen in love with the occupation so many years ago. It was knowing you can't be wrong, knowing your team is there to help, and knowing when to hold the patient and fix them, and when to fold them and send them to some other specialist.

Skyler smiled, she couldn't believe that Tate and her shared similar philosophies. She still laws worried about Tommy. It was female nature to worry. He was her second ankle case and he was the worst. She grabbed a bottle of water and went back out to man the chutes again. She wanted to find Kale to apologize for her rude behavior towards him. She realized he was lowering into the chute on Rapid Revolver. She couldn't talk with him now. She suddenly couldn't think straight, what happened if he got hurt too? What happened if she never got to tell him thank you?

Sweat started dripping from the brim of her hat. She took her hat off and used her sleeve to wipe away the sweat beads. It seemed like Kale was in the chute for a lifetime. In one swift movement of time Rapid Revolver shot straight out into the arena. He had been like a bullet from a Revolver. The dirt kicked up behind the chutes like gun smoke. She couldn't believe for the bulls' size that he could kick so high in the air. She found out for the first time why Kale loved riding bulls. He had the perfect counteraction, he seemed glued to the center no matter which direction Rapid spun. This Revolver was out of rounds and out of luck. Kale had conquered him in what felt like a historic moment in bull riding history. He had only been the second guy to cover him in Rapid Revolvers two years on tour. As the dust settled she could see Kale smiling. He had overcome one bull thus far. She knew he had two more to conquer before he could take a buckle home. She couldn't fight the urge to scream so she did "Way to go Kale!" she smiled as he turned and smiled back. The loudspeaker crackled with the sound of the announcer's voice.

"Well....well ladies and gentleman I know you thought that ride was exciting, too. How about a 90.0 point ride for Kale Weston, Greensboro, let's show him off." The announcer whistled as the roar of the crowd became an inferno of screams.

Kale

A smile felt cemented onto his face as he approached the rodeo clown. He threw a few quick jabs before walking over to him and giving him a high five. They had performed this duet often after Kale's successful ride. It wasn't only Kale's way to showcase his boxing skills and get a laugh from the crowd. The sound of the loudspeaker continued to echo in his hears. 90.00 points had been far from his grasp for too long. As he exited the arena he ran into Brayden.

"I guess you owe me three hundred dollars then." Brayden interjected as he gave Kale a hug.

"Sure do, a deals a deal. Three hundred dollars ain't worth nothin' as the feelin' of ridin' Rapid Revolver." He sounded out of breathe as he pulled from his friends embrace.

"Yeah, I'm sure man. Right now you are in bliss mode." Brayden knew the euphoric feeling. He could sense Kale's triumph with him.

Brayden tipped his hat to Kale as he wiggled his way through the crowd lined up to congratulate him. As the sea of riders slowly tampered off he spotted a black Stetson hat heading his way. As B.J. turned to leave she appeared in front of him. Smiling in front of him was Skyler he could see the excitement in her eyes.

"Nice ride cowboy. About earlier, thank you for catchin' me. It could have been embarassin'." Her face glowed like a light bulb.

"You're welcome; I just did what I was supposed to do. Thanks for the support." He wanted to pull her close but knew if he did it would probably scare her off.

"I give credit to those who deserve it, you cowboy could have been higher out there had you spurred a little more, but its okay." I understand you're not a flashy rider." Skyler admitted with assertion.

"Kale didn't know what to say, her eyes spoke words she didn't speak. Her smile, her mesmerizing smile hypnotized him.

"So, what are you doin' tonight? I saw you talking to Matt earlier." He didn't want to pry into her life too much.

"Yeah, we were. We talk a lot. He is like my big brother; it's weird. I'm not sure, more than likely goin' to check on Tommy."

"Oh, I see. Well, I guess I'll see you tomorrow."

He couldn't believe it, he blew her off. Why didn't he ask her to go to the after party with him? He didn't he hug her?

The perfect moment had risen, and he let it fall. He went walking down the long hallway and found Dakota rubbing down Hectic Handful.

"What did Cade have to say? He was pretty impressive out there." Kale wanted to know everything.

"Pretty impressive, eh? He posted the second highest score in the round. He wants him in Albuquerque. Cade and TJ both and you know as well as I do that only the rank bulls make TJ Mason's event.

Kale hugged her, "I knew you could do it. Make it to the big leagues and knock the socks off of Cade. This tour can't beat you or your bulls."

"Thanks Kale really, I don't know what to do. I want to scream, I want to kiss Brayden but I think he's worried about something. I want to meet that Skyler girl. Don't think you will get out of this mister."

"You can't, she left. She went to check on Tommy with Tate. I have to go to the locker room and meet up with Jace and Brayden. We'll meet you back here before the after party." Kale turned as he continued to explain his situation to Dakota.

"Alright, keep him in line. Don't let any of them buckle bunnies try anything." She yelled hoping Kale was paying attention.

"I won't" trailed behind him as the door to the locker room closed. The locker room seemed quit as he entered. He had no clue why a hush seemed frozen over the room. He went to his duffle bag and found a note sitting on top of it. He gently unfolded it to reveal a letter.
****

You did amazin' tonight. I couldn't believe how great your ride was. I will be at the after party tonight. Find me. I'll be in the color of envy, but for you think John Deere tractor. I'll have a drink in my hand. It would be hard to miss me, when my eyes have met yours. Don't forget, the littlest details.

∎••∎
Signed,
Scarlett O'Hara
****

"Who do you think it is Kale?" Brayden wasted no time asking the tough question.

"Well, I'm flattered and all. I just don't know who it could be. Only a few girls have access back here. Does she know it's impossible to find people at after parties?" Kale seemed a little flustered. He didn't want this to be one huge joke but again he couldn't help but wonder who it was.

"Kale, it ain't hard to pay someone to get back here and slip a note or something." Jace responded as he pulled his bag out of his locker.

"True, your girlfriend does it all the time. Why would she have signed it Scarlett O'Hara?"

"Kale, it's in a book. *Gone with the Wind* you ever read it. I guess she wants to be your southern belle or something. She sure has a brain on her though." Matt seem to find a convenient time to chime in.

"Scarlett O'Hara, huh? Well, she won't be a secret for long."

Kale and the rest of the guys exited into the arena to sign autographs.

"Awesome ride tonight Kale," rang from a fans voice.

"Thank you, I appreciate it." He took a quick glance at her eyes, and felt nothing.

He had a strange feeling about the note. He wanted it to be Skyler. She said she was going to see Tommy, but she didn't say she wasn't going to the after party. As he finished signing autographs and taking pictures, he approached Matt.

"So, can you tell me anything about Skyler?" He knew other than Tate. Matt would be the closest to get answers from.

"Great, Smart, and Athletic. Why? You think she is Scarlett O'Hara." Matt tone didn't settle well with Kale's heart.

"I don't know. I guess kind of, or at least I hope it's her." His voice held a hint of hope.

"Kale, Skyler has a few more events, then back to school to graduate. Tate doesn't have an opening on the team right now. More than likely, after graduation Skyler is going to be back on a Boeing 747 to Billings, Montana. Don't allow yourself to get your hopes up." Matt turned to leave Kale with his own thoughts.

Kale didn't understand Matt or anyone else for that matter. He was exactly the same as Dakota, and Brayden. What about the possibility? Tate could lose someone, Skyler sure seemed to get along great with him, the spot was hers guaranteed. However, that wasn't true. Tate had liked most of his interns; he had a large pool to work with. Skyler, however was at the bottom of the totem pole.

Skyler

Entering the hospital with Tate made Skyler feel a little uneasy; the last time she had been in a hospital was the day her grandmother died. It was a feeling that still held her prisoner. She tried to shake it off, but she knew her body language spoke differently.

"What's wrong Sky, don't like hospitals." Tate mustered.

"No, it's I haven't really been in one since my Grandma died. I know they help people, but they couldn't help her. It's a wound I haven't let heal up because I know the pain it's left for my Grandfather."

"Skyler, you wear your heart on your sleeve. You're the most genuine person I know, and here I haven't asked you anything about your life. I only ask about school, and ask you to prove to me your worth it." Tate seemed a little disappointed in himself.

"I thought that's what internships were, job skill training. I didn't know that the person you are interning for needed to be able to write a biography over you later. I don't hold it against you Tate. I do need to prove myself. How else do you see the passion?" Skyler was determined to let Tate know he had done nothing wrong.

"Skyler, you're funny. No, I guess what I meant or was trying to say was I wanted to get the person behind the smile. I know you have passion Skyler. I don't have to pressure you into showing it to me. If you didn't have passion for it you wouldn't have tried as hard as you did. You also wouldn't have spun around the first day and befriending Matt and the others would be far from your mind. I have seen the passion, determination and drive. Now, I want to get to see the inner Skyler." Tate knew he had sparked something in Skyler's mind.

"Well, sir, you would be in for a long night. Plus, this isn't about me. It's about how Tommy is doin'." She politely declined the offer to spell her guts to him.

They walked into Tommy's room. He was sitting up and smiling.

"How are you feeling?" Tate asked.

"Fine doc, I feel as if I can ride tomorrow." Tommy wanted to try his best to convince Dr. Feldman that was a true statement.

"To bad you can't, but, Skyler here can put together a program for you. You can start it after the bones heal. I trust her, and I think you should too. She is smart and I don't say that about anyone you know. I mean it too Tommy. You and Skyler can exchange numbers and Keep in touch." Tate's assertiveness made Skyler feel good inside. Skyler scribbled down her name and number.

"Start the healin' process cowboy, the faster you heal the faster you can be back to ridin' the rank ones." She said with assurance.

Tate and Skyler left the room as the nurse walked in.

"You sure do have faith in these guys don't you?"

"I believe you should have faith in everyone, Tate. Some people, well, they will surprise you, but a surprise is better than nothing. Without believing and faith, where would this world be?" Skyler sensed that she had nailed Tate to a wall he was unfamiliar with.

'I don't know Sky, I don't know. I will see you tomorrow night though, kiddo. So have fun tonight, don't go gettin' into trouble." He wrapped his arms around her. It didn't last long before she pulled away laughing.

"I won't sir, I promise I won't. I'll be with Matt and Walker. I am sure they will keep me in line."

Skyler exited the hospital and searched the parking lot until she found her truck. She drove back to the hotel in silence. The parking lot was full of guest and fans coming to celebrate the BRA's legacy of rank rides and even ranker parties. She ran upstairs as quick as she could and opened her room. The dress lay perfectly on the bed. Waiting for her to slip into it, as she lifted it over her head she could feel the material start to hug her body. After straightening her hair and putting on make-up she closed the door and walked down the staircase. She could see the overflow from the room that was specially designed for the BRA's after party. She had no clue if in the swarms of people she would be able to find Matt and Walker. She also doubted she would find Kale. She didn't even know if Kale got her note, what if he thought it was a joke? She walked over to the bar and waited in line to get a drink.

"What can I get for a pretty lady like you?" The bartender said in the way any Casanova would.

"A jack on the rocks." Her voice stung with disgust.

"You're telling me a beautiful girl like you can drink Jack straight up?" He seemed a little flabbergasted.

"I ordered it, didn't I?" She cocked her eyebrow and threw a bit of attitude his way.

The bar tender was astonished by her reaction. He turned around and made he drink.

"That'll be $6.00" He snarled.

Skyler took out eight bucks and slammed it on the counter. She walked away, hoping she would find Kale. She soon ran into B.J. Jones instead.

"Hey, how's Tommy?" The words couldn't have come out of his mouth any smoother.

"Hey, B.J., he's doin' fine there's nothin' to worry about. His bones need to work some magic. Who knows? Before too long he will be back ridin' bulls like Hectic Handful." Skyler wanted to assure B.J. but she also didn't have all the facts which made it hard.

"Sky, you um you sure know about rodeo. I don't want to impose but why?" The alcohol was starting to settle in.

"My father was a bull rider. You know him, but I don't want to say his name. I'm sure you would figure out real quick if you wanted too." Her half smile seemed to spark a game with B.J.

"Well…I have…kinda….sortaaa…heard, you may be Ben Pendle…Pendleton's daughter." The slur was becoming quit pronounced.

"Those ain't rumors B.J. they're facts, but let's keep that out of the rumor mill, alright! I'll see you tomorrow cowboy." Skyler winked knowing B.J. was likely to forget by the morning who he had talked to. She figured by now, his own name was becoming fuzzy. She was on a mission though. To find her Romeo, but had a feeling he wasn't looking for Scarlett O'Hara. He was probably playing a drinking game with Brayden, or dancing with some buckle bunny. For all she knew he could be in bed with a buckle bunny. She didn't want to think about that too much. She walked around aimlessly for an hour when Matt and Walker approached.

"Hey guys, fancy seenin' you here." She smiled. She could find her way to Matt and Walker with blindfolded and her hands tied behind her back. It was something about the three of them that tended to gravitate towards each other.

"More like fancy seeing you here. Look at that dress, you sure clean up nice. Those are definitely your colors sister; all that green and yellow following perfectly, to the ruffled bottom." Walker was doing his best to make her laugh. He couldn't help but grin.

"Thanks! You two don't look bad yourselves." She smiled trying not to laugh.

The three of them found an empty table and went to sit down.

'Sky, you're pretty distant tonight what's wrong?" Matt was a little concerned.

"Ah, nothin' really. Takin' in what this after party thing is all about." Lying threw her teeth was not one of Sky's fortes.

"Skyler, you can't hold things in forever. You know that right? Sometimes you have to let it out." As Matt spoke Walker shook his head to back up Matt's statement.

She couldn't believe how they could both make her smile. Though the both pressed the hard questions she knew they cared. She knew they wanted what was best for her. Something she hadn't had seen Loren. She decided to tell Matt the truth.

"Why can't I, but, I guess if you need to know...it's this guy. He drives me crazy. Not bad crazy, but crazy. He seems to have some force field around me. It's annoyin' 'cause I can't run from it. I also obviously can't hide it." Skyler felt weird confessing everything to Matt and Walker. She knew her secret was safe with them and leaving the name for them to figure out was all part of her plan.

"Well thank you, Skyler; you can drive me nuts with your knowledge sometimes." Walker commented sarcastically.

"Funny Walker, you're really funny. I guess I haven't experienced enough to know if he likes me or not. I shouldn't be tellin' you guys this. Really, you don't find this weird?"

"What's so wrong about it, because this would be classified as girl talk in some circumstances? Well Skyler, unlike popular belief, cowboys have a high cognitive ability.

No I don't find it weird because you're my friend." Matt expressed with conviction.

"It's not that, it's awkward. I haven't really told anyone but Loren things that were on my mind. I guess it was a comfort thing, and now, well, I still haven't gotten comfortable with a ton of people knowing my business." Skyler felt like a freak. Matt and Walker wouldn't judge her no matter what. She was certain of that, but, her heart still closed like a safe; so unwilling to open up for anyone even Matt and Walker.

"Ahh, so that's why you don't tell us you're related to Ben Pendleton?" Matt didn't want to press her buttons.

"It's not that, it's. Many people believe he cheated his way to a world championship, and I'm tired of havin' to defend him. I'm flat tired of dealin' with it." The whiskey had amplified her frustration with her father.

"Sorry, Sky. I can't imagine what you go through with all those rumors. You know they ain't true right. Your dad he won it fair and square." Matt wanted her to see that if she let the rumors eat her up that it wouldn't help her any.

"Geez Matt, don't go getting all mushy on me. It's not really a big deal. I need to let it go, but for some reason I can't. I have learned to deal with it though. He is my father, I adore him, and he is goin' to be my Dad forever so."

Skyler's words seem to emanate what her heart felt but her mouth never spoke of.

"True." Matt and Walker added.

Skyler smiled, "Well guys. I think I'm gonna head back to my room. See you tomorrow at church." She pushed in her chair and exited before she could hear there response. She couldn't stick around any longer and obviously, Kale had disregarded the note. She didn't blame him; maybe he didn't believe there was really a girl. It could have easily been a prank now that she thought about it.

She opened her hotel door, as she walked in she saw flowers on her nightstand. Her jaw dropped. Who in the heck send her these? She wondered as she slowly approached the flowers. A small card laid neatly on a stand in the center of the flowers. She pulled the card from its base and opened it.
■■

You looked so beautiful tonight. I hope you had fun. I hope these flowers will remind you of your beauty.
Rhett Butler
****

Skyler was floored. She couldn't believe it. Similar to what she had done to Kale. This couldn't be Kale? She thought he had no clue she was Scarlett O'Hara. Or did he? She pulled out one of the yellow roses and fell on her bed. If Loren was still alive she would have called her screaming. So, Skyler did the next best thing.

"So Loren, who is it? I know you can't tell me, it's all about the mystery. I can't believe it. I never even thought anyone could be my Rhett Butler except for Kale. That's not true though, he doesn't even know I'm Scarlett O'Hara. I'm sure of that. Lor, you think I can solve this mystery before I go back to school? I want to Loren; I want to know who this gentleman is. I hope you're having a good night Loren. Sweet dreams angel.

Kale

He couldn't believe she hadn't shown up. She said she would be there dressed in the colors of a tractor: a drink in her hand, and her hair all done. None of the girls he encountered seem to create the same feeling he imagined he had with Ms. Scarlett O'Hara.

"Brayden, I wonder if the note was all a joke." Kale's voice quivered.

"Maybe, Scarlett O'Hara got busy. You believe in Skyler so much, so maybe you should believe in this Scarlett O'Hara character too." Brayden was tired of Kale's whining. If he wanted Skyler then he wanted him to go for her without hesitation. If he wanted mystery girl, then he wanted Kale to pursue her.

"I believe Scarlett O'Hara is Skyler. That is why I sent flowers to her room tonight." He hoped his last minute attempt would catch her attention.

"Maybe she did go, who knows; maybe she got caught up in something. People forget sometimes." Brayden rolled his eyes.

"Skyler wouldn't forget, though. She couldn't have forgotten." Kale shook his head. He couldn't see why Skyler would play games with someone. That is why his mind told him he was wrong though his heart to him he had the right thought.

"She could have Kale. She is human. So many people come to after parties. It was her first time. Maybe she lost hope in finding you. Why don't you ask her yourself tomorrow at church."

Kale couldn't believe Brayden. He only believes in the things he wanted to believe. Skyler was something he couldn't understand. She was too intelligent to lead him on. She was too sweet to play tricks on him. As he climbed into the truck, he started to doze off as he starred out the window. All that encompassed him was Skyler's hazel eyes and the mystery of Scarlett O'Hara.

Skyler

The morning came swiftly as the sun peaked over the horizon. Skyler was dancing around her room trying to figure out what she would wear to church. She searched her bag until she found a cute skirt, her blue button up. She then went to pack her bag for work; throwing her jeans and work shirt quickly in the bag. She took mousse and scrunched her hair. She applied a little make up and stood at the mirror in disbelief as she gazed at herself in the mirror. She checked her watch and realized it was time for her to leave. When she arrived at the arena, she smiled as she saw Pastor Trent Price and his wife.

"Good to see you again, Skyler." Pastor Trent said shaking her hand.

"It's great to see you guys, too."

She walked in and found an empty seat a row up from Matt and Walker's families. She looked to her right, and there sat Kale. He looked sad, she hoped it wasn't from the note she left him. She had tried to find him, but she didn't try hard enough. She glanced down at her watch again to check the time. She decided to go to the restroom. She would then decide if she would move near Kale.

She stood in the bathroom talking to herself.

"Skyler, do it. Go sit next to him. He won't bite; he's real sweet. Don't be such a wimp."

She had been so caught up in psyching herself out that she didn't realize anyone had walked in.

"You talk to yourself in mirrors too," interjected Dakota who had a smile on her face.

"Yeah, sometimes when I don't know what to do. I guess it's a habit I acquired." Skyler couldn't help but laugh. She was a little embarrassed but it didn't seem to bother her.

"Well, if you're looking for a place to sit you can always sit next to my husband and I, we have a friend in town from Texas." She wasn't sure if it would give it away or not.

"Sure. I'm Skyler by the way." She continued to smile.

Dakota's jaw dropped discreetly. "So, you're the mystery girl I've been hearing about. I'm Dakota."

"What do you mean?" Skyler scowled as retorted the question back to Dakota.

"Nothin'. We better go take a seat; we don't want to miss anything." She didn't know if the cover up would work.

Skyler found a spot between Brayden and Kale.

"Hey Sky, fancy seeing you here" Kale said somberly.

"You too. Good morning and God bless." She could feel her hands sweat.

"Yeah, you too." Kale was happy to be seeing her.

As they started to sing Skyler was scared Kale might think she had a terrible voice. She had always been shy as she sang. The main reason was she didn't feel her voice sounded as great as everyone else. Though when it came to singing hymns she couldn't help but find herself slowly belting them out. When the singing was over she sat down and looked in Kale's eyes. Something was wrong, something was tearing him up inside. She didn't know what, but she did know she cared about him. She thought about a way to ask him after church about the flowers. However, se the sermon and prayers ended so did her chances.

"Kale, can I talk to you," she asked in a shy tone.

"Sure."

As everyone was exiting the arena, they were the only two who remained in the row.

"I'm really sorry about being so mean, and being so caught up in the moment. I wish I could make it up to you. I was wonderin'; do you know anyone who sends yellow roses to a stranger? Actually this mornin' I found it odd.

There was one single red rose hidden in the thick of them all."

"No, actually most of us on this tour don't know our flowers. We couldn't tell the difference between a dandelion and a daisy. Are you sure it's not someone from school." Kale wanted to cover his tracks up. He didn't want her to have any thought in the world it was him.

"No, I'm not sure that's it thought. I want to find this Rhett Butler character, he has great taste." A smile illuminated her face.

Kale face lit up. He could tell by the sparkle in her eyes he had did good.

"Well, Skyler, I hate to do this to you, but I have to go. Dakota, Brayden, Jace and I have plans to go out to lunch."

"Well, you don't want to break your plans. Have fun."

Kale turned to leave the arena. She couldn't help but stare at his butt. As he climbed the stairs to the concourse she couldn't help but smile. Sitting next to him at church made her feel safe. He again seemed so prefect.

She couldn't believe it had slipped her mind. There was her chance to ask Kale if he was Rhett and she let him leave. It seemed more and more that all they would ever be were a convenience to one another. She didn't want to be Kale's convenience. She wanted to be Kale's Scarlett, his one true love, everything he ever dreamed about and more. Skyler wanted to be with Kale, but she was too chicken to try anything with him.

Kale

He couldn't believe she had sat next to him in church. He loved hearing her angelic voice sing *Amazing Grace.* He also couldn't believe he hasn't asked her to come to lunch with them. He knew that Dakota probably had things to say about her, but he didn't want to hear it. He didn't want anyone to change his mind. He wasn't going to let anyone change it for him either. Skyler was a great girl, even if she didn't open up to others.

"So Kale, Skyler is a sweet girl," Dakota commented sincerely.

"Yeah she is. I can't believe you met her anyways." Kale announced.

"I can, most of you guys see me as a little sister. I know everyone around this tour. It was about time I met the intern, too. She reminds me a lot of me is the funny thing. You should have asked her to lunch."

"I'm sorry, I didn't know I could." Kale figured playing dumb would help his case.

Brayden had no problem stepping in. "It's not that you didn't know you could, you were scared to ask her." He knew it was true. Kale had been acting scared to even talk to her before now.

"I wasn't scared; I figured it was all four of us hangin' out like old times."

Jace couldn't help but laugh, "Bud, you sure do need to lighten up and go for it. Who cares what happens; she would be dumb to reject you. Plus, she is a hot mama; you never know who may try for her if you don't." He winked as if encouraging Kale that if he didn't try for Skyler then he would step in and do it himself.

"Thanks, Jace, really it doesn't matter. She is only here for a short time. I think I got caught up in her pretty face." He was trying to mask the feelings he once exposed to his friends.

Dakota couldn't believe how stupid Kale was sometimes. She saw the way he looked at Skyler. She saw the way he squirmed when Dakota brought her into church, but she also had no room to be pushing him. Dakota looked at her watch.

"Well boys, the three of you are due to the arena here soon. So we better get going."

All four of them exited the small diner and walk to their vehicles.

Skyler

She checked her watch. The round would start in forty five minutes. She had heard the guys thrashing through the hallway. Sometimes she thought they were louder than the bulls bellowing in the back pens. She couldn't help but wonder what she would see on her last night in Greensboro.

She heard the door to the room open.

"Hey Skyler, I was wondering if you had anything to numb my elbow." Her heart quivered as his voice echoed threw her ears. It sent a small shocking pulse throughout her body.

"Sure we do Kale, come sit down. Is there a brace you are supposed to wear?" She figured there was but didn't want to interrogate him.

"Yeah, it's in my bag. I wasn't goin' to put it on." He knew the last statement probably wasn't something he should have told her.

"Well, if your elbow is bothering you then you should put it on. If you want me to help you I can, you wanna go get it? I'll make sure it's fitted right." The stern look on her face prompted Kale to get up and go to the locker room.

Kale exited the room. She couldn't believe she started to see him everywhere now. She didn't mind however getting to see him. He provoked giant butterflies inside her stomach to flutter. She turned to get the numbing medication out of the bag and hoped the butterflies would calm themselves. When she turned around Kale was there.

"So, let's put this on your elbow first. I'll wrap it and then we'll mobilize it in your brace." She sounded like an old tape repeating what you should do in case of an emergency.

"Sounds good to me, but Skyler, you don't have to tell me what you're doin'. I trust your medical judgment." He looked her straight in the eyes. It was the truth and he wanted her to know that.

"Thanks, it means a lot to hear that from you."

She continued to massage the medication into his elbow. She couldn't help but think about how it would be like giving him a massage after a long weekend of riding or cuddling with him and having his strong arms wrap around her.

She took the shrink wrap and slowly tightened around his elbow. The awkward silence was starting to cause her to feel uneasy. What was he thinking? Was he ready to get out of there? Was she wrapping to slow? So finally she decided she needed to ask him how the wrap felt.

"That doesn't hurt does it? You can still bend it a little bit, right?" Her voice came out of her mouth trembling with wonder.

"Yeah, it's prefect." He said trying to assure her she was doing a great job.

Her hand met his as they both moved to roll down his sleeves. Skyler's face reddened and her eyes widened.

"I'm so sorry. I should have known you could do that."

Kale couldn't help but laugh. "Sky, it's fine really. You have two hands, so I'll let you finish."

She could feel her hands clamming up. She didn't want to sweat all over him so she wiped her hands on her pants. She then carefully unrolled each fold in his sleeve. Gazing into his eyes she couldn't help but ignite the fire raging in her heart already. Her heart was screaming to her at this point but she couldn't find the words to tell him. As she got to the end of the sleeve she softly snapped the button.

"Okay, so for the next step you'll need to position the brace where it is most comfortable. Make sure the black circular plates are lined parallel to each other." She stood back as he stood up and grabbed his brace.

"Aye-Aye Capitan, I think I can do that." He pseudo-saluted her like any second in command would do.

As Skyler watched him maneuver his arm in the brace, she couldn't help but feel the urge to laugh. She gingerly bit the bottom of her lip trying not to say anything to him.

"What Doc? What am I doin' wrong here?" Kale smiled. He could see by the look in his eyes she loved to hear him ask questions.

"You're bendin' your arm to much. You slide it on with your arm straightened."

"You didn't tell me that in the instructions." Kale cocked her a little bit of attitude.

"Sorry, it's your brace I figured you wore it every now and again." She shook her head side to side trying not to smile.

"Yeah, right! I barely wear it, maybe that's my problem."

"Could be? Maybe you would get a few more qualified rides with a stable elbow." Her sarcastic nature was starting to show through her shy exterior.

"Okay! Geez, don't dog on me now." He looked at her as if he was mad at her.

"I ain't doggin' on you I want to help you." Skyler exclaimed with a smile. She took control like she always did in many situations. She aligned the brace like it was supposed to be and gently tightened it around his arm.

"Does that hurt? I can loosin' it." She couldn't help but keep a hold of his arm.

"No, feels good actually. Thanks." He slowly removed his arm from her hand. He knew he had to get into the alleyway in a few short moments.

"You better hurry cowboy. Ya'll are about to get announced to the fans of Greensboro."

Kale smiled, "thanks Sky, you're a lifesaver."

"I'm doin' my job. You really should get out there. Good luck, hope you win."

"Thanks," faded behind the sound of the door closing.

Kale

Standing under the lights during the national anthem, Kale could feel the heat radiating off his skin from his heart. It was something about Skyler. Was it the way she could always speak to his heart? Maybe it was the way she got embarrassed when she thought she was doing something wrong?

As they dispersed behind the chutes, all he wanted to do was ride both of his bulls to impress Skyler. He knew she would be watching on the monitor in the Sports Medicine room.

"Hey Kale, how's the elbow?" B.J. asked.

"Fine, it doesn't even hurt. I swear Tate needs to hire Sky." Kale's face lit up with the simple sound of her name.

"Yeah, she's real nice. Tommy says he is truly excited to work with her." B.J. wasn't quite sure about Kale's infatuation with her.

"Who wouldn't? She's beautiful!"

Kale nodded to B.J. and walked back into the locker room. He picked the note in his duffle bag. He could swear it came from Skyler. The way the words flower together, the way the "s" curved, everything screamed Skyler to him. Even the scent of the paper seemed to invoke thoughts of Skyler.

He wanted to ride so bad. He wanted to ride so bad. He wanted Greensboro to scream his name. He laid the letter back into the bag and entered back into the arena.

"Dude, you keep disappearing." Brayden stated as if he was a little pissed off at Kale.

"Sorry, I had a moment. I needed time for myself."

"How much time do you need pretty boy? You're riding in about five minutes." Brayden sounded stern with him.

"Brayden, I'm ready. I'm gonna win this." Kale's confidence couldn't be scattered.

"Keep telling yourself that bud." Brayden followed Kale up the stairs behind the chute. As he approached the Jack Daniels chute he met face to face with his opponent. Tombé was a large American breed bucking bull. He was crossed with a Texas longhorn. Kale didn't want to let his name fool him. Tombé means "to fall" in French, and falling was far from Kale's mind. He lowered himself down into the steel chute. Tombé leaned against Kale's left leg. Brayden took the wooden block to try and push Tombé off of Kale's leg. Kale knew there was no easy way to keep the bull still in the chute so he nodded his head and out into the arena they went.

It was like a war dance. One strong move counteracting another, one strong attitude colliding with another. For once, Kale wasn't thinking about himself or the ride, he was thinking about Skyler. How her smiling face shined brighter than the lights he was riding under. The dance ended in perfect form. The buzzer sounded and Tombé bucked off Kale. Landing on his feet he smiled. Everyone in the arena was on their feet. Kale removed his helmet swiftly and smiled. He felt so good.

It was his first win of the season and it couldn't felt better.

"Geez Kale, where did that come from?" Jace wondered. Normally, it was Jace on the top of the leader board but tonight in Greensboro it illuminated with the name Kale Weston.

"I don't know Jace. Somethin' inside of me told me to hold on, so I did. I made sure Tombé wouldn't make me fall." Kale cracked a smile and took a deep breath.

"Good Job. Congrats." Jace shook Kale's hand.

"Thanks Jace! Thanks for all you and Brayden do. I really wouldn't do great on this tour without you two." Kale said in a appreciative tone.

"No, need to thank me, I know I'm brilliant." Jace muttered cracking his shit face smile.

Kale walked down the alleyway and walked into the Sports Medicine rom. As he opened the door he saw Skyler packing her bag.

"Hey Skyler, I just wanted to tell you thank you. This win is for you!" He felt nervous that she would find his comment weird but he waited patiently for her response.

"Thank you, but I definitely think it was God and you who deserved it. I just wrapped you elbow." The words rang from her mouth modestly.

"Well, still thank you, you definitely are a big help."

"You're welcome Kale, truly welcome." She smiled as she stared into his blue eyes as if she was searching for something.

"I wanted to come by and thank you, but I'm sure you busy getting' ready to leave. Have a safe trip back to Texas. See you in New Mexico." He wanted to hug her goodbye but felt that leaving would be more appropriate.

As he opened the door he heard her voice once again, "You too, don't let anyone take your money cowboy you earned it."

Kale exited the room and walked back towards the locker room smiling.

Skyler

She had a smile radiating from her face. She couldn't believe he thanked her. She couldn't believe he thought she helped him win. It made her feel good. It made her wonder if he was possibly Rhett. He had denied it at church, but maybe that was to keep the mystery going. She picked up her bag and flipped off the light switch.

She exited the arena in the afternoon heat. She slid her sunglasses on and decided to head back to the car rental place. She smiled as she saw the man who had rented the truck out to her.

"How was the truck miss?" He asked with wonder.

"Amazin', it was truly amazing". I will have to get me one of these when I'm done with school."

"Definitely, have a nice trip home."

"Thanks, and you have a great day."

Skyler waited for the airport shuttle bus to pick her up. She pulled out the note that had been attached to the flowers that were not being pressed in her diary. She wanted to know who Rhett was. Something told her it was Kale. She wanted to get close with him, but she didn't know what she would do once she went back to school and he was traveling around the states. He treated her different from the rest of the guys. She only had one major league tour left, and Albuquerque. She trusted Kale though, he was a Christian: he was sweet: and he knew how to make her smile. She sat on the bench trying to figure out what exactly she could do to catch Kale's attention.

When the bus appeared she had two plans, neither of them she liked. She knew she should be up front with him, but her shyness seemed to block her ability to do that. She wanted nothing more than to get back to her grandfather's ranch. She wanted to go on a long ride. She knew that could help her determine the next step to take with Kale, but she also knew it could hinder it.

She couldn't help but think of what Kale would want. Maybe Kale, didn't want to be with her. Maybe kale was already in a relationship, and he didn't know how to break her heart. The clouds outside resembled the clouds floating in her brain.

She wanted courage to ask Kale, to approach him with one simple question. She couldn't find it though. She had another week to devise a plan or a whole week to forget the whole idea. She knew something wouldn't allow her to forget. She softly whispered to herself:

"Loren, I know you find this really childish, like I always was when it came to guys I like. I don't even know if Kale is worth it. To me, he is more than worth it. How many times have I been wrong, thought, Loren? A million times! I'm scared that the same thing will happen with him as it's been with other guys. I feel something more with kale though. It's something about the way he looks into my eyes it drives me nuts Loren. It about time for me to get off this plane so I'll talk to you later Loren; I miss you so much Buckle bunny."

Kale

Getting off the airplane in Dallas, he figured it would be like a normal return home. Though as he turned from the luggage carousel he figured it wasn't. A three year old little girl came running towards him. Her curly blonde hair bouncing as she smiled. She stood about thirty six inches tall and had her pink cowboy boots on. He was astonished to see his niece.

"Uncle Kale, Uncle Kale," Screamed his McKenzie.

"Hey there Kenzie, what are you doin' here beautiful." He murmured a little shocked to see her.

"What do you think I'm doin' silly, I'm here to pick you up and take you back home. I wanted to be the first one to do this." McKenzie leaned in and Kissed Kale's lips.

"Well, to let you know you were the first, and you're goin' to drive me home huh? I guess I better have you sit on my lap then or somethin', no way your feet are reachin' the pedals." He smiled as he tickled his niece playfully.

Kale then caught a glimpse of his mom. She stood at five foot four inches tall, he sandy blonde hair was cut short. Her eyes made up with eye shadow and her smile glistening underneath the lights. Standing next to her was his sister. A five foot six inch beauty, her long hair was straightened and fell to right below her shoulder. She also was smiling in her white t-shirt and blue jeans.

"Oh, I guess I forgot to tell you Grandma and Mommy were here too!" McKenzie looked at him innocently, her small hand resting in his.

Kale laughed. It was great to see them all.

"Great job, little brother," his sister retorted as she wrapped her arms around him. Kale gave her a bear hug.

"Thanks." He kissed his sister's forehead.

McKenzie jumped into her mother's arms. Kale's mother smiled at her son. Giving him the motherly eye she could tell he was a different man then the little boy she had raised.

"Come over here, Kale."

Kale walked over to his mom and wrapped his arms around her tightly. It felt so good to embrace her. It had been awhile since the last time he had seen her. She gently pulled away.

"So, are you comin' to dinner tonight at our house? I know you don't want to go home when you have so many people who want to congratulate you." She tried her best to lure him in.

"Well, I'm goin' wherever you guys are goin'."

Kale's mom smile widened. It was great to get to spend time with her son. McKenzie got down from her mothers' arms and ran between her uncle and grandma.

"I love you Uncle Kale." Her blue eyes sparkling like stars.

"Love you too Kenzie. Let's go get in the car and go to Grandma's." He squeezed out as he lifted her into his arms. When they reached the car Kale buckled McKenzie into her seat and slid in next to her.

"So, what have you been up to Ms. Kenzie? Anythin' excitin' goin' on with you Kenzie?" He gently pressed his finger against her belly. She let out a small laugh.

"Nothin' much... Mommy and I made cookies for Grandma and Grandpa. Also, we got a new doggy, his name is Rascal. He's a lot like your doggy Cooper."

"Really? Sounds like you've been busy, and where are my cookies?" His curiosity showed as he looked at her with his eyes widened.

"Mommy said you didn't need cookies, or else you would get a tummy ache. We don't want you havin' a tummy ache." McKenzie concern for her uncle melted his heart even more.

"Did she now? Well next time, make me a few cookies okay, so I don't get a tummy ache." Kale glanced at his sister and rolled his eyes.

"Okay, Uncle Kale I will do that." Kenzie leaned over and kissed Kale's cheek.

"Thank you, sugar. You're the only girl I need in my life."

"What about Grandma? You need her too." McKenzie scrunched her eyebrows a little confused by her uncle's statement.

"True, you're the second girl I need in my life!" He figured the correction would make her stop contorting her face.

"What about Mommy?" She tilted her head waiting for his answer.

"Mommy doesn't count, 'cause she has your daddy." Kale hoped he had cleared up the whole situation.

"Oh, so when you get married, Grandma won't count?"

"No, she will always count, but the girl I marry comes after you and Grandma. She will be the third most important girl in my life." As he spoke he knew that Skyler wasn't worthy of a third best title. She deserved to be number one. He didn't want to jinx himself.

"Oh well that's good!" McKenzie exclaimed.

Before too long they were turning into the Weston Ranch. Kale couldn't wait to see his Dad and show him his buckle. The ranch stood the same it had for all of eternity. The white picked fence surrounded the house, cattle gates had been left open as all the cattle were sleeping peacefully in the barn. The grass was a lush green. The pale blue house stood in stark contrast to the bright red barn that had been repainted last year. As Kale stepped out of the truck the air smelled like it was about to rain. It wasn't long before he turned the brass doorknob into the house. They walked into a long entry way and Kale could hear the TV on in the living room. It wasn't long before Kenzie took off in that direction.

"Grandpa, Grandpa, look who we brought home." Kenzie squealed.

"Who did you bring back, sweetie?" he said looking her straight in the eye.

"Uncle Kale, Uncle Kale."

"Well, I knew you would be a good decoy to lure him here. Thanks sweetie." He dug in his pockets and pulled out a twenty. He gave it to McKenzie as he kissed her on the lips.

"Thanks Grandpa, it was a pleasure doin' business with you." She looked over the twenty before runnin' off to the kitchen.

Kale shook his head in disgust. "I see now, you're usin' my niece for business matters. Shame on you Dad."

Jake got up from his chair and walked near Kale.

"It was the only way I could get you here. You didn't answer you cell phone."

"Sorry, I didn't mean to, I got caught up in things this weekend." His eyes told the whole story. He's dad could read him like an open book.

"Caught up in what? Is there a girl getting' brought home to us real soon?"

"Not really, we are friends, Dad. How did you know there was a girl?" Kale seemed a little shocked. His dad had the hardest time telling when his mom would get a haircut, but he hit the girl thing like a hammer to a nail.

"The way you're tryin' not to smile, same thing I did when your mother stole my heart."

"She didn't steal my heart, she well….stole my heart." Kale had a hard enough time lying to himself about Sky. There was no way he could lie to his dad.

"Well, what's her name? When will we be meetin' her?" His dad wanted to hear everything about Skyler. Kale on the other hand wanted to give him as little information as possible. He didn't want to be the one to feed the rumor mill.

"Never. She has on major league tour event left and back to school she goes. I don't even know what school she goes too. Her name is Skyler and her dad is Ben Pendleton." Kale knew his father would have some wise remark.

"Ask, Kale. You won't get anywhere without askin'. Don't be scared son. If she means a lot to you, ask her."

"Dad, I know, it's well…it's well." Kale's voice shook as the words left his mind blank and his mouth stuttering.

"Well what son? What's wrong with her?" His father took a sip from his glass as he waited for Kale to speak.

"Nothin' is wrong with her. She's busy all the time. Plus, like I said, I don't know if she has a boyfriend at school, how school is for her, or if she will even have time for me." Kale thought his answer would be good enough.

"Kale, listen, you have to take risks. You take the risk of your life by climbin' on bulls. Let your heart take a risk with this girl. I can see it in your eyes, she has stolen your heart away, and now you're left wonderin' how to get it back."

Kale loved his dad's advice. It was that advice that had told him to start bull riding professionally. It was his advice that always gave him strength in hard times. They hugged each other and made their way to the kitchen for dinner.

Skyler

The night couldn't seem anymore calming from the barn. There were no horses stirring; only her light to write by flickered against the chipped wooden barn. Out of the loft door she could see the stars scattered for miles in the night sky. She tried to figure out the pattern they were following but each star, newly recharged, and changed her way of thinking. She held her diary in her hand and flipped through it. She uncovered past stories she never completed: stories whose lives were lost somewhere between a loss of inspiration and her misguided heart. She had the urge to write. She wanted to write of enchanted love, where she would be taken away by the noblest prince in the land, or maybe a knight defeating all evil for her delicate hand in marriage. She couldn't help but laugh as she remembered all the fairy tales her father told her as a little girl. She drew up her pen; she was armed for battle against the blank page. She was going to find a way to solve her Kale problem by writing. She had no clue what would flow from her head but hoped it would be a masterpiece. As her hand started writing she felt taken away into an uncharted fairy tale.

~~~~~~~~~~~~~~~~~~~~~~~~~~~~~~

Sir Wimbledon was the fiercest knight on a journey to slay the vile dragon named Hectidimus, the foulest dragon in all of Textosiaca. He had stolen his beloved Skylark, the fairest of maidens in all of Textosiaca. He had flown in by night's eerie darkness, and plucked her from her bed of golden acorns. Sire Wimbledon could hear her screaming. From the mountain top he heard her voice shirk calling for help. What he wanted to do most was to save her from Hectidimus evil plans. He had no idea what Hectidimus had in mind but as he thought of the possibility he trembled in fear at the thought of losing his Skylark.

Sir Wimbledon started his ascend on the highest peak of Textosiaca, Mount Dragon Tear. It housed all of the evil dragons in Textosiaca. It was a place of evil doing and also was the darkest place in all of Textosiaca. Sir Wimbledon had no clue how he would rescue Skylark. Would he jab his sharp dagger into Hectidimus's beady black eyes, or would he go straight to his chest and into his cold blooded heart.

~~~~~~~~~~~~~~~~~~~~~~~~~~~~~~

Skyler dropped her pen as she heard the sound of the barn door opening.

"What are you doin' out here Sky? It's cold." Her grandpa couldn't help but worry about her.

"Just catchin' some fresh air Grandpa, I'll be in the house in a minute. Oh Grandpa can JB and I do the mornin' tasks by ourselves tomorrow." She knew he would probably object but it was worth a shot.

"Sure can sport, but are you sure you don't need help. Hun, if this is 'cause your mind needs time to think of this cowboy. I'm gonna give you all the time in the world, but Sky, you need to give time to your own self. I know people say it only takes a year to heal from the loss of someone, but Skyler every day I wake up and wish your grandmother was by my side, and every day I talk to God and her. I see you do that with Loren sometimes. You stand in the kitchen gigglin', and no one is there. When you make cookies I can see you turn to the sink as if you were about to hand Loren something' to wash. Skyler it's okay to do it, and if you're out here because this is the place you held your secret meetings…well I understand. Sky, I heard some of those secrets and I know how hard you are pushin' to complete those secrets and dreams. I see it in your hazel eyes daily. Remember Sky, Loren was a huge part of your life, but Sky you also can't freeze your life 'cause she ain't here hun. I love you." He felt as if he was lecturing her; although, sometimes he felt as if he needed to speak to her in that way to get it through her thick head.

"Yeah, I am Grandpa. Thanks for everythin'...I love you too. Good night."

Skyler didn't like the feeling of blowing her grandfather off like that but every thought of Loren ripped the seams of her heart back open, and out flowed heartache, frustration, and tears. She heard him exit the barn. He could hear his boots sink into the grass. When she could feel that he was most of the way to the house she let out a big yelp. Tears started streaming down her face. Why did loving Kale, make her think of Loren that much more? She knew it was the fact that Loren wanted her with a bull rider; Loren wanted her with a man who could make her happy. Kale was that man, but as she wiped the tears from her cheek she still hadn't solved the problem of how she would get her attention. She dug back around for her pen before she decided to blow out her candle and lay down. As she lay down she looked back at the stars. Wishing there was some kind of address, that way she could send Loren a letter. Requesting for help on how to get Kale's attention; she knew Loren was trying her best to help, but she also was more confused than before.

Kale

He heard a whisper in his ears and felt a small hand rubbing his back.

"Wake up Uncle Kale. I want to make breakfast with you."

"A few more minutes, Kenzie. Please give me a few more minutes." He tugged the covers back over him as he tried to fall back asleep.

"If you don't get up and help me now, when everyone gets up there will be no breakfast." She let out a little attitude.

"Okay, I'm comin' right after you." Kale pushed the covers off the bed and sat up. Kenzie took off towards the kitchen. He stretched quickly before getting up and chasing after her. They ran down the steps towards the kitchen.

"I'm gonna get you." He picked her up and spun her around.

"Uncle Kale, I love when you play with me. It's sad we can't play more." Kenzie face showed her sadness.

"Good, I love to play games too. I promise we will find more time to play once this season is over with." Kale kissed her forehead.

Kale was caught off guard when McKenzie started asking him questions.

"Uncle Kale, when are you goin' to have a cousin for me?"

"Hard question, I have to find you an aunt first. I guess I ain't lookin' hard enough." He felt as if his answer was appropriate but knew by the look on her face it wasn't the last.

"What about the girl you were yellin' at in your dream? She had a pretty name, Skyler I think it was. I imagined this really beautiful girl, and I bet she would make a wonderful aunt."

Kale took a deep breath. Sometimes he hated talking in his sleep. He didn't know how to explain to McKenzie that Skyler and he were nothing but friends. He also didn't know himself if she was in a relationship. So he tried his best to answer her question truthfully.

"Hunnie, I think she would too, but she is a busy person and still in school. Plus, who knows, maybe she is gonna be someone else's aunt soon." He could feel his heart breaking inside.

Kale sat Kenzie on the countertop. He leaned in close to her. "It would be great for her to be your aunt Kenzie really. However, God is pickin' your aunt and if it's Skyler well great.

"You sound mad at God, Uncle Kale."

"Not mad, I'm wonderin' why I keep feelin' my heart danglin' on a string." He knew she would have no idea what he was talking about.

"That's impossible, God wouldn't do that. He loves all of us."

Her naivety comforted Kale. "He sure does. So what was it that you wanted to cook for breakfast, little miss, 'cause we better get started."

"Grandma told me you make a good breakfast burritos; so, I thought those or pancakes. Those are my favorite."

"Well, pancakes hmm. I could do that." He picked McKenzie up and put her back on the ground. "Go grab me the box mix out of the pantry over there. Then we can get started." He pointed to its location and watched as she ran to the door. She carefully brought the box to Kale.

"Okie dokie Uncle Kale, what's next?" She was ready to get started.

"This." He picked her up and sat her on the counter again.

"I'm gonna add these messy eggs, and you're gonna stir as hard as you can. You got that?"

McKenzie nodded. Kale slowly cracked the eggs helping McKenzie stir before he added another one.

"I didn't know pancakes looked like this before they were on the breakfast table." Her face revealed a little disgust for the building blocks of her breakfast.

"Yeah, nothin' comes the way it looks." He assured her.

"Yeah, well these are funny lookin'. Are you sure you didn't mess them up?" She asked a little concerned at her uncle's pancake making ability.

"I'm sure. Let's keep stirring you little rugrat."

"I'm not a rugrat. I don't live under the rug, and I know I'm not a rat."

"It was an expression Kenzie, but its okay. You're my little pumpkin."

"Uncle Kale, stop with those 'pression things, you're not very good."

Kale laughed. He didn't know it would take a simple thing like making pancakes with his niece to realize that he was stressing out way to much about life. God had given this little girl the prettiest smile, the most beautiful eyes, and a charm all her own. He couldn't help but imagine what she would be doing someday.

"Uncle Kale, can I get down and set the table? I think it's time to get that pan hot, and I don't want to get hurt."

He picked her up and held her over the sink to wash the excess batter off her hands. After drying them he laid her down on the floor.

"Uncle Kale, can you get the plates down? Please?"

He reached in the cabinet and gave her five plates.

"Thank you." She said smiling.

Kale quickly started to cook the pancakes as he heard the rest of the family stampede down the steps.

"Mmm....smells good, what are you cookin'." Jake asked Kenzie.

"Silly Grandpa, don't you know what pancakes smell like?" McKenzie muttered.

"I guess my sniffer is off."

"That's okay Grandpa, 'cause they smell so good." She licked her lips as she finished speaking.

McKenzie climbed up into her Grandpa's lap and watched as her uncle accumulated a pile of pancakes. Kale turned off the burner and took them to the table.

"Breakfast is served, thanks to this little one right here." He replied as he scrunched his nose against McKenzie's

They sat in silence enjoying the sun peaking through the windows, and the mound of pancakes on the table.

Skyler

The heat from the sun never felt better. She hadn't left the barn and she hadn't minded the peace and quiet from the sounds around her. She climbed down from the loft, and went to feed the horses, As she placed the lead rope around JB the only thing she wanted to do was ride him far away, but she knew they had a lot of work to do.

Once outside, she quickly prepared him for the days' work. After fastening the saddle to him, she pulled herself on up. JB had always been a little skittish when the rider first got on, but for the first time, Skyler realized how good the ranch had been for JB. It gave him a sense of pride, she figured that much. The round ups, all the fence checks, everything her did made him one more necessity to the team. Something his previous owner didn't realize about him.

JB softly neighed as they stopped along the creek. She saw no problems with the fences surrounding it and JB had no problem with the crisp Creek water. She gave him a small rub down and went to look at the shape of her old tree house. It was rundown. The boards had rotted. It didn't seem so much of the escape that she and Loren had made it to be.

On Sunday afternoons they would come back from church and have picnics in the tree house. They would ride JB and Gunner out, find a nice place for them to graze and climb into the tree house. She remembered it was late June, and the only thing on their minds was the rodeo occurring the next weekend. To them, rodeos were the holy grail of sports. There was nothing tougher than cowboys and cowgirls, gritting their teeth for a chance at a gold buckle and a few measly dollars to pay for their next go around. Loren's take on their obsession always fascinated Skyler. To Loren, it wasn't only an obsession; it was also there way of keeping the west alive. Something Skyler had started a crusade for at their high school in Billings, and no one caught on to the trend, except for Loren. It seemed as if any goofy idea Skyler thought of Loren was right there along side of her.

"So God, I bet you're listenin', I wanted to say thanks, thanks for the opportunities. I know I've been real selfish lately, I want to fix that I really do, but God I want to do what you have sent me here to do. Which I think I'm doin'? I don't want to fall for Kale unless it's the right thing to do, but I'm fallin'. So is it right? Well, I wanted to thank you for all these wonderful and beautiful thing I see, for never leavin' me. I know you never will. You and Loren both."

Tears again graced her face. It had been a long time since she let the pain surface full force. She was taught that cowgirls don't cry, and that was something she had let eat her inside. How was she supposed to move on with her life, if tears weren't supposed to come rolling down after an event like losing her best friend. She started to brush her face against JB's mane. She never believed that he would bring so much joy to her. To her JB wasn't a horse, he was an unforgotten piece of Loren that no one realized but herself. She felt JB life his head and she slowly moved her head out of his mane.

"Ready to head back boy? I know you are you can get a treat. I know how much you like food, you big boy."

She didn't care that he didn't answer. She knew all the answers in her heart. She mounted him and like a speeding jet plan they were off towards the barn.

Kale

The week at his parents' house seemed to fly by and the only thing left was Albuquerque. He didn't want to show too much excitement but the thought of seeing Skyler, for what could possibly be the last time scared him. He wanted to stare in her hazel eyes and tell her everything about the battle raging inside of him. The first time she walked in on him may have been an embarrassment for her, but for him it was a moment of fate set into perpetual motion. It was the start of something new for him. He finally realized things her valued and Skyler overflowed with those values. He couldn't imagine not having to catch her falling down the stairs, or directing her down hallways anymore.

"Well Kiddo, you go show TJ Mason that you're better than any assembly of bulls he has."

"Thanks Mom, and when Kenzie comes back over I left something for her in my old room. Tell her it's important she wears it at all times."

"Will do hunnie. You don't know how much she looks up to you Kale; she wants to be so much like you. She only wants you to be happy."

"I know mom. Where's dad? Is he goin' to come give me his normal pep talk?" Kale was actually hoping the pep talk included more to his father's plans of snagging Skyler.

"He had to run to the feed store, but if you can wait a few minutes he will be back soon." His mother could tell he was ready to leave and something else was on his mind.

"Yeah I can wait. The plane doesn't leave until seven and the airport ain't that far away."

"Kale, its only noon, how are you fully packed? Are you sure you ain't sick?" His mother wondered. Normally, it was the last second before he was out the door.

"No Mom, I'm not sick. More like anxious." Kale had to try everything from jumping up and down.

"Is it that girl again? She sure has brought out a side in you I haven't seen."

"No! It's not Skyler, Mom. Can we forget Skyler even came into my life, okay? It's not goin' to work out and I need to move on." Kale knew what he was saying didn't match the way his heart felt. He wanted to be with Skyler, he wanted to remember how she came into his life.

"Are you tellin' me that, or are you foolin' your heart into believing the words you're sayin'. When you said 'I need to move on" your eyes sparkled. Son, you can't fool your own mother, I know how much she is consumin' you. I want you to do one thing for me. Find a way to keep in touch with this girl, anyway that's possible." She knew her demand may or may not be met but she still couldn't help herself from trying her best to convince him he needed to talk to Skyler.

"Will do."

Kale's dad walked in through the door.

"Can you help me move some bags of feed, superstar?"

"Sure can." He replied following his dad out to the truck. He picked up a few bags of feed from the truck bed.

"So, I hear this year TJ's bull choices are even harder, so be careful. You know TJ if the bulls can't cause a commotion they ain't in." His dad's voice held a tone of concern in it.

"Dad, I will be. I take a million safety precautions." Kale knew though at times one of those precautions could fail.

"I'm worried about your elbow Kale, so wear your brace alright."

"I can do that Dad." He laid the bags of feed next to the rest of them.

"Well son, I think you're ready. I have nothin' else to say except for maybe get to know that Skyler girl."

"Dad, like I told Mom, Skyler isn't goin' to happen." He knew he couldn't hide his feelings that well but still he tried.

"Keep tellin' yourself that Kale. I have a feelin' she may be feelin' the same thing you are."

Kale's eyebrows peaked up as if he was interested in what his father was saying. How in the world did he know that Skyler was feeling the same thing?

"Right, 'cause all I get is an anonymous note from a Scarlett O'Hara who never meets me and here I'm sending flowers under the alias Rhett Butler."

"Hmm…what do you mean you sent flowers?" The curiosity was growing in his fathers' eyes.

"Well, I sent Skyler flowers in Greensboro, and paid the hotel to have flowers in her room when she arrived back from the after party."

"Son, you're far more romantic then I was. Don't let your mother know the things you're doin'."

Kale laughed. "Don't worry Dad; I won't hurt your romantic status with Mom."

"Good to know. Now go on; get out of here." His dad hit him on the butt.

Kale hugged his father. Kale looked up to his father. He wanted the world to see him as they saw his father; full of heart, full of passion, as well as one of the greatest bull riders to walk the earth.

    Kale climbed into his truck and waved to his Dad as he left. It felt like he was creating a new beginning; a beginning which felt uncertain to him. Was he supposed to do all the things he wanted too, or was he supposed to hold back, and wait for things to fall into place?

    He stopped by his favorite western store. It had been a long time since he had been inside. He decided maybe he should add something other than the flowers to Skyler's room. He knew he would be there before her, since he was leaving a day early. He didn't think there would be a problem in the execution of his plans. He went to the glass case containing jewelry. He wanted to get her something special, but nothing too extreme to scare her off. He saw it gleaming in the back at him, screaming Skyler's name. It was a horseshow on a chain with a small cross behind it. He knew that Skyler held her faith high and that she retained many of the qualities a woman in the old west would have had. He couldn't help but imagine how beautiful it would look when Skyler wore it.

    He called the lady over and purchased it. He couldn't wait to see Skyler's face when she found it on her desk in the Sports Medicine room. He knew he would have to fake an injury in order to see the shock on her face. He hoped all the trouble he was going through would be worthwhile to both him and Skyler.

He arrived at the airport and his anxiety level rose. What if he went a little too far with everything? What if she walks into the hotel with her boyfriend and he sees the flowers? What if she couldn't feel the same way about him? He knew that all what ifs would eat him alive, but he couldn't help but play every possible scenario in his head. He boarded the plane and found his seat. He was surprised when Matt sat down next to him.

"Hey, Matt." He said politely.

"Hey, Kale. How's it goin'?"

"Pretty good, real excited to get to the event and keep last weekend's streak alive."

"Yeah, I'm sure. You'll do fine. Why you sweatin'? What are you nervous about? I'm sure that the pilot knows how to fly." Matt watched as Kale wiped the sweat off his forehead with his sleeve.

"It's not that Matt, its Scarlett O' Hara. Her note has had my mind boggled for the last week. I kind of hope she's in New Mexico."

He could feel Matt's eyes searing through him. He also knew how Matt felt about his assumption that it was Skyler.

"Maybe she will be who knows. Kale don't let yourself get your hopes up."

They both put in their headphones to their I-pods; Kale figured that Matt was listening to the bible. It was fine with him, but it seemed as if every song on his playlist emanated thoughts of Skyler. He placed his head against the window and drifted off to sleep.

Skyler

After packing everything, she was ready to go to New Mexico. It would be her first time experiencing the New Mexican desert, seeing the rankest pen in BRA history. TJ Mason had a reputation for assembling the rank pen. Cade Larsen also had an eye for the eliminators. TJ"s event normally was nicknamed the massacre for the fact that the greatest injuries in a season came from his event.

She ran downstairs and found a note from her grandpa.

****
Meet me in the barn.
****

She couldn't help but wonder what was going on? Grandpa usually talked to her directly and never led her on a wild goose chase. She got her jacket and ran as fast as she could to the barn.

She didn't see Grandpa anywhere, what the heck he meant by meet him in the barn if he wasn't even there. She heard the sound of his truck and wondered what horse Grandpa had sold this time. Her grandfather slowly walked into the barn.

"Who are you sellin', Grandpa?" Skyler didn't want to know, but at the same time she did.

"What do you mean, who did I sell? I didn't sell anyone." Her grandpa seemed confused.

"Oh, so what am I doin' out here in the barn waitin' for you?"

"Makin' a home for a new friend of yours; he can't sleep in the house or outside in the pasture."

Her grandpa pulled a blue heeler puppy from behind his back.

"A Puppy! Oh my gosh, Grandpa. He is gorgeous. He will be a good ranch dog once he gets a little bit bigger." She brought the puppy to her face.

"Believe me, Sky. I can see he will be." He patted the dog on his head.

The puppy's eyes sparkled and were the prettiest brown she had ever seen. She kissed him on top of his head. The puppy took the liberty of licking her.

"Hey Shooter, stop that. That won't make the cattle see you as mean."

"Shooter…huh? So we got ourselves a Gunner and a Shooter."

"Yeah, Dad's first horse was Shooter. It also makes me think of shootin' stars. That is definitely what Loren is, my shootin' star."

"She sure is, sport. You better make him comfortable. Then, I'll run you to the airport."

"Thanks Grandpa, so much. I'll be ready in a few."

She took Shooter to the corner of the barn and piled up fresh hay. She found joy in Shooter's little quirks, like trying to eat the hay as she laid it down. She found one of her bandana's a tied to JB's saddle horn and wrapped it around Shooters' body. She found a small bowl, and went to fill it up with the dog food grandpa had left her. She went in search of a water bowl for him and found a small bucket.

"Now Shooter, Grandpa is a little iffy on dogs. He usually likes larger animals, as you can tell. If you are real good this weekend, maybe we can get you a friend. You have to be a good, okay boy?"

Shooter barked in recognition of his task.

"You're too cute. I'll see you late Sunday, boy. Be careful okay? Don't wonder off; some of these horses don't like me even. So leave them alone."

She walked away from Shooter and he sat there staring at her. She walked over to JB.

"Hey you have a new job. Make sure Shooter don't get into trouble, will you boy? Make sure he doesn't bite Grandpa."

She gave him a rub down, and before she exited the barn to find Grandpa she gave him a kiss on his nose.

"Ready to go?" Jesse said.

"Sure is Grandpa, I sure am."

The ride to the airport was quite silent, except for the sounds of classic country.

"Skyler, remember to have fun okay."

"I will Grandpa, but I have to work too. That way when a spot comes open after graduation I can go tourin' full time, and stay Texas.

"Sky, don't worry about that stuff. Worry about now, and live now."

He leaned over to kiss his granddaughter.

"Be safe, if you get delayed somewhere call, alright."

Skyler rolled her eyes before she responded. "I'll be fine, Grandpa."

She climbed out of the truck, and got her bag. Her eyes met his weary ones. She knew he only wanted the best for her, and he knew that Kale meant the world to her, even if she didn't tell herself that. She smiled, shut the truck door, and ran into the airport.

Kale

The New Mexico heat sent warmth up his body. The heat made him excited for the event, and for the possibility of what could come. After grabbing his bags he went to rent a car. He picked up the keys to a truck and hopped in.

He didn't want to be riding alone, but knew there was no way to convince Skyler to go for a ride with him without creeping her out. He could only imagine the sparkle in her eyes when she would get the first glimpse of her horseshoe necklace. He only wanted Skyler to be happy, and if she was happy by the little things he did for her.

He walked into the hotel and grabbed his room key.

"Sir, I was wonderin' if Skyler Pendleton checked in?" his voice has a sense of excitement in it.

"No she hasn't, she has check-in at seven o'clock tonight, and would you like me to send her to your room?" The guy smiled at Kale.

"No thank you, I was wondering if flowers I order had gotten delivered to the right room." He wanted everything to be perfect for her.

"They did sir. You enjoy your stay here."

"I will, and thank you." He tipped his hat to the guy as she turned to go upstairs.

He ran up the steps anxious to hear Skyler talk about the mystery things she received. When he opened the door he saw Brayden's bag. He figured it was like normal, Brayden didn't reserve a room and asked the guy at the front desk where Kale was. So Kale slowly shoved his stuff into drawers, so that Brayden didn't know he was there. As he exited the room to go for a run, he ran into Matt again.

"Where are you goin?" Matt was curious about Kale's new found excitement.

"Goin' on a run to catch some air, why?" Kale usually didn't get confronted by Matt, but didn't feel he had to tell Matt anything.

"Oh well, we are havin' bible study later your welcome to come."

"Thanks Matt, I will have to see what I'm doin'." He knew if he went he would get to see Skyler.

"Okay." Matt continued walking to his room.

It's not that Kale didn't want to go to bible study. He knew a lot of great people would be there but the only person he could focus on was Skyler. Skyler, he thought would be there and talking about him in a non-direct way. As he continued to walk down the stairs he only wondered what Skyler would do when she walked in and on her nightstand sat a dozen beautiful flowers.

Skyler

Although the plane ride seemed to go smoothly, she didn't feel so good. Her head was pounding and the only thing she wanted to do was crash. She went to pick up her bag. She was thankful that it didn't get lost this time. She wondered over to the car rental place and got the keys to her rental car. She didn't want to go straight to the hotel, but she felt that a nap before bible study would probably help relieve the pain.

She pulled into the hotel parking lot next to another rental car. She looked in and thought she saw someone but she didn't know who it was. She got her bag out of the backset, and entered in the hotel. She approached the desk as Matt and Walker approached her.

"You are comin' to Bible study?" They both asked her.

"I wouldn't miss it. What time?" She loved seeing Matt and Walker. The whole talking in unison was actually becoming easy for her to deal with.

"Does 7:30 work for you?" Matt asked hoping it would be a great time.

"Yeah it does. Where am I goin'?" Skyler was unfamiliar with the hotel setup and hoped it wouldn't be far from her room.

"The meeting room over there. If you see cowboy hats, you're in the right room." Matt narrated as Walker acted the directions in his own crazy way.

"Thanks guys." Skyler said trying to hold in her laughter.

"See you later, Sky." The dynamic duo continued to leave the hotel.

She walked upstairs to her room. She flipped the light switch and found a dozen red roses on her night stand. She was starting to get suspicious about the man leaving her the flowers. She walked over and plucked the card from its place.

****

Shakespeare said that Romeo would always love Juliet, and the same is true with me. I will love you until the last rose dies. Remember this pledge my darling Scarlett.
Rhett

****

She was flattered two bouquets of beautiful roses but who was Rhett? Was it true that he would love her until the last one died? The excitement fell from her face. It was replaced with a feeling of melancholy as she realized that the gorgeous blooms would only last a week. As she started the smell them she found a small wooden red rose nestled among the other eleven.

She started to cry. Who could think of her so much to please her like this? Who was this guy tugging at her heart; the guy who obviously held her to such high esteem? She could only imagine what he Knight looked like.

He was tall, she knew this for sure. She knew that he could ride the wildest horses. That he loved her like all knights should love their maidens. Who was this noble knight? Could she call up King Arthur for the knight's name, or was it unknown? Was he too young of a knight to be praised for his deeds?

Skyler let herself drift away into a fairytale.

Kale

He grabbed his bible out of the rental car and went to bible study. When he walked in the room he saw Matt, Jace, Walker,

Brayden, Dakota, and a few more of his fellow riders.

"Nice seenin' you here, Weston." Jace said in his normal joking tone.

"You too, Montgomery although I didn't expect to be graced by your presence this evenin'." Kale always had a way to fire it right back at Jace.

Dakota walked up to Kale and gave him a hug.

"How have you been, Cowboy?" She questioned wrapping her arms around him for a second time.

"Fine. Fine really, ready to ride this weekend." Kale was actually more excited for the events that were about to take place at Bible study.

"You're only fine, well that ain't no good."

"I will be great here in a few minutes, wait a minute and I promise I'll be better." Kale smiled as he saw Skyler approaching the room.

"Dude, seriously, could you make it any more obvious?" Brayden couldn't help but shake his head.

"Sorry Brayden. You can't help it when the light of her eyes draws you near."

"Uh Kale, you are getting to be too mushy for my liking. If you talk like that again, I will have to slap you."

Skyler interrupted Brayden and Kale's conversation as she opened the door. "Sorry, I'm late ya'll." She was a little out of breathe.

"Skyler, you are only a minute late," muttered Walker.

"Yeah, well I'm still sorry."

She walked over and took the empty seat next to Kale.

"Nice to see you at bible study," Kale whispered.

"You too, it's always a pleasure to worship with God-fearin' people." She smiled.

Kale shot her a smile back, "yeah, it is."

He watched as Skyler flipped to the first passage on the sheet. He wanted to say more, he wanted to tell her the flowers were from him, but he couldn't. He didn't know how.

As bible study concluded they all headed back to their rooms to sleep, except Kale, who exited the hotel and went on a walk.

"Kale you're so stupid. He said to himself. Why in the world won't you talk to her? What makes her so intimating, huh? What, Kale? She is a woman, and not any woman but the one of your dreams for goodness sake."

After returning from his walk, he went upstairs and quietly climbed into the extra bed in the hotel room.

The morning light didn't take any time to rise above the horizon.

"Wake up, Brayden." Dakota whispered as she kissed his cheek.

"A few more minutes, babe. Can I have a few more minutes?" He asked her in a whining voice.

"No, we need to go check on the pen, and I need you to come with." She softly shook him. Dakota kissed him again. She sat up and saw the sheets on the other bed moving.

"Brayden. Who is in the other bed?"

"It's me Kale, Dakota." His voice was still groggy.

Kota couldn't believe it. This was supposed to be her and Brayden's weekend and here was Kale in the other bed. Dakota jabbed Brayden with her finger.

"You, mister, are sleeping in the bull trailer tonight, and you can take him with you." Her voice was stern. She was pissed. It had been a long time since they had been alone together.

"Hunnie."

Dakota interrupted. "Brayden don't hunnie me. This was supposed to be our weekend."

To try and prevent any further problem he leaned up and kissed her.

"Could you guys quit doin' that seriously?" Kale asked as he put a pillow over his head.

"Kale, you better get up and get out." Dakota commanded with a snap of her fingers.

Kale threw the blackest on the floor, sat up in the bed, and then stood up to exit the room. He had forgotten that he was only in his boxers. When he saw the door open, he was shocked to see who was coming out.

"Mornin' Kale, nice boxers," She complimented him as she tried not to laugh.

"Mornin' Sky, um thanks. Where are you running off too?" His face was pale. He was comfortable in his skin but Skyler added a whole new level to being comfortable with one's self.

"To the ice machine. I can't have hot water for breakfast you know."

"No that would be a shame. Mind if I come get ice with you?" He knew this would probably be the best time to capitalize on his opportunity with her.

"Sure, I don't have any rules. The hotel may, but I'm sure boxers are appropriate clothing." She was trying all that she could not to laugh.

"It's a long story actually, but I'm sure you would get bored with it." It wasn't that she would get bored with it. Kale really didn't want to tell her about his embarrassing room situation.

"How do you know I would? How do you know I don't like stories?" She playfully asked him.

"I don't know. Brayden and Dakota were sleeping and I found out this mornin' that they were supposed to have an alone weekend, which is impossible when they are sleepin' in the room I reserved." He had a tinge of anger in his voice.

"Sorry, cowboy, but when people wanna be alone, you gotta give them time."

"I didn't even know they were in there."

"Ah I see. Well, maybe you all should coordinate times for those things." Skyler didn't want to come off as a know it all, but she knew that to Kale this was a crisis when really it wasn't that big of a deal.

"Won't have to worry about that tonight, I have to sleep in the bull trailer with Brayden."

"Oh, that sounds awful." She mimicked. She couldn't help herself but she let out a small laugh.

"Skyler, this really isn't a laughin' matter." Kale's blood was boiling threw his veins.

Skyler couldn't help but sarcastically laugh at him. "It isn't? Are you sure?"

"What's so funny? Don't you and your friends have issues like this?"

"Actually, no. I don't have many friends, mostly my horse, and my new puppy, and of course, my family."

"Are you tellin' me this is the first time you hung out with people your own age?" Kale was flabbergasted. No wonder she seemed way more mature than most girls. This explained her determination, her outlook on life, and her undying passion that she kept wrapped up inside of her.

"No, I used to have a best friend. She passed away when I was nineteen years old. I haven't been able to make many friends since." She could feel sweat bubbling up on her skin as she spoke to him.

"Well Dakota sure thinks you are pretty cool, she thinks you're a little goofy too."

"Nice to know." She blurted out as she pressed the ice cup against the machine.

"Maybe you should hang out with her." He knew if he proposed the idea that maybe she would take the bait.

"Yeah would be fun, but I'm sure we both are busy. She has a bull tryin' to make a name for herself and I'm tryin' to make my own name."

They walked back down the hallway in silences. As she turned to walk into her room Kale broke the silence.

"See you later Sky."

"Yeah, and cowboy, I recommend actually gettin' dressed for an event." She shot a crooked smile his way. Her eyes sparkling as she stared into his blue eyes.

"I will, don't worry. See ya."

He opened the door and walked in. He finally knew how Skyler felt before, when it had been her in his shoes. At the same time he was caught up in the moment. It had been awhile since he had spent even a minute of time with Skyler.

"Where have you been?" Brayden asked.

"I went to get ice with Skyler. Why does it matter?"

"Kale bud, don't lie to me."

"Brayden, you ain't the only one who can smooth talk the ladies."

"I can hear that," Dakota replied as she brushed her teeth.

"Sorry Kota, I was just sayin'." Kale didn't want her to be upset but he also wanted Brayden to realize he wasn't the only one who could get a women's attention.

Kale dug through his bag quietly for his competition gear.

Skyler

She couldn't believe they always met in the craziest situations. Though, it felt good to see him smile. It had been in her dream last night, and was a smile she wanted to see all the time. She dropped a few cubes of ice into her glass.

She climbed back into her bed, and found the remote to the TV. She flipped through channels until she found an old rodeo event. It had been the last year her Dad was riding. She could see his tall lanky body behind the chutes. She couldn't recall the location. She also had no clue if it had been one he had taken her too. She could make out numerous guys behind the chute next to him; TJ Mason, Scott Wilkens, James Mathis. They were guys who defined the sport of bull riding. Guys that Kale, Brayden, Jace, and others strived to imitate.

She sat in awe of how things had changed since the time her Dad rode. They were no were near superstars, though guys like Jace Montgomery, Brayden Carter and of course Kale Weston, were on the fast track to superstardom. She turned off the TV and thought about the offer Kale proposed.

Maybe a night with Dakota wouldn't be so bad. Maybe, she would have numerous stories about the three amigos. She had already acquired plenty of things on Kale, but why not chat with an insider. All these thoughts swirled around in her head.

She went to take a shower since she knew that Tate would want her at the arena early to help unload supplies. The water felt good running down her body and it didn't help that all she wanted to do was go back to sleep.

She quickly brushed her teeth and turned off the water. She hadn't realized how cold the hotel was until she stepped out of the shower. She found her work shit, quickly threw up her hair, and applied a little bit of makeup. She felt a little overdone to go work with Tate, but it hadn't been the first time she had retained this feeling. She grabbed her purse and out she went to the arena.

The drive proved to be calming. New Mexico had so many unique sights and sounds, and to Skyler each new sound represented a new part of herself. She had recalled coming into this internship as a scared little girl and now knowing what she did she was leaving more confident than ever.

She remembered Grandpa's comment about how she shouldn't think of the future, but it was really hard for her to refrain from such thoughts. She could only imagine the life on the road. Every stop would hold a new experience. Every stop would help her become who she was supposed to become.

She pulled into the arena parking lot. She maneuvered into a spot next to another rental vehicle. She was astonished by all the fans already standing outside. These were die-hard bull-riding fans. She could see it on their faces. She grabbed her bag and went around looking for the medical equipment van. She spotted Tate and moseyed on towards him.

"Hey, Skyler! Good to see you; ready for this weekend's events?" Tate asked in his ever so doctor like tone.

"You bet. I take it the can isn't here yet. What are they thinkin' we have a room to put together?" Skyler always seemed to have an opinion. Punctuality was something she relied on. She figured everyone should be like that.

"No. it's not. I don't know what they are thinking. I have a question for you too." Tate always seemed to have the right words to say.

"Fire away boss." She had started to show Tate and the staff a more relaxed side of her.

"When do you graduate?"

"This comin' December, with a doctorate degree in Athletic trainin'." She told Tate with pride.

"Abilene offers that? Wow, you sure seemed to have weight out your options." Tate couldn't help but smile.

"Yes, sir. I wasn't goin' to let any opportunities pass me by."

Skyler felt a little suspicious after Tate's question, but maybe all he wanted to do was weight his options.

"So Skyler, I forgot to ask in Greensboro, but want to watch full time out of the box."

"I would love that! Thanks, Tate." His face lit up with excitement.

The van arrived and they hurried to set up a makeshift medical room. Tate knew guys would be coming in earlier than they had before, and he wanted to be prepared.

Kale

He arrived at the arena, and only wanted to do one thing. Fake that his elbow was hurting him so he could see Skyler. He had asked one of the producers from the television station to leave the necklace on the supply desk so Skyler could find it, but the only thing he cared about was her reaction.

He dropped his bag off in the locker room and grabbed his brace. He quickly walked to the Sports Medicine room. He couldn't help but smile as he saw Skyler move towards the supply desk.

"Hey Sky, are you guys busy?"

"Not yet, cowboy! Why you ask?"

"Havin' difficulties with my brace again, if you could help, but if you need to count supplies I can wait." Kale knew his acting chops were weak but he could tell he was reeling her in slowly.

"Nah come on now, we're never too busy to do our jobs. Go sit down. I'll be over there in a second."

Skyler spotted the box on the supply desk; she opened it thinking it could contain medical supplies. She saw a necklace inside with a note.

****

Beauty is only skin deep. What others cannot see is that everything about you is beautiful; not only because you are a beauty, but because inside, you're also beautiful.

Rhett

****

Kale watched in silence as Skyler stared at the necklace.

"Want help puttin' it on?"

"Sure, I really need to find this Rhett character. He deserves a million 'thank you'."

"I'm sure whoever he is wants nothin' more than to see a smile on your face." He didn't want to give himself away.

"Well, he will when I thank him."
Kale smiled and whispered, "You're welcome."

"What did you say?" Skyler asked.

"I asked if it was too tight." Kale wondered as he clasped the necklace around her neck.

"No, it's fine, really. Thank you for puttin' it on." Skyler was amazed at the necklace as it hung from her neck.

"You're welcome Skyler."

"Let's get this brace on cowboy, so you can take another victory."

"Okay."

Skyler and Kale laughed as Kale tried to make it difficult for her to put on his brace.

"Geez cowboy, sometimes your quite a pain."

"I can't help it. You're the expert on this." Kale loved to joke with Skyler. As he repositioned the brace he tipped his hat to her. Skyler winked back as Kale exited the Sports Medicine room.

Skyler

She didn't know what it was about Kale. Was it his playful nature, or was it the fact he had so many things she wanted? She wondered all of this as she went to counting supplies. She figured that they wouldn't have time to do it if a ton of wrecks occurred.

She checked her watch and told Sam that she was heading out to be with Tate. As she walked down the hallway to the arena, she wondered what Kale had really said before. Did he know who Rhett was, or was it that he was and wanted to keep the secret going for one more day?

She couldn't help but get excited for the round. She knew that Dakota's bull Hectic Handful would be out, and she loved everything about him. He knew how to outsmart the riders. He didn't need time to make up his mind out of the chute. He could read the riders every move.

"Glad to see you escaped the box." Tate replied bringing Skyler out of her mind.

"Yeah, wasn't hard. I told Sam to stay, and we would get him if anything horrific happens."

"With the bulls in the round, we may need all the help we can get tonight." Tate stated somberly.

"Yeah, I'm pretty ecstatic for tonight. I have only seen the rank pen on TV, so it will be quite an experience to see it live." Skyler loved bull riding as much as she loved medicine. The ranker the bulls the better the event was for her. Although, it also scared her a bit. With bulls of such caliber of bulls Skyler knew anything was possible.

"Skyler, sometimes you're a little dorky." Tate added.

"Thanks Tate. It's the way God made me. So, I'm okay with it as you see."

"Glad to hear it. Nice necklace." He mumbled in a sarcastic tone.

"Thanks. I got it today from a mystery man who calls himself Rhett." Skyler cheeks flushed.

"You're the apple of someone's eyes, huh? I should have known I hire a girl straight out of Texas and I'd start some sort of frenzy among the riders."

Skyler laughed. She didn't know what to say back to that. She hadn't started any type of frenzy; she had fallen for a guy and hoped he was the Rhett character. She quietly sat watching Tate. He was so calm. He never fret about what was going to happen, but was like a cheetah on the prowl. Whenever he was needed he pounced.

In all Skyler's observations of Tate she hadn't seen the wreck. All she saw was an instant replay showing Stephen Wilkins getting stomped in the abdomen by Hectic Handful. A part of Skyler laughed as the other part quickly followed Tate into the arena.

"You're going to be fine Stephan." Tate said with conviction. "Skyler come talk to him while we wait for the paramedics."

Skyler did as she was ordered. "Where are you hurtin'?" She asked.

"My abdomen, didn't you see the ride." He shouted back at her.

"Hey cowboy, don't get riled up. We are tryin' to help. Breathe slowly." What Skyler really wanted to do was injury him herself. He had no right to snap at her. She was doing her job was all?

The paramedics came in and out went everyone from the arena. Skyler spotted Dakota before she walked through the alleyway. Skyler smiled at her and was surprised when she received on back. When they arrived to the room, Tate immediately sent Sky back out into the arena.

"If you need me, use your walkie-talkie okay?" Tate could sense Skyler's apprehension.

"Alright, Tate. I'll do what I can." Skyler tried to muster all the confidence she had in her five foot five inch frame.

Skyler was petrified. She was to man the back of the chutes by herself it seemed. Sam and she were to watch for any injuries and to treat them effectively.

As she came up to the chutes she saw Dakota standing against the back railing.

"Nice bull you've got there." Skyler casually stated.

"Thanks, he sure is turning out to be exactly what I imagined him to be." Dakota retorted.

"Yeah, except for the eliminator part right?" Skyler softly chuckled.

"Exactly, but it wasn't his fault, Stephan rolled underneath him." Dakota commented in Hectic Handful's defense.

"I noticed that in the replay. Don't worry Stephen, looks like he is goin' to come out with a bruised abdomen. Nothin' serious, except his pride was hurt in the process." A sting was left behind the chutes after Skyler spoke.

"I take it you don't like Stephan much." Dakota enquired.

"No, it's a long story though. I was wonderin' what you were doin' tonight after the event." Skyler could feel a lump building in her throat.

"Nothing, going to take care of Hectic Handful and make sure he is in tiptop shape for the championship round." Dakota was oozing with excitement as she spoke about her bull.

"They are puttin' him in the championship round, that's awesome." Skyler's face lit up. She always loved when people's dreams started coming true.

"Sure is. Why did you ask?" Dakota pondered the reasons in her head.

"There ain't many girls on this tour, or married to the tour, that I like, but you're an amazing stock contractor. Thought maybe we could have a sleep over. Talk about bulls, cowboys, anything you want to talk about actually." Skyler bit her lip nonchalantly.

"Yeah, it sounds like fun. Although, I think Brayden wants to go to the after party for a little bit. You should come. You know Kale; well he is a great dancer." Dakota felt good adding the plug about Kale. She also knew that would be the only way to get Skyler to go along with it.

"Will do, so where do you want me to meet you guys?" As she spoke all she could think about was possibly dancing with Kale to prove Dakota's theory.

"It's a bar not far from the hotel, so we can all meet in the lobby."

"Sounds good. Dakota, when you're ready to sell Hectic Handful, I'm ready to sweep him up." Skyler couldn't help but add the last line about Dakota's bull.

"Don't even think of it cowgirl, I ain't selling him." Dakota sternly replied.

"If you change your mind my offer stands." Skyler always had to get the last say in a conversation.

Skyler walked away to catch up with Sam. It felt good to be able to talk to someone like her. Who understood the circuit as much or if not more than she did; someone who didn't care about the glamorous side of bull riding, but loved the nitty gritty side.

Kale

He couldn't help but think of Sky's smile as he situated himself aboard Twisted Angel. He knew the bull from the college circuit, and he had finally broken into the big leagues. Kale never had a chance at him while attending Texas Christian, but he was excited about the chance of riding him now.

He couldn't help but visualize himself riding for a ninety plus score. What would the look on Skyler's face be at that moment? He made sure Brayden pulled his rope tight, and then he nodded his head. Out went twisted Angel. He spun hard to the right, and in about three seconds had made a hard left and off Kale went.

He was mad at himself. He should have adjusted; he should have ridden that bull. The round was over and to Kale it felt like his chances at a repeat was over as well. He walked back to the locker room and threw his helmet against one of the lockers.

"Whoa their bud." Brayden retorted.

"What? Brayden, you saw that ride. It sucked!" Kale fired back with anger.

"Actually it didn't suck you weren't in the zone." Brayden explained.

"Thanks for tryin' but can I have some time by myself?" He asked politely.

"Yeah, don't forget to put on your happy face, you have fans out there waiting for you cowboy. I'm going to go head out there so Dakota and I can leave and get ready for the after party."

"Okay, have fun." Kale snorted.

Kale didn't want anything to do with the fans. He wanted someone to come in and tell him that he didn't blow his chances with Sky. He had no clue if he did. The smile on her face may have been from mere shock, something inside of him knew that she was glad to have received the necklace. He huffed and puffed for a few moments before getting up, and realizing he needed to go sign autographs.

Brayden and Jace weren't that far ahead of him. He could see Dakota standing on the arena fate. He couldn't help but over hear what Jace and Dakota were talking about.

"I love you, Dakota Carter." Jace yelled.

"I love you too, Jace Montgomery." Dakota mimicked with a smile on her face.

"I love you more, Kota." Jace assured.

"You're wrong cowboy, I love you more." Dakota restated.

"Girl, I think you got it all wrong." Jace demanded.

Brayden came up from behind Jace and pulled him off the arena gates. "Quit flirting with my wife." Brayden said blowing steam from his ears.

"Geez, Brayden, I was having a little fun." Jace ensured.

Dakota smiled. She loved when Brayden in things in her honor. As he made his way in front of her, she leaned over and gave him a kiss.

"You don't love Jace more than me, do you, hunnie?" Brayden asked a little insecure with himself.

"Of course not, Jace and I have that funny friend thing about us. We joke around Brayden. Don't forget that. You hold my heart cowboy." Dakota kissed him again to make it stick in his head.

Brayden couldn't help but smile. "Ya hear that Jace, I hold her heart."

"Whatever, Brayden! She is tryin' to make you happy."

Dakota laughed. Jace was Brayden's best friend. He meant a lot to her, but nothing like what Brayden did. Jace was the playful one, while Brayden was more reserved. She couldn't help but want to scream at Brayden as he rounded the corner.

"I like your butt in them Wranglers, Brayden Carter." Dakota added a whistle after her comment.

Brayden turned around and shot her back a wink.

Kale finally made his way in front of Dakota.

"You are nuts." He assured her.

"Yeah, well, I guess Skyler will get to see that tonight." She taunted him.

"What do you mean; Skyler?" Kale was confused.

"She is going to the after party with us, than we are having a girl's night. No Cowboys Allowed!" She continued to mock him.

"What? Are you serious? What are you going to do?" Kale's mind started running a mile a minute.

"Kale there is unwritten rules of girls' nights that girls cannot discuss with the opposite sex. Although I assure you, cowboy, I will be questioning her a lot tonight."

"Don't scare her away, Dakota, please?"

"Me? Scare her away? You're more likely to do that in the hideous excuse of a western shirt you got on cowboy. You probably should change into something nice before the after party." Dakota smirked.

"Why? I like this shirt?" Kale was flustered.

"Trust me Kale won't. It looks like Twisted Angel snot all over you." She was brutally honest sometimes.

"Thanks, Dakota. I will reevaluate my outfit after I sign autographs."

"Good, 'cause cowboy you need all the help you can get."

He didn't care what Dakota said. He thought of her like a little sister and like most big brothers took some of the things she muttered as irrelevant.

He rounded the arena, and found no sign of Skyler. He knew she had probably run to check on Stephan, or maybe she made her way back to the hotel. He would try and run into her anyways. So, he walked quickly down the hallway and went into the locker room. Sitting on top of his bag was yet another note.

****

You don't know how special you are. You can't see what's underneath. You wonder if I see the real you and I do. You're courageous and strong, you're gentle but not weak. You think before you speak. You're a ladies' man, but you don't play games. You can find strength if you look above. You can believe in love, if only you see it too. If you

have a little faith, maybe it's come to you. You wonder who I am and I sign it so true. I'm a cowgirl waiting for my outlaw to come. So outlaw, will you take me away.
Hope this never ends,
Scarlett O'Hara
****

He couldn't believe it. She had struck yet again. It gave him more evidence that Scarlett O' Hara was Skyler. He couldn't confront her thought. They were going on a date, well, kind of. He picked up his bag and walked towards the sports medicine room. He saw Tate leaving.

"Hey Kale, how's the elbow?" Dr. Feldman asked.

"Fine actually Dr. Feldman. My heart well that's another story." Kale confessed.

"You okay?" Tate was a little confused.

"I think that I'm in the position to lose the best thing in my life in a few short days." Kale started to sweat.

"Sorry, wish I could help. I sure know something that would. Go have fun with your friends. Sometimes the best remedy is the one they can come up with."

"Thanks Doc. I was wonderin' has Skyler left yet." Kale could feel his body heating up from the inside out.

"Yeah, a few minutes ago. You may still find her in the bull pen. She has taken a liking to the animals. Harley and Donaldson let her feed their cattle, so she has taken on a few more jobs around the circuit you can see." Tate couldn't help but smile. Skyler was like a daughter to him and he loved that she wasn't there just for the medicine aspect of it all.

"Okay, thanks Tate. See you tomorrow." Kale peeled out from the conversation as fast as he could.

He figured Brayden and Dakota were probably done with Hectic Handful. So he went to check to see if he could find Sky. He peaked in and saw her standing not far from Rapid Revolver. He could tell the bull loved Sky's treatment.

"Hey Sky. What are you doin'? You're goin' to make him a sissy bull if you ain't careful." Kale joked.

"No I won't. Weston, the next time you get on, he has a new move especially for you." Skyler glared at him for a few seconds.

Kale could feel the heat from her eyes melting his heart.

"Does he? Well, I'll have to wait and see." He retorted in a cocky fashion.

"Oh Kale, I'll probably be late to the after party, so you guys go on without me."

He tried his best not to let his smile fall into a frown. As his heart sunk lower into his chest; "Are you sure? We can wait? It's no problem for us to wait." He had to pull out all the stops, though would Skyler buy it was all he worried about.

"I don't want to ruin y'alls fun. So go ahead I'll catch up." Kale could see something was on Skyler's mind; he had no clue what it was. Her hazel eyes were starting to fade in their natural sparkle.

"We'll wait. We ain't in any hurry." Kale hoped to reassure her.

"Alright, well I'll see you later then." Her eyes seemed to have been recharged and it was something that Kale loved to see.

"Later Sky." He said with a huge smile on his face.

Skyler

Skyler washed her hands as she exited the back pens. She had fun babying Rapid Revolver, but was excited to spend the night with the Carters, and Kale, of course.

She drove back to the hotel. She was anxious. What would she do if she tripped? What would she do if Kale didn't like her dad? What would happen if someone else asked her to dance? All these questions swirled around in her mind until she arrived at the hotel.

"Sky, don't worry, things will happen that are supposed to happen. Give fate a chance Sky. Don't hold back," she kept repeating over and over to herself.

She ran upstairs to her room and pulled clothes from her bag. She found a blue silk shirt, black jeans and her favorite pair of high heel boots. She pulled her hair back and put on a bit of makeup. She grabbed her purse and left her hotel room. As she walked down the steps she saw kale standing in the corner of the lobby.

"Hey, cowboy, are we ready to go?" She asked with a sensual tone in her voice.

"Sure are. We have to wait for Brayden and Dakota."

"It's fine with me. Where are they anyways?"

Kale pointed as Brayden and Dakota came down the stairs holding each other's hands.

"Let's go party?" Brayden yelled.

The four of them walked around the corner to the bar.

Kale

It was hard not to grab Sky's hand and hold onto it. It was something he wanted to do more than anything in the world.

"So Skyler, is this your first after party?" Brayden asked.

"No, I went to the one in Greensboro. It was kind of awkward actually. I guess I didn't expect everything that happened."

"Yeah the first one is always the weirdest. You learn to get use to it."

"Thanks, Brayden, I trust your advice." Skyler confessed.

"Good to know."

They walked into the bar, following Jace and BJ.

"Want to dance, hun?" Brayden asked Dakota.

"I would love to dance." She placed her hand in his and followed him onto the dance floor.

Kale saw Skyler gazing at Brayden and Dakota dancing. He also couldn't help but notice her tapping her toes to the beat. He felt bad for leaving her alone while Brayden and Dakota danced. He slowly approached her. He had to find the courage to at least ask her to dance. Her smiling face was visible to him as he approached the table.

"Sky, you want to dance?" He could feel his palms sweating.

"Of course I do."

Skyler placed her hand in his. He felt chills run up his arm. What was it about Skyler? Was it the way her eyes sparkled, her shy smile saying things he couldn't understand or things she wasn't ready to unveil to him. He looked her straight in the eyes, hoping to provoke conversation, but all Skyler did was smile.

As he led her out on the dance floor his favorite slow song started to play. He didn't want to come across as dorky, but as the chorus came around he could help but sing it to Skyler.

"I tip my hat to the keeper of the stars. He sure knew what he was doing when he joined these two hearts. I hold everything when I hold you in my arms. I've got all I ever need. Thanks to the Keeper of the stars." He felt her melt within his arms.

"You have a great voice, cowboy, and I ain't lyin'." The words came pouring from her lips.

"Thanks, it means a lot, comin' from you." He couldn't help but glance in her eyes. They captivated him.

"Well, I'm honored to bestow such a compliment." She softly tightened her grip around his neck.

"Skyler you're such a dork." He was shocked at himself. He could have said anything but he said that.

"Why?" She looked at him with confusion.

"It's you; you sounded like some royal person knightin' someone or something." He hoped he had covered up his tracks and didn't offend her.

"So, how do you know I ain't royalty?" She wanted to twist his mind a little.

"True, I don't know that." He lowered one eyebrow wondering what she was getting at.

"Right, if I was royalty I would not be fraternizin' with a commoner." She replied with a little attitude behind it.

"Someone has her head up her butt." He said taking one of the hands from around his neck.

"Sorry, I was playin' the part." She shrugged.

"You're good at it to say the least."

"I did a lot of actin' in high school."

"I can only imagine what that was like?" He admitted jokingly.

"I was good cowboy, believe me. I was the best Annie Oakley in Billings High history." She couldn't help but start a stare down with him.

"Sure you were." He sarcastically added.

Skyler saw as Brayden and Dakota made their way back to the table. Kale could see her eyes shift from him.

"Want to go sit?" He asked a little disappointed in himself.

"Yeah, these boots are kind of killer." She admitted.

Brayden looked over at Kale as they approached the table.

"We probably should let the girls go have their night."

"Sure, so we can go hang with the guys." Kale responded.

Dakota leaned in and Kissed Brayden. "Be good, Cowboy. I have eyes and ears everything." She reminded him as she laughed.

"I know you do, but that's why I love you so much." He proclaimed.

Kale and Skyler rolled their eyes at each other as Brayden and Dakota kissed. Kale couldn't help but feel some intense connection to Skyler.

"Let's go Skyler, We have a lot to do."

"Okay. Bye Brayden. Bye Kale; thanks for the dance Kale."

"Bye." Brayden replied.

"See you later Sky, and it was my pleasure." Kale mumbled as he smiled at her.

Skyler
She and Dakota walked out of the bar.

"So Skyler, what do you think of Kale's dancing?" Dakota insisted on getting a truthful answer out of Skyler.

"You were completely and honestly right. He is a great dancer. Somehow you forgot to mention he has an incredible singin' voice." Skyler face showed the colors of love. She was smitten. She knew that Dakota could read her like an open book. She didn't care. She was tired of caring what the world thought. She was irrevocably in love with Kale Weston if only she found a way to tell him.

"That's because I've never heard him sing." Dakota was a little shocked. Kale never showed an interest in singing before. It gave her an indication on how much Kale truly adored Skyler.

"Awe, well you sure missed out, he almost brought me to tears." Skyler couldn't help but bite her lip again. She knew she was showing Dakota a little too much of herself.

They entered the hotel, and went up to Skyler's room.

"I'm going to go run and get my pajamas, I'll be right back."

"Alright, I'll be changin' out of these clothes into something comfortable."

It wasn't long after their brief conversation that Dakota came knocking on the door. Skyler pulled her tank top over her head and went to open the door.

"Those pajamas are cute." Skyler muttered. She always was a sucker for an oversize t-shirt and shorts.

"Thanks, it's Brayden's shirt actually, and these are his boxers too come to think of it." Dakota chimed in.

"must be nice gettin' to raid someone else's clothes, always havin' double the options." Skyler couldn't help but be engrossed in the girl talk.

"Sometimes, it's real great. Especially, when you can find a ratty t-shirt to go out and clean the barn in."

"Sure Brayden appreciates that." Skyler couldn't help but laugh a little.

"It doesn't matter, he loves me. You'll find that out when you find the love of your life." Dakota let a softer side of her shine through.

"Hope I find him, he must amazin' at the game of hide and seek. I feel like I've looked everywhere and been left with a huge goose egg." Skyler knew she wasn't being truthful. Kale wasn't a goose egg, but she also hadn't made much progress with him.

Dakota thought, *no he isn't.* She didn't want to cause tension between them, all she could find herself doing was smile.

"So, Sky? What was it like growing up in Montana?" Dakota knew she had to start somewhere with the questioning.

"It was amazin'. Funny thing is there are more animals in the state then people in some places. That what makes it so great; all the green pastures, all the animals grazin'. The sense of the old west is surly alive in Montana."

"Must have been nice. Like a scene out of a movie or something."

"It sure was. So how'd you meet Brayden, Jace and Kale?" Skyler was nervous; she didn't want to get on Dakota's bad side. She also didn't want to do anything that would make Dakota tell Kale about.

"Long story: here it goes. I met Kale when I lived in Texas. We went to the same church camp and the nerd followed me around the whole time. He was in awe of my superior rodeo knowledge. I met Brayden and Jace when my Mom got a new job in North Carolina. Started going to school with Jace. The next thing I know I'm going to a rodeo to support Jace and this guy walks over to me at the dance. He's all like 'Hey, I'm Brayden Carter.' Needless to say he didn't have to use a pick up line to get me." Dakota face flushed. She hadn't told a lot of people about how she met Brayden. It was good to have a little girl talk.

"Sounds like a great thing for an E! True Hollywood Story if you ask me."

"Oh, my life is one big soap opera." Dakota couldn't help but add a little dramatic moment into the conversation.

"I doubt it mine could be turned into a Lifetime movie." Skyler scoffed. She knew it could be more than that, but she also knew she couldn't complain. Her life had been far from eventful, but it also had shaped her into the women she was.

"Why you say that?" Dakota was intrigued. Skyler seemed the least likely to open up about anything. She was now unveiling a part of herself to a stranger.

"I'm sure you've heard I'm a Pendleton. My dad supposedly cheated his way to the top while he rode bulls. Stephan Wilkins and his crew have never let me live it down. He thinks my father cheated his from the glory he deserved. If he is anything like his son he needs to earn it as much as anyone else." Dakota could see the steam floating around in Skyler's eyes. It was a touchy topic for her, and she now realized why Stephan's wreck seemed less important to Skyler.

"Stephan is weird. He has always been that way. When Jace started on the tour, he felt his own pride slip. When Brayden moseyed his way into the top ten I think Stephan started a riot against North Carolina."

Skyler laughed. She never heard Stephan or his family described like that.

Though, she knew the way that both Jace and Brayden rode. It would scare any guy that competed against them. Although, she also thought Kale had a chance too. Though, she could see that Dakota didn't seem to care about Kale all the time.

"Yeah but the Wilkins have been in the rodeo business a long time, so everyone tends to respect them. That much I have found." Skyler didn't know how to defend her side of the feud. She felt as if the Wilkins's were the Hatfield's and the Pendleton's were the McCoy's.

"Screw um. Seriously, your family has had a bigger impact than their family ever will." Dakota sent chills up Skyler's spine. She had never had her family defended before. Normally, they were the bad guys.

"Thanks Dakota. Sure didn't think anyone liked my family, but I guess I was wrong." Her face lit up. She was happy to know that the world hadn't lost respect for her father.

"A little heads up, your dad is Kale's hero."

Skyler looked like a deer in the headlights. Why hadn't Kale told her that? Though, it now made sense to her why he treated her so nicely.

"What? No way. I guess that's why he's been given me so much attention this summer."

"Partly but Skyler he is also a great guy. He seriously thinks you're a great doctor." Dakota had to find a way to score some Kale points with Skyler.

"Yeah, he is. Sure wish I had enough guts to tell him."

"Why don't you? I saw the way you guys were looking at each other tonight." Dakota raised her eyebrows as if she wanted Skyler to explain their behavior.

"We were dancin' we weren't doin' anythin' else. Other than enjoyin' each other's company, I swear that was all we were doin'." Skyler defensively muttered.

"Maybe to you, but to the world, it sure set off an alarm." Her eyes widen as she spoke. Skyler was utterly confused. To her it felt as if they were dancing in their own little world. Now Dakota made her think that everyone knew about her crush on Kale.

"Right Dakota seriously, we probably look awkward together. I bet people were like what is that buckle bunny doin' with that cowboy."

"No, you guys don't at all actually. So Skyler Pendleton, what else is there to know underneath your tough exterior?" Dakota was now digging her claws into Skyler for answers.

"I don't know, what do you want to know? I guess I can start with the fact I'm a hopeless romantic. I want a romance like Rhett and Scarlett, Johnny and June, Romeo and Juliet. I also want my life to revolve around this tour. It's been a big part of my life and I don't want it to be any different now. I'm a girl trying to find a balance between the old naïve version of her and the new and totally experience self. That would be great also." Skyler's felt naked. She had bared some of her most intimate secrets for yet another time in her life. She had let the chains fall to the ground. She had given Dakota the rawest view of who she was, and what she was about. She anxiously awaited Dakota's response.

"Well I'm sure both Skyler's are great girls. Plus, if they both like cowboys, than I'm sure they both have been eyeing Kale Weston."

Skyler blushed. She knew she had made some things obvious. She now knew at least Dakota knew about her crush on Kale.

"Skyler, we all fall in love with the wrangler butts. It's inevitable for a cowgirl."

"Brayden told me that was what made you fall in love with him." Skyler couldn't help but leak her and Brayden's secret.

"Ha Ha. Brayden thinks he is so funny doesn't he." Dakota declared.

"Yeah, he really isn't as funny as he thinks." Skyler had to add in her two cents.

"Glad someone else believes me." Dakota mustered in as she got up to slide in a movie. It wasn't too long into 8 seconds that the girls were fast asleep.

Kale

He felt breeze across his face and the sound of Brayden snoring. As he lifted up his head, he couldn't believe that they had taken refuge in his rental truck. Kale's head pounded and he had no clue how many beers he had drank, but knew it was more than he had ever drank before in his life. He looked at his cell phone and realized that Cowboy Church would start in an hour.

"Brayden, get up. We gotta go inside and change. Church is goin' to start in an hour." He said trying to shake Brayden awake.

Brayden soon sprung up and hit Kale in the face.

"What are you telling me, Weston. I bet Dakota is worried about me."

"Highly doubt it, and thank you for the mornin' slap."

They jumped out of the truck bed, and ran inside the hotel .They saw Dakota and Skyler laughing on the couch in the lobby.

"Lookin' real good there, Weston." Skyler mocked him as she laughed.

"Hold that thought, we will be right back." Kale replied in a panic. He and Brayden dashed up the steps.

Skyler turned to Dakota. "The boys obviously had fun without us."

"Yeah, I don't want to know what kind of fun."

"As long as it was nothin' like that gay cowboy movie, I'm okay with whatever happened." Skyler added.

'Same here, I doubt they did, but they sure did run upstairs real fast together."

They could help but laugh. Kale came out of the hotel room buttoning up his shirt. Skyler tried to discretely bite her lip. Kale looked good, she couldn't deny that.

"How do I look now, Ms. Pendleton?" Kale said in a charming fashion.

"Sharp, like you're ready to go to church."

"I can take you to church and the other two can go together."

"That's good. Brayden takes longer than a girl to get ready." Dakota interrupted.

"I don't want to miss talkin' with Trent." Sky mentioned.

'Well let's go." Kale anxiously added.

Skyler smiled at Dakota. "save you a seat Dakota. Hurry that boy up."

"Will do."

Kale and Skyler walked out to the rental truck.

"So, did you have fun last night with Dakota?" Kale asked in a wondrous tone.

"Sure, we had fun." Skyler smiled. It was good talking to Kale. It felt natural.

Kale opened the door for her.

"Thanks, you're a true gentleman." Skyler climbed into the truck in silence.

"My momma raised me right." He blurted as he climbed in the other side.

"So what did you and Dakota do?" Kale wanted to know every detail. He knew if he asked Dakota he would get nothing. So he tried his best to pry his information from Skyler.

"Laughed a lot and I found out some pretty cool things about Brayden and Jace." He could see it in her eyes that she was trying to make him squirm for more information.

"Oh really, that's cool." He played it cool.

"Kale, I want to thank you again for dancing with me last night. I haven't done that in a long time. It was a lot of fun."

"No problem, it was my pleasure.' He could hear his heart beating in his ears.

They sat in silence as the music played from the radio. Kale turned into the arena parking lot. He took the imitative to restart the conversation with Skyler.

"This should be a great sermon." Kale hoped talk about church would spark Skyler's attention.

"Aren't they always great?" Skyler was perplexed. She always loved Trent's sermons.

"Yeah, the ones I don't fall asleep during." Kale was honest. He had fallen asleep a few times. Though he wanted to change people's perception of him, he wanted to be a better person not only for himself but for Skyler as well.

"Kale that is bad. Today I'm gonna keep you up. You have to listen to God's word." Skyler showed Kale a look of determination.

"Good because I had a late night last night. I need a little baby-sittin'."

As they entered the arena; they walked up to Trent. Trent gave Kale a look of surprise although he shook his hand like he did to all the church goers. They both got a program from Matt. Although, Matt also gave Skyler something extra: a hug. Kale was a little jealous. He knew they had nothing but a brother and sister bond. He wished however that he could be the one hugging her. Sure last night being close to her was more than he expected. Although, he hadn't gotten enough of being close to her; he quickly followed her as she went to find a seat in church.

Skyler

She couldn't help but want to tell Kale how she felt. She didn't want to leave things unfinished with him. She didn't want Kale to think she didn't care about him. Her heart told her to spill her guts, while her mind told her she needed to stay cool and let fate play its role.

She smiled as Dakota made her way to seat next to her.

Skyler turned to Dakota as she sat down. "Jace wanted me to tell you hello. He was running to the locker room to get something out of his bag."

"Thanks, I hope it's something for me." She jokingly responded.

"Who knows? He sure does treat you like his little sister or secret mistress." Skyler retorted.

"Yeah, well you get used to it. It exactly the way Matt and Walker treat you, minus the mistress part. They don't want to see you get hurt, so they watch out over you." Dakota couldn't believe what was coming out of her mouth.

"You have Brayden? So what's Jace for?" Skyler gave her a confused look.

"To help me keep Brayden in line…when I'm not around."

"Ah, gotcha never thought about that." Skyler hadn't thought about having a guy as a spy. She had listened to Dakota's spiel on love, but didn't love require trust.

They stood up to sing. This time she wasn't as worried about Kale hearing her. He had shared his gift of singing with her last night. She felt comfortable. To Skyler Cowboy church was a comfort. It was a time for her to be around people exactly like her. She didn't care if this would be her last service as an intern; she only wanted one thing, to remember the summer. As Trent started to preach she looked to her left. She saw Dakota and Brayden, two people she never imagined she would encounter. To her right she saw Kale, the guy who hadn't even opened up to her, but yet she knew everything she needed to know about him. Two rows in front were her big brothers Matt and Walker, who kept her on the straight and narrow. She couldn't think any more about the future. At that moment she wanted the world to stop and to be surrounded by those people forever.

As church ended she turned to Kale.

"What did you think about the sermon?" She was interested in hearing Kale's response.

"It was great, Sky. Maybe it will help me ride my bulls this afternoon." Kale stared straight into her eyes. He was searching for something that he couldn't find quit yet.

"Good, I hope it does. Kale, thanks for everything this summer. You made it a memorable one for sure." Her face was brightened by her smile.

"Sky, I should be the one thanking you. Without all your help I would be in worst shape on this tour than I am now."

He hugged her. She felt weak in the knees as he wrapped his muscular arms around her. She didn't want the moment to end, but knew it had to.

"Hope you don't have to work to hard you last night, cowgirl."

"If I do, it wouldn't really matter; it would top off an amazing summer."

She smiled at Kale. She wanted so badly for him to ask her, but she could see it in his eyes that he was focused on the bulls he would be getting on. She didn't want to break his focus.

She walked up the steps and out into the hallway.

"Hey Trent, I wanted to tell you thanks for puttin' up with me this summer." She gave him a quick embrace.

"Sky, it wasn't like you were a pain, well…maybe a little bit." Trent joked with her.

"Thanks, it means a lot to me to know you care."

"I do care; if I didn't care I wouldn't tease you. I'm glad you didn't leave without saying goodbye to your favorite pastor."

"I couldn't do that. It would almost be like a sin. I won't be gone for long though."

"Good plan to me, maybe I can talk to Tate for you."

"No, you really don't have to. You have done enough for me." She loved the thought of Trent helping her out, but he already helped her out with all the spiritual uplifting.

Trent smiled and Skyler knew he was happy to hear that he had made an impact on her summer. She really couldn't believe everyone who had.

She made her way to the Sports Medicine room and took a notebook out of her purse. She thought of writing another note as Scarlett O'Hara but she couldn't put the pressure on Kale now. Not hours before he was to ride. So she jotted down a few things to remember.

~~~~~~~~~~~~~~~~~~~~~~~~~~~

<u>This summer things to remember!</u>
1) Things aren't always what they first appear to be.
2) Don't let fear keep you from living in the moment.

3) Falling in love is as much an adventure as it is a mystery.
4) No one care where you come from, all they care about is where you're going.
5) Good friends are hard to find, but even harder to forget.

~~~~~~~~~~~~~~~~~~~~~~~~~~~

    She circled the last one seven times. There had been seven amazing people to touch her life this summer. Matt who had been her hero for so long, turned out to be her big brother; and there was Walker, who never ceased to amaze her with his funny jokes, his carefree spirit, and an intellectual mind. Dakota, the only girl of the eight, but the most important; she taught Skyler that loving someone means giving your heart to them a hundred percent. She also taught Skyler that a girl can dominant in a man's career. Dakota was confident and that's what made so many of the riders captivated. Of course there was Brayden who taught her how to laugh again, even with his lame jokes. Brayden was trumped by Tate, who showed Skyler that even the wisest person in her dream profession can see Talent, hard work and determination. There was also Trent. So much like a father she hadn't gotten to know. He kept her spiritual on track, as well as always brought a smile to her face. She couldn't leave out Jace who taught her how to live again. Who taught her to walk with an attitude and who had been in her life for the shortest amount of time? Though, the one who weight heaviest in her heart was Kale. The man who stole her heart and who had been there through every embarrassing moment she faced. He held her captive in love, a captivity she didn't want to break free from.

Skyler didn't want this summer to end, but knew in less than two hours it would be her last event. It was a bitter-sweet moment.

Kale

He walked into the locker room. He could see most of the guys preparing for the event, but that was far from his mind. He hadn't told Skyler how he truly felt and he was lost in a world of emotions. No words in his vocabulary could explain to Skyler the strange, yet exhilarating, feeling she provoked within him. He pulled out his rope and stated spreading resin on it.

"Hey Kale, What are you doing after the event?" B.J. asked as he approached Kale in the locker room.

"Nothin' really B.J., Why?" Kale wondered what was on B.J.'s mind.

"Thought me, you, Brayden, and Tommy could go eat or something."

"Well, Dakota's here and I don't know if she will want to get Hectic Handful back home. That would be something to ask Brayden. I'm in though definitely."

Kale didn't want to impose the idea on Skyler. He knew like most events she would run back to the hotel, grab her things and head back to Texas. He wanted to do the same but he didn't want to let B.J. and Tommy down.

"What's wrong, Weston." B.J. sensed something was wrong.

"Nothin', tryin' to keep my head cleaned and Jones you have Rapid Revolver according to an unidentified source. He has gotten ranker." Kale warned.

"Good the ranker they are the better I perform." B.J. assured him.

Kale couldn't help but think about his bull. He wasn't going to get outsmarted again. He wasn't going to let Skyler go back to school without seeing the real Kale in action, the fearless cowboy who attacked each bull with all his might.

He walked out and prepared for the introduction. The lights dimmed in the arena and all Kale could hear was the beat of his heart. He was ready to prove to New Mexico that he was the cowboy for the job, but forty-four other guys wanted to lay their name to the claim. One by one they entered the arena, and Kale couldn't help but tip his hat as they called his name.

"The cowboy from Cool, Texas: Mr. Kale Weston." The announcer said in his southern drawl. To Kale it didn't matter how many screaming people he head clapping. He knew one person was clapping for him and she was the only one who mattered.

He ran into Brayden behind the chutes.

"B.J. wants us to go to dinner with him and Tommy tonight. What do you say?"

"Well, I have a felling Kota wants to load Hectic Handful up tonight and start the trek home." Brayden declared. He knew his wife hated to stay around two long when her bulls were involved.

"I told him that may be the case, but try and convince her to stay another night. What could it hurt?" Kale wanted to beg Brayden to stay but knew he didn't want to be on Dakota's bad side.

"My wife is a stubborn woman; she only wants the best for her animals. Kale there are things you won't understand until you're married."

"If you love her enough, you will ask." Kale taunted.

"Alright, I'll ask but I'm not sure she will want to." Brayden repeated himself.

"Good, I think Jace needs your help. He's nodding at you like he thinks you're hot or something." Kale tried his best to tease Brayden.

"Funny, Kale. You're real funny."

"I learned from the master himself."

Kale watched as Matt climbed aboard Lunatic. It was another new bull and he was intrigued by the bulls' calmness in the chute. With a name like Lunatic he figured the bull would be leaping out of the chute but he didn't.

Kale couldn't help but anticipate his own ride. He slowly walked over to the chute harboring Toxic Poison. He only had to ride him for an 88.00 to get back into the middle of the championship round. He climbed over, lowered himself down and took a deep breath.

He didn't want to be one of Skyler's patients her last night working. B.J. pulled his rope tight.

"Good Kale? Is it okay?" B.J. asked hoping he would say it was perfect.

"Great." He said wrapping it around his riding hand in suicide fashion.

He centered himself aboard Toxic Poison and nodded his head. Toxic spun left and took a few jumps to the right and 8 seconds later, Kale had a qualified ride. Kale untied himself and ran towards the shark cage in the middle of the arena. The rodeo clown ran over near Kale and he threw his signature punches. Kale smiled as he heard the crowd roar. He knew the ride wouldn't give him a ton of points because of the sloppy finish but he felt confident that he would get back into the championship round. He looked up at the Jumbotron and saw an 84.25 score posted. He knew he wasn't making it to the championship round; he felt a ping in his heart. He was glad he at least covered one bull. He wanted to go check in on Skyler, but knew she was probably busy. He wondered how the summer was going to end.

    As he walked down the alleyway he remembered how it all began.

    He had decided to run the gambit of tours. From the challenge to the elite, it didn't occur to him until Dallas that this summer wouldn't be like any other. She was a petite girl with auburn hair, her hazel eyes emanated from her soft face. Her cheeks reddened quickly, and her voice was soft. She seemed shy, but her soft voice rang out with confusion. He directed her to where she needed to go and every time he saw her after that it was like the tides of his heart came crashing on the shores of love. Shores that were unknown to him but shores he wanted to explore. It took a few short meetings for her to steal his heart and took as much time for him to get the courage to do something nice for her. She wore her necklace with pride. He remembered it dangling from her neck as they danced. She smelled like wildflowers that night, he eyes shone underneath the dim lights of the dance floor and she smiled. It was one more portal to her soul for him. He couldn't believe that he sand to her but his heart told him things would be okay and they were. She complimented him. Thought it was her last night here he couldn't think of anything to do. He was going to wait, wait for her move to show him that all his efforts were worth it.

He was jarred out of his daydream by Brayden.

"Dude, why do you have to scream in my ear like that?" Kale asked trying to shake the echoes from his ears.

" 'Cause I said your name twenty times and you remained in la-la-land. That's why?" Brayden seemed a little on the edge.

"Sorry, I didn't know you were tryin' to talk to me."

"Yeah, I figured I would like to tell ya that I'm in the lead." Brayden boasted.

"Way to go, maybe you can win some money." Kale joked.

"Yeah, don't want Dakota to bring home all the money."

"Sure you don't. You probably should go get ready for the championship round. I have a feelin' it will be down to you and Jace."

"Jace ain't got anything on me." Brayden told Kale with a little anger behind it.

'I didn't say he did. I wanted to make you aware of the possibility that this won't be an easy win."

"Get up, cowboy. Who else am I going to trust to pull my rope?"

Brayden and Kale left the locker room in silence. What Brayden didn't know was that Kale was still engulfed in the thoughts of Skyler but he knew Brayden didn't seem to mind. The only thing floating around in Brayden's head was an event win, and rightfully so.

Skyler

Her last night seemed slow, but as the event rounded down to only the top fifteen, she felt her summer internship coming to a close. She looked over at Sam napping on the bench, and knew that Tate was probably sitting on the back of the chutes sipping coffee and talking with whoever walked by. She hadn't imagined that her summer would have turned out so amazing. She had gained the trust of her medical hero Tate, she had won the respect of the cowboys, and she had found a great passion for Sports medicine. She could hear the roar of the crowd, and she knew that the championship round was one of double standards. Some guys would rise to the occasion, as others would crumble to the dirt. She knew that Kale was beating himself up for his performance but to Skyler it didn't matter how many bulls he covered, as long as he made it out of the arena safe from harm's way.

Skyler listened carefully as the crowd started to scream. She heard Brayden Carter's name resonant from the rafters. She couldn't help but smile. Brayden was a great bull rider, although, like Kale, he could be lost in the sea of riders. She went to give Sam a hug to bid him farewell. She hoped it wouldn't be long before she saw him again.

As she heard the clanking of spurs she decided to go say her final goodbyes to the guys who had become like her family. As she entered the locker room she encountered Matt and Walker.

"Come over here short stuff." Walker said in the same fashion he always did. "Sure going to miss you, half pint."

"I'm goin' to miss you too Walker. Keep Matt in line alright. Good luck for the rest of the season."

Matt smirked at her and then gestured her in his direction.

"Keep workin' hard Skyler. You'll be back; I ain't worried about that." Matt said as he hugged her.

"Thanks Matt. Keep climbin' your way back to the top superstar. You'll get there; I have faith."

Sky made her way around the locker room, giving hugs and shaking hands. As soon as Brayden walked in she ran over to him and gave him a hug.

"Good job tonight Carter, keep up the good work. I see a big gold shiny buckle in your future." She teased.

"Thanks Sky, you keep pushing on too. I see a sheet of paper in your future." He always knew how to throw it right back at her.

She couldn't help but laugh. "Yeah, the most valuable sheet of paper in my whole life."

As she was about to approach Kale she saw Dakota moving outside the locker room.

"Dakota you can't leave without tellin' me goodbye, cowgirl."

Dakota walked into the locker room.

"Keep your head high cowgirl, and don't be afraid to come back to the tour when big bad school kicks you out." Dakota sarcastically replied.

"I won't Dakota, you keep them bulls comin' Hectic Handful is goin' to need a travelin' partner."

"Sure is. Thanks for having a girls night with me."

"I should be the one thanking you. We will have to do it again more often when I come back." Skyler added.

"Sure will."

She smiled at Dakota and walked over to Kale who was throwing stuff into his bag.

"Can that wait cowboy?" She asked in an innocent tone.

"What? I'm almost done." He was pissed and it was easy for Skyler to see that.

"Kale Weston, turn around now." Skyler demanded.

"Hold on."

She stood behind him tapping his toes. She contemplated ripping his arm and turning him around but she didn't want to make him any madder than he was. She knew Kale was probably tapping his toes as she circled the room.

"What Sky." He asked leaving a burn on her heart.

She wrapped her arms around him. She couldn't believe what she was doing. She wanted to hold onto him forever, and knew she couldn't. She could tell by the look in his eyes that he was a little surprised as well.

"Stay strong cowboy. When the goin' gets tough, keep pushin' on okay?" She had the urge to kiss him, but all she could do was tilt her head to give her statement added effect.

"Will do Sky, will do. Don't forget about us alright?" His eyes started to cloud. She could see small tears blur over his eyes.

"Weston, I will never forget about you guys. Don't go forgotten about me now, ya hear?" His face lit up a bit, but she could see disappointment still in his eyes. She hoped he hadn't done anything to disappoint him.

"No way! Never!" He smiled and pulled her a little closer.

She loved being close to Kale but she knew she had to leave.

"Remember Weston, arm straight as you slide in into the brace." She said pulling away slowly.

"I won't forget." He assured her as he released her from his arms.

She left the locker room smiling. She couldn't believe that she had touched their lives. Let alone how close she had gotten with Kale. Unfortunately not close enough for her liking. She grabbed her bag and slung it over her shoulder. She was heading back to Texas, and this time, unlike the rest, she was unsure about her future with the BRA.

Kale

Her scent lingered for awhile as he zipped his bag up in silence. He wanted to go run after her; his heart was bursting into flames inside of him. He had let her go. He lost the only thing that mattered to him, more than bull riding. He would have to go home to his parent's house. He knew his mom would question him about his encounter with Skyler, and Kale, felt ashamed to tell his mom that nothing further had or would happen with her. He hadn't even tried though. He danced with her, sure. That was his newest breakthrough, but he had nothing else to account for then a hug, a short ride to the arena, and those glances from her mesmerizing eyes. He caught up with B.J. and went to eat.

It seemed like forever until they got their food. Kale hadn't gotten much of an opinion from B.J. and Tommy about Skyler so he thought he would ask as they ate.

"B.J, how's everythin' with Michelle?"

"Great. I love being married. Why you ask?" B.J. looked at Kale with pondering eyes.

"I want to know what a single guy like me could do to snag the woman on his dreams."

"Wait …Kale. The right girl will walk in and your world will turn upside down. You'll have thoughts of forever, which is probably the scariest part, but knowing that you'll be together forever is the best part." B.J. clamored.

"So, Tommy, what about Jessica?"

"Most amazing women in the world, wouldn't trade her for no one else."

Kale couldn't help but laugh.

"Why are you asking so many questions Kale? You know our wives?" They both declared to him.

"Yeah, I was wondering however, if I let the door shut on an opportunity."

"Why Kale? 'Cause Skyler is going back to school?" B.J. insisted.

"No, it's not Skyler." Kale defensively stated.

"Come, on cowboy we all saw the look on your face when she wrapped her arms around you." B.J. mocked. He knew he had putting Kale in a corner and couldn't wait to see how he would try to escape.

"So, she smelled good. Didn't y'all get to experience that yourself?" Kale knew he couldn't fake it, he knew everyone could and would figure out he was madly head over heels for Skyler.

"Right Kale, we really believe that." Tommy retorted. He and B.J. could tell by the look in Kale's eyes that he was lying through his teeth.

"It's true, she did smell good. She is a great girl, but someone else probably had her heart. Why wouldn't someone else already stake their claim to her? She is one of the best catches out in this sea."

B.J. couldn't help but laugh. "If someone had her heart; then why was she on this massive search for this Rhett guy all summer?" B.J. started a stare down with Kale.

"Rhett? She was searchin' for Rhett all summer?" Kale was shocked but he couldn't let them see it.

"Yeah obviously some guy gave her flowers, and a necklace. She sure was falling for him." B.J. could sense the wheels in Kale's head turning.

Kale smiled. It made him feel good that he made Sky's summer by doing simple things for her, but he also didn't want to leak out that he was Rhett.

"Kale, are you Rhett?" Tommy asked out of sheer curiosity.

"What if I was?" He knew he couldn't hold his secret any longer. Tommy and B.J. were hot on his case.

"Why didn't you tell her?" B.J. blurted out.

"I couldn't do it. Every time I wanted too it got harder. Then we danced guys I sang to her. I even got lost in her eyes. I don't know what to do. She graduates in December the next possible chance of me seeing Sky is in January." He was anxious to hear what they had to say in response to his mini monologue.

"Not unless you find out where she is going to school." Tommy suggested.

"I can't do that. I know it's somewhere down in Texas."

"Well, ask Tate. I doubt he is sworn to secrecy." B.J. suggested.

"Guys, I'm goin' to wait and see how this plays out."

Kale knew he wouldn't get an approval from his move. He couldn't bring himself to go searching after her though either. The mystery of the possible boyfriend back at school still lingered in his mind. They didn't understand that maybe she was searching for Rhett to thank him and to tell him to leave her alone. He couldn't deal with the thought of rejection from Skyler. He put his knife down on his plate and waited for the reaction from the peanut gallery.

Both B.J. and Tommy shook their heads in disapproval.

------------ ------------------
Skyler

The flight back to Texas seemed to drag on. She didn't know if it had to do with her excitement for her last year of school, or her undying need to be back on the ranch. She missed it a lot when she traveled, but didn't realize it until she had idle time. She picked up her diary from her carry on and scanned her summer page again. She wanted so bad to conclude the summer with something grand, but he summer was ending. She would have two weeks of ranch work, before school would start again. It was a matter of time before she would be out of school, searching the great unknown for a job.

As she got off the airplane she could see the sparkle in her Grandpa's eyes.

"Welcome back." He said in the same raspy southern drawl he always had.

"Thanks Grandpa. I sure missed you." She had to admit it. She missed being around him, learning his lesson, and of course being babied by him.

"Now that we are admitting it, I missed you too."

Skyler loved when he was a wise crack. She couldn't help but laugh. Of all the people in the world she felt alike, the first was her mother. The second happened to be her grandfather.

Skyler and Jesse were straddled when they heard a foreign voice.

"Hey Jesse! What you doing here?" A voice came from afar.

An older woman started to approach. She had sliver-grey hair cut short. She had stark brown eyes and her skin was tanned as if she had spent her winter in Florida. Her face displayed the map of her life. Every laugh line, frown line, and age spot told of her life story.

"Ilene, I haven't seen you in forever. I'm here to pick up my granddaughter, Skyler." Jesse pulled Skyler close to him.

"Didn't know you had children even. Maybe would have known if you showed up at a class reunion once and awhile. She is almost a spit image of her grandmother. How's poor Lanette doin'?" Ilene questioned. The crackle in her voice gave the place an eerie feeling to Skyler.

"She passed away ten years ago." He responded trying to keep from falling apart in front of Ilene.

Skyler could see this conversation was tearing him apart. He had a hard time talking about the loss of his loving Lanette with his own family. Let alone some high school friend who had forgotten about him.

"Sorry to hear that Jesse. Everyone knew you guys would be together for a long time."

"Yeah we were; it's getting' late and we have some early mornin' ranch work to get done. It was nice seenin' you Ilene." He muttered as she tugged on Skyler's shirt sleeve. They exited the airport in silence.

"Whose Ilene, Grandpa? One of the girls from high school grandma always talked about who wanted you?" Skyler tried her best not to come off as if she was prying into his business.

"No, she was one of those girls who wanted to be. I saw your Grandma Sky and knew we would be together forever. We will, we always will. Ilene, on the other hand tried hard to get your Grandma to believe I was a scum, but it didn't work. Funny how strong love is. If it's meant to be it will find a way."

"Grandpa, I think you opened my eyes." It was true. He had opened her eyes. She had been so bummed about Kale, but if Kale was meant to be. God would find a way to make it happen.

"What do you mean hunnie?" Her grandfather was confused. He knew he felt the exact way he had spoken, but how did it open her eyes? He wondered.

'Durin' the plane ride I was feelin' bad that nothin' ever happened with me and a certain bull rider. I pitied myself for not being a strong woman and takin' the lead. Grandpa, I don't want to have to take the lead if a guy loves me. I want the kind of love Grandma always talked about. How you walked into the room and your smile made her melt. I want a guy who can say my name and send chills up my spine. Is it wrong to want love like a fairy tale?" She could feel a ping in her heart. She knew it was wrong to expect anything that wasn't right, though she loved the thought of Kale. The thought of him being the cowboy to finally take her away into the wild blue; although her heart ached thinking about the possibility that it wouldn't happen.

"No, as long as you have limits. Not everythin' is going to happen. Doesn't mean none of what you want will. Is this about the bull rider from around here?" Her grandpa's curiosity on this mystery man was growing steadily.

"This state yes, but I'm sure he never went to a bull ridin' school of yours. Believe me, Grandpa he doesn't have your form whatsoever."

"Skyler, we all ride differently. What's this bull rider's name?" He asked hoping she would tell him.

"Grandpa, his name isn't important. He exemplifies the stereotype at least for the most part."

"Skyler, don't make me ground you." His stern voice echoed in the tiny Ford Ranger.

"Ground me." She lightly chuckled. "The last time you said that, Loren was here. We snuck out to go to a bonfire. You told us to stay home 'cause one of the cows could possibly calf while you were in town. Loren kept provokin' me to go so we left. We got back in the nick of time, to deliver the calf ourselves. You said we would be grounded and for a good job you took us out for ice cream. So, if I remember correctly, groundin' is a good thing." She smiled. She couldn't help but remember that moment. He had been furious at first that the girls had snuck out to the bonfire. Though, his frustration was replaced by gratitude for delivering the calf safely.

"I was never too good at modern parenting or grand parenting obviously. It's not that I want to go pull up this guy's criminal records, but I will if you want me too." Grandpa Jesse admitted.

"No Grandpa. No need to go senile yet. His name is Kale Weston and, if you want to know, he is a Christian." Hoping the last statement would ease her grandfather's mind a bit.

"Good. Pretty necklace you got there. Where did you get it at?"

"Complication to the Kale story so there is this Rhett Butler floatin' around the circuit, sendin' me flowers and givin' me jewelry." She still had a strong connection that it was Kale. Although, a part of her wonders why Kale wouldn't have admitted it; why he wouldn't tell her? She would have told him she was Scarlett O'Hara but the timing wasn't right. She also knew she had left him an extra surprise.

"How do you know Rhett ain't Kale?" Her grandpa gave her the cowboy stare.

"He told me. He said he had no clue about the flowers in my room. He assured me that it wasn't him." Her heart sank in her chest as she recalled hearing the news.

"Sky, you are goin' to believe everythin' you hear?" He had taught her to always be thinking. He knew she had many ideas spinning in her head, but hoped she hadn't lost hope on this Weston kid.

"When I trust him, yes."

"Skyler let me give you some advice kiddo. When a guy is in love, they lie a lot. Not intentionally, more like white lies. We avoid our inner feelings Sky. We have a hard time tellin' people what we feel. Maybe, this Kale Weston character didn't want you to know his inner feelin's about you."

"Yeah right Grandpa." She said as she reached to turn on the radio. She was mad that her grandfather was defending Kale. Obviously, he didn't care for her. Sure, they had danced and the best night of the summer was that night. Though, he only ever asked her to treat him. He never let her in and he still happened to be the guy who she walked in on. She wanted to believe what her grandfather was rambling. She wanted to believe that fate would bring her back to Kale, that he was masking some sort of feelings for her. Though, something inside of her told her to stop being foolish. To settle for the fact that she had let Rhett and Kale slip away.

A song kicked on the radio as she twisted the old dials. She couldn't believe this song was playing at a time like this. A time when she was torn between a man she danced with and a man she didn't know. She had played it many nights while she was a sophomore at Northeast Montana State University. It was a song that gave her courage when she felt lacking. It was a song that made her think of Loren and their crazy antics. It was a song that somehow fit in her complicated life.

She couldn't help but start belting out the words.

"I can tell you his favorite colors green; he loves to argue, born on the 17th. His sister's beautiful. He got his daddy's eyes, if you ask me if I love him. I'd lie.

First thought when I wake up is my God he's so beautiful, so I put on my makeup and pray for a miracle. Yes, I could tell you his favorite colors green, he loves to argue and it kills me. His sister's beautiful. He has his daddy's eyes. If you ask me if I love him, If you ask me if I love him, I'd lie."

"Skyler, why would you lie about something like that?" Her grandfather was a bit confused. He knew he had raised her to be honest about her feelings. He taught her to be in tuned with nature and the world around her.

"I wouldn't want the whole world to know, Grandpa. It's a song too, Grandpa. Maybe, I wouldn't do it in real life." She assured him with a smile.

"So, let me get this straight. You didn't try anythin' with this bull rider, 'cause everyone would know your human and fall in love? Am I right?" He raised his cowboy hat up as he raised his eyebrows.

"It's not that, I didn't want girls thinkin' I was only into him because of the wranglers, or buckles. Grandpa, I like Kale in ways he doesn't even think about and ways I ain't tellin' you, that would be to awkward. I want the world to see me as a cowgirl, a doctor, and not as a buckle bunny." Skyler had the worst taste in her mouth as she said buckle bunny. In most applications of the word, it stood as an insult. Not when she referred to Loren of course. She knew how people felt about a girl who threw herself at a rodeo cowboy. She knew the history behind those who engaged in such acts. She wanted to be held with respect. She had been raised with respect; she had given respect to those who deserve it. The last thing she wanted was to be stereotyped into a class she didn't belong.

"Fair enough, remember Sky, if this Kale Weston is meant to be with you. God will allow it to work out in his own time. Remember, the verse about love is patient. Apply that here."

Skyler smiled. She often times lost touch with the word of God. She knew everything her grandfather was saying was true. If Kale was meant to be with her, God would find a way to make it happen. Be patient, she repeated to herself before she responded back to her grandpa.

"Thanks Grandpa," she murmured as slide out of her side of the truck.

------------------   ------------------

Kale

The morning flight home made him anxious. He couldn't wait to be back in Texas. At the same time, it was a reminder of a missed opportunity with Skyler. He had been crazy about her; at least that's what he learned from B.J. and Tommy. He dug through his carry-on. He compared the two notes he had received from Scarlett O'Hara.

As he tugged on them to free them from his bag, a sealed envelope with his name on it fell out.

He gently busted the seal as he picked it up. He was hoping to be more careful as to not rip the contents. He found a note in the same handwriting as the other two.

****

Summer may be coming to an end, but my memory will never die. My memory of you will live on. I hope one day all the barriers in our way, will be removed. Love cannot be caged: it cannot be forbidden, it cannot be harnessed. You may never see the love from my eyes, but know that all the love that fills them will never leave me. For I know, someday, we will be together.
Love: XOXO
Scarlett O'Hara
P.s. Farewell beloved.

****

He knew that Scarlett O'Hara was Skyler. The way each word flowed in the same passionate way, the way he envisioned her writing such words brought tears to his eyes; he had been given a sign all along. She was the one to make the first move, and here he was being a dumbass. He couldn't believe he had missed everything. He wanted so bad to find her, but feared fate wouldn't lead him back to her. He sighed. How could he have been so dumb, how could life being closing in on him.

As the plane landed he was relieved to finally be home. It seemed as if the whole plane ride was a reminder of what he should have done. He knew before too long the end of the season would dawn upon him. He knew he needed to get focused if he wanted to be in the race for a world buckle. Sitting in tenth place, he thought it would be impossible that the BRA name him World Champion. Though he mentally calculated the points left, and he knew under miraculous circumstances that it could be done.

He walked out of the airport and saw his Dad waving him over.

"Hey Kale, tough break this weekend. Believe me son; sometimes those judges are blinder than bats." He mentioned as he scooped his son up in his arms.

"It's alright Dad, really. My mind wasn't in it like it should have been." He shamefully admitted.

"Been bitten by the love bug, huh, son?" He could see it in his son's eyes. He was lost in self pity. What he should have done, consumed him. As he thought of what he did do.

"Sure have, I know there is no cure for it, except for her." His face got long. He wanted to scream, or cry. He didn't know. He knew only one thing that could solve his pent up aggression; his punching bag.

"Her? You mean Skyler, don't ya?"

"Yeah Dad, that's who I mean. She left me another letter. I found it in my bag today."

"Well, what did it say?" His father was intrigued by the girl's game plan.

"That she knew that it didn't work out like she had wanted it to. That if we were meant to be then fate would make it that way again."

"She's a smart girl, this Skyler. She knows what real loves all about."

"Dad, she isn't smart, she is beyond smart. I can't believe I was the dumb one. I was jaded, Dad. Jaded by some farfetched possibilities. I guess they weren't so farfetched after all." He looked his dad square in the eye, hoping to find the answers he was searching so long for.

"Son, nothin's too farfetched."

Kale climbed into his dad's truck.

Skyler

The heat of the sun beamed down, as Grandpa and her prepared for the round up. It was time for some of the bulls to get their shots, and it was Skyler's duty to help round them up for the morning's festivities. She always loved round up's with her grandfather. They were days when he told stories, mostly about the stories his grandpa told him, but sometimes, it was stories of experience.

"Skyler, every time I see you on these round ups I remember when your Grandma was learning. Owin' a little farm is much easier than this big old ranch. Sometimes she would sit up in the saddle on her chestnut Quarter Horse, Catalina. She would watch me go after the cattle, and her eyes would light up." He was easily swept back to the memory like the wind swept through the trees.

"I can only imagine Grandpa. I watch you 'cause I'm learnin', not to check you out like Grandma did." She knew he wouldn't appreciate the sassy comment.

"Skyler!" His face seemed mortified at his granddaughter's comment.

"What Grandpa? I'm sayin' what I'm hearin'. Grandma had eyes for you and only you, old man."

"Skyler Kay Pendleton. I AM NOT AN OLD MAN!" He felt the steam come out of his ears.

"Maybe inside Grandpa, but the outside screams early seventies." She knew there was a possibility she would be in the doghouse with such a comment, but she let it fly anyways.

"Sometimes, I wondered why I told your mother I would take you in." He mentioned with a tinge of frustration in his voice.

"You needed help out here, you love me, and she didn't want you to be lonely. I'm your only granddaughter as well." She batted her eyelashes. She knew deep down inside she was grandpa's baby girl. Wither he admitted it to the world or not.

"True, but sometimes I wonder if my ideas were right."

"Grandpa, they were. When you're gone I will be able to handle the ranch by myself. You won't have to worry."

"You know this how?" He demanded.

"Grandpa, I ain't leavin' Texas." She reminded him.

"Skyler, what were the terms about you comin' here?"

"If Tate says no, I go home." She felt disguised as she repeated it. Why should her life in Texas depend on one doctor? She could always find a job at any other clinic but that didn't run through her grandfather's mind. Skyler hated the thought of going back to Billings.

"Yes and Sky, don't think of me as a bad guy. I know what kind of life you would have if you stayed here. Believe me hun, it's a life I don't want you to have." He looked at her remorsefully.

"Grandpa, what is so shameful about being a ranch hand anyways?" The blood in her veins started to boil to the surface.

"Skyler you're too young to realize it, it's a hard profession. You only work on two small ranches. You have uncertainty. What happens if the ranch you are workin on goes belly up? Skyler, you're goin' to college to better your life. To try and make somethin' of yourself you understand that right? I know you and Loren dreamed of workin' this ranch, but Skyler, it's impossible to live like that, and impossibility I don't want you to have to face." He took a deep breath.

"Grandpa, where did you get your logic? Nothin' is impossible. One thing Loren and I lived by." A tear slowly leaked from her right eye as she spoke.

"So, it's settled. You're marryin' Kale Weston 'cause me ain't goin' to let the ranch be without a man!"

Skyler started to bit her lip. She was furious. Where did he get by on saying who she married? Her ears started to twitch as she replayed the comment in her head. She could work this ranch better than most men in Texas, which included Kale.

"Grandpa, I can run this ranch. I can run it right too. I learned from the best. You even told me that had it been you to go before Grandma, you would have trusted her. So why can't you trust me. This is my home as well." She turned JB so that he and Gunner would be nose to nose.

"I do trust you Sky. Sometimes I think you focus too much on your career and not enough of what's really important. When was the last time you made amends with your father?"

She could feel her grandpa stepping over unnecessary boundaries.

"Grandpa, we talk on and off. I'm sorry I have been a little focused on school. Plus, I realized this time that it doesn't matter what he did on tour, he is still my dad, and to some guys he is a hero."

"He has always been a hero, he is your hero." He had no problem reminding her of that fact.

She tried effortlessly to keep the tears from pouring down her face. It was true, every word was true. He was her hero. He was her superman. Her father could do no wrong in her eyes at least until the rumor shattered everything they had.

"He was Loren's too. It took me awhile to realize it. I aint goin' to let moments slip away from us, Grandpa. You said your biggest regret was never being with the ones you love. I ain't goin' to let those moments go." A stream of tears flowed down from her misty eyes.

He smiled at her, knowing he had raised her well for the last four years.

Three
Months
Later

Kale

It seemed like forever since the last time he saw Skyler. It was November and the last weekend of the World Finals. He had waited for the last weekend because like normal Jace and Brayden were duking it out, but B.J. wasn't going to let them be the only two. He also couldn't wait to see Dakota. Hectic Handful was among the bulls chosen for the finals. He would be bucking in the weekends' rounds. He heard his phone ring and went to pick it up.

"Yo, Brayden! What you doin'?" He asked trying to be cool.

"Laughing my butt off we need you to get back to the back pens. We need your helped." He urged as he hung up the phone on Kale.

He walked to the back pens and saw Dakota laughing so hard on the ground.

"What's goin' on?" He asked.

"That bull sure lives up to his name." Brayden said trying to gasp for air.

"What do you mean?" Kale asked a little confused about the whole ordeal.

"He almost ran Dakota over when she opened the trailer." Brayden said as he finally found composure.

"Dakota, you okay?" Kale asked concerned about her safety.

"I'm fine. He sure doesn't like long trips. I can't blame him. He is taken after Brayden I suppose. You know Brayden he gets so whiney after long trips." She stood up and dusted off her butt.

"I don't get whiney." Brayden mentioned trying to defend himself.

Dakota rolled her eyes.

"It's sure great to see y'all. Again, what's it been, a week?" Kale chimed in.

"Yeah, how's Vegas?" Dakota questioned.

"Not helpin' me fill my pockets. Kind of hopin' after this weekend's event is over that someone else gets lucky."

"Kale, you can say her name. We know you mean Sky. We know you want Tate to hire her." The Carters said soundly.

"Yeah, 'cause she deserves it. She deserves a lot more than a job on tour, too."

"Right, you want to fix everything that didn't happen this summer." Brayden said in a mocking kind of way.

"Yeah, kind of. Now let's get this bull settled in. We can't let his chances of being bull of the year get ruined by the long trip."

They all took different tasks to make sure Hectic Handful was a little more settled in.

As the weekend dragged on Kale knew that Jace Montgomery would be crowned

World Champion. He also predicted that Hectic Handful would be the first bull to win both bull of the year honors as well as bull of the finals. The lights shined down upon the arena and the energy from the fans made the arena feel over 150 degrees. He knew that Jace was preparing for his glory; being the second guy in BRA history to win the finals and world championship buckles; right behind Sky's hero and big brother, Matt. He was happy for Jace, as he climbed on the only bull that stood in his way of the buckle. Warrior had been on the tour a long time and claimed two world championship buckles himself. He was looking for his third and knew his only way of achieving it would be to buck off Jace Montgomery.

    The eight second buzzer couldn't have sounded sweeter to Kale. It was the perfect ending to a historic ride. His friend was the world champion and rightfully so. He searched around for the bull sheets, and found Dakota clenching one in awe.

    He snuck a peek. He couldn't believe it. She had surpassed all expectation; claiming the three most prodigious honors that a stock contractor could receive.

    "Congrats. Three buckles. How you plan on wearin' all of them? Harley and Donaldson now know they have stiff competition, Stock

Contractor of the Year." He wrapped his arms around Dakota.

Dakota returned his embrace. She turned around to her husband, who was awaiting his kiss.

"I'm proud of you baby, you did way better than me, at least on Carter is leaving Vegas a champion."

Brayden picked her up and spun her around. As he placed her back on the platform she smiled.

"Hunnie, I'm leaving Vegas with three buckles." She said as she laughed.

Brayden kissed her forehead. "Go get your picture taken champ." He swiftly slapped her butt.

Kale smiled at Brayden and they both stormed the arena to jump on Jace.

Skyler

It was awfully warm for December. She was graduating. Her Dad, Mom and Grandpa were all sitting in a row, waiting to hear her name called. She couldn't help but start to tear up as they said.

"Dr. Skyler Kay Pendleton."
She had a hard time believing it. She had finally hit her goal, and she knew as the rain

suddenly came pouring down that she had people in heaven proud of her too.

"Grandma sure is proud, look at those rain drops." Her grandpa insisted.

"She sure is, Grandpa." Skyler mentioned before kissing his cheek.

"Loren ain't far from her bawling her baby blues out." Sky's mom added.

"I know, Mom. She needs to quit it. It's not a big deal."

"Not a big deal? Skyler Pendleton, you did it. You are a doctor, and if you don't think that's anything special than you haven't seen all you had to do to get here." Her father was determined to show her how amazing her accomplishment was. He wrapped his arms around his daughter. They swayed as he held her tightly.

"No Dad. I know it's amazing. I'm glad y'all are here to share it with me." She looked up at the grey sky.

They walked back to their vehicles and headed back to the ranch. Skyler picked up her cell phone; she had to call Tate. She had to see if she had a job for the next season.

The phone seemed to ring forever and the voice she wanted to hear finally answered.

"Dr. Tate Feldman, how may I help you?"

His voice sounded the same on the phone as he did in person. It sent sparks up

Skyler's spine. She wanted him to tell her she was in, though, by the length of pause she had added to the conversation she was a bit concerned.

"Tate, its Skyler. I graduated today and was wondering if you had an opening on the Sports Medicine team."

"Congratulations, Skyler! Or should I say Dr. Pendleton. Although, I don't want to make you're exciting day bad, but I don't have an opening right now. Sky, go get your hands dirty in the field, I'll keep you in mind the next time I need someone okay."

"Okay, I hope you have fun relaxin' before you guys have to hit the road again. Take care." As she hung up the phone she could feel the lump in her throat migrate to her heart.

She couldn't believe it. The job she dreamed of since she was fourteen years old suddenly was gone.

"What's wrong Sky?" Her mother asked.

"I didn't get the job with Tate." She still couldn't believe it as it flowed from her lips.

Her Grandpa knew exactly what she was thinking inside. She wasn't ready to leave Texas and he knew that. He couldn't allow her to be less than her best.

"You didn't rent my room at." She asked both her parents. Ashamed that she would be ending back on the ranch in Billings, she didn't want to go home though she couldn't fight it.

"No Sky. We actually cleared the back 150 acres. We built you your own little cabin, and when you're done with it, your dad will kindly take it off your hands." Her mother mentioned.

She tried to put up a strong front. "Thanks, it means a lot."

Her heart still fought her about going home to Billings. She had adjusted to life in Texas. She had adjusted to small town Abilene.

Five
Months
Later

Kale

The season seemed to fly by in Kale's eyes. One minute it was the first event in New York and now he was getting ready to head to Montana. He was excited not only because of the event but he knew Matt's mom would be cooking for all the guys. She started the tradition not long after Matt joined the tour, and to Kale anything free was a great thing.

He quickly packed his things and ran downstairs. He knew he had someone important to pick up before he could head to the airport. As he parked in her driveway he smiled as she ran to the truck.

Out came a five foot six blonde bombshell. She had the perfect figure since she was a model. She had gone to college with Kale and before he knew it she had come back into the limelight of his life.

"Ready to go to Billings, baby?" He asked in a sweet tone.

"Sure am, hun." Tiffany said in her nasal tone.

They drove to the airport in silence. She was tired from her trip to Spain for a photo shoot, and he, was focused on getting them to the airport safe. When they arrived, they quickly went to check in and climb aboard the plane.

"Hun, is it goin' to be cold up there?" She asked really concerned about the clothes she packed.

"Don't know. Sometimes it's freezin' other times there is great weather. Most beautiful state you will ever see though."

"You goin' to win, baby; show Brayden whose boss."

"Goin' to try Tiff, I'm goin' to try."

They both fell asleep, holding each other's hand. As Kale slept he could only imagine how the event would go. Billings's venue was beautiful. He also couldn't help but remember Skyler. He knew she was originally from Montana. He knew that Tate had declined her offer to be on his team. He hoped wherever she was, she was doing what she loved. He hoped that if she was drifting around Montana, that she wouldn't show up in Billings. He didn't know how he would handle her seeing him with Tiffany.

Skyler

She couldn't believe she was attending a Bra event as a fan again. It would be her first time in the grandstands since Loren passed away, and it was a weird feeling. She quickly checked her purse for her ticket. She hoped she was close enough to see the action, and maybe even close enough to talk to the guys again. She had missed them a lot. Working in Billings was nothing like the summer she had worked on tour. All the amazing people she had met, all the grotesque injuries she got to repair. To her, working in Billings was boring. Most injuries she dealt with came from football and baseball. She didn't care though. She figured that she would never get the same rush she did that summer. Tate tended to keep people on his staff for a long time. She knew it would be a long time before her chance would even come around.

She ran downstairs.

"Where are you going speedy?" Sky's dad asked.

"To my other house, I think I left my make up over there."

"Must be nice to have two homes. Sorry we didn't get it heated."

She smiled. They had done everything they could to welcome her back to Billings. Her Dad could feel that they were no longer going to butt heads over his past. He loved having her home, but most the time she was off to work or running around.

"No Dad, it's great. I love it out there really. I also love living in my old room though, too. So I live in both, but dad. I really need to go get my makeup. I don't want to be late to the event."

"Ride JB out there. He needs some exercise." Her dad insisted.

"Thanks Dad, always lookin' out for my horse."

She went to the barn and mounted JB. She could tell he was ready to be out. He galloped towards the cabin. The ride was one of JB's favorites, he got to jump over tree trunks and of course there was a little creek to splash through.

She dismounted him and rubbed him down.

"Boy, what would I do without you?"

He nickered as if telling her that she would be lost without him. She knew it was true. She opened the door to the cabin and JB stuck his head in.

"Boy, you know you can't come inside. You won't fit. I'll be right back."

She rummaged through her bathroom and found her backpack full of makeup. She shut and locked the door to the cabin. She turned around and mounted JB.

"Ready to go back. Boy?

He nodded in agreement. They rode back off into the distance to Sky's parents place.

Kale

He nudged Tiffany.

"Hun, we are here."

They both stumbled off the plane.

"Where we goin' now, baby?" She whined.

"To rent a truck so we can go to Matt's moms' house." He murmured to her as he kissed her cheek.

"Oh yeah, you told me she is a great cook. Then we go off to the event?"

"Exactly... what are we doin', baby?" He said smilin' at her.

They walked over to the car rental place. Kale's eyes lit up as they gave him the keys to a brand new Ford F-250 Super Duty.

"Baby, do we need a truck this big?" Tiffany scoffed.

"Yeah why not, test drives it. We don't know if we want one so why not test it out?" He looked at her with sad eyes.

"Okay, if you say so."

Kale and Tiffany climbed into the truck and drove off towards Matt's moms' house.

They were the last two to arrive. Kale could see Brayden and Dakota in the corner.

He slowly made his way holding Tiffany's hand through the slew of riders.

"Hey guys. How's the bulls?" Kale asked hoping to get a response.

"Hectic Handful's great like always. In contention for another championship no doubt, and Joker well, he is going to make a joke out of you Kale." Brayden mentioned.

"Why me?" He was a bit confused.

"Cade told me you drew him." Brayden added with a smile on his face.

"Nice, I can't wait to test out you new one."

Dakota inserted a comment in the conversation.

"Why did you bring her?"

"She's my girlfriend I wanted her to come to Billings."

"Dude, her and Dakota don't get along." Brayden reminded him.

"Yeah, little skanky clad buckle bunny. Trying to break into a new scene or something?" Dakota was ready to pounce.

"Dakota, she ain't a buckle bunny. She is great on horseback. Sure she models, but why does that matter?"

Tiffany ran off to the bathroom crying.

"She is disrespectful, plus I didn't know you could forget about Skyler. She was way better than tiffany anyday." Dakota didn't care if she was hurting Tiffany's feelings nor did she care if she reminded Kale that Skyler still existed.

"We weren't meant to be Dakota. If we were things would have happened." Kale knew that was a weak excuse.

"Like what, Tate would have given her a job. She didn't obviously get a job with Tate. That doesn't mean you have to settle down with Tiffany."

Dakota stomped away to find Jace, she was tired of confronting Kale. She knew that Skyler was the girl for him. It wasn't only because of their short time together, but because she knew Tiffany was only in it for Kale's money.

"Whoa, slow down, snarl nose." Jace said.

"Jace, I ain't a horse."

"I know. Don't go storming out, we're about to have dinner, unless you need to leave to check on the bulls. Then I'll cover for you."

"No, I'm staying but as long as I don't have to sit next to Tiffany. I swear Jace, if I sit next to her, she is gonna get hurt." Dakota was furious.

"Dakota, don't ruin your job over her. Besides, I was waiting to show someone this." He pulled out a newspaper article from his pocket.

The headline read Dr. Skyler Pendleton may have found the right combination of rest and recovery for concussion patients.

"Jace, where did you find this?" Dakota wondered.

"In the grocery store, look at the city." Jace put his finger on the second sentence.

"Billings! Oh my gosh, Jace. Are you trying to tell me she is in Billings?"

"Yeah, exactly what I'm telling you. You know as well as I do a rodeo comes to town, a cowgirl comes running." Jace's eyes widen as a crazy scheme started brewing in his head.

"Jace, you're a genius." Dakota hugged him.

"I'm not a genius. I have a feeling she will be there and that we have to find a way for Kale to see her."

"Don't say a thing Jace Montgomery. I'll find Skyler at the event. I've been meaning to talk to her anyways."

Dakota hugged Jace again and started he walk back to Brayden. She was happy to know that Tiffany would be long gone after Kale looked at Skyler. She also knew with the article Jace had, Tate was more likely to hire her on. She couldn't believe that everything she had been wishing for was coming true.

She found Brayden standing in the corner of the kitchen.

"Everything alright, baby?" Brayden asked concerned about his wife.

"Sure is. I Love you, you know that right?" She stared at him with a smitten look on her face.

"Sure do, but I love it when you say it."

Brayden leaned over to kiss her. Walker made a groaning sound from behind them.

"Walker, shut up." Dakota said jokingly.

They all filed in through the kitchen and made their plates. The sound of praying echoed through the old house.

Skyler

She finished applying her make-up and walked down the steps.

"You look gorgeous, hun." Her mom said from the kitchen.

"Thanks Mom, a doctor of my standing should look good every once in awhile."

"Speaking of that, Sky, look what you're father found in today's paper."

She flipped to the local news to find her research study and an article about it. She started to read it aloud.

"This small town girl turned into a big time star, proposing that each concussion and each circumstance should be treated differently. This isn't a new proposition, but her techniques are new and engaging. Dr. Skyler Kay Pendleton, 25, of Billings, Montana is among the newest young guns to hit the medical field. Pendleton treats every patient with the same respect. Skyler's fascination came from bull riding; a sport that the men in her family have long been involved in. When asked at a conference why it impacted her study she simply replied,

'Ain't many golf players that get concussions? I saw my father get numerous concussions. I have seen friends get them. Believe me, they are an endangerment to the life of athletes, but with proper treatment and proper teaching, the world of concussions will go from black to white. Right now we are in the grey. I'm tryin' to move it forward.'"

"Skyler, congratulations," both of her parents said with smiles on their faces.

"Thanks, guys. I can't believe it."

"Well, hun, you're going to be late for the rodeo, you better go. We can celebrate later." Skyler's mom wrapped her arms around her.

"Okay, love you mom." She said pulling away from her.

Skyler left the house and climbed into her truck. The air smelled like rain, and Skyler loved everything about rain. As sher turned into the parking lot, she saw the stream of fans waiting to get inside the arena. She found a parking sport next to a Ford Super Duty. She climbed out and moseyed her way to join the rest of the anxious fans.

Kale

He could feel the heat rising within him. He was out to prove he could ride alongside the big dogs. Many people were in disbelief that he was in the top three. He, however, was out to prove to the world that the underdog could finally pull through. With a win under his belt already, he felt pretty confident that he could string four bulls together in Billings.

"Hey Kale, are you ready to go ride?" asked Rylan.

Rylan Cummings was a hot shot rookie. He stood five foot eight and had shaggy blonde hair that curled at the end under his cowboy hat. Rylan had won rookie of the year last season and now seemed to be gunning for Kale ever chance he got.

"Yeah Rylan I am. Are you ready to be schooled?" Kale looked at him like there was no way Rylan could beat him.

"Come on Kale, we all know that I will be the one schooling you. Besides, that pretty little thing in the Sports Medicine room last summer ain't here to bring you luck."

Rylan's comment struck Kale in the heart like a knife. He knew Skyler wasn't there. He knew he had screwed up with her. He had no doubt in his mind that she was married somewhere. He had to shake Skyler, he couldn't let her cloud his memory.

"I don't need luck, Rylan. I have talent." Kale defensively stated.

Rylan smirked and walked away.

"So Kale, you going to ride one tonight?" Jacob Harley asked.

Jacob Harley was a tall lanky gentleman. His hair was cut short and rested underneath his white Stetson. He had been Kale's friend in school and his dad Jordyn Donaldson used to run Kale to rodeos whenever his father couldn't.

"I drew one of Dakota's bulls. So I better ride or she is going to laugh me out of this place."

"Yeah, that new little Mulley she has is quit the bull. He is like a sprinkler or something when he gets into that spin."

"Yeah, that happens to be my draw. His name is Joker."

"Good luck then Kale." He said shaking Kale's hand.

"Thanks. I think they are getting ready for introductions. Don't want to be late."

Kale walked through the alleyway and to the back of the chutes.

Skyler

She couldn't believe how close to the alleyway she was. It had been a dream of Loren's to sit there. So when Jace would walk out she would scream his name, trying to get his attention. Skyler wasn't going to try that. She liked Jace sure, but only one name was on her mind. The lights dimmed in front of her eyes, and she knew it was time for the show to begin. The announcer's voice seemed faint until he moved to the four riders stationed on the shark cage. As the arena lights oscillated she could make out the faces of the four. She could never forget Matt's face, and standing right next to him, was the one man she wanted to see. Kale stood tall; he stood with pride, something Skyler hadn't had the chance to see. Next to him was none other than Brayden Carter, and standing to his right was Jace Montgomery.

As the announcer made his way around the shark cage, she could finally hear his southern voice.

"Sittin' in the number three position thus far in the season is Kale Weston. This cowboy hails from Cool, Texas, and comes from a linage of bull riders. His daddy is the great Jake Weston, and his granddaddy was the amazing Justin Weston. This kid has already taken a buckle this season, so let's hear it for Kale Weston."

Skyler couldn't help but scream. She knew he couldn't make out her scream from the other billion. As the announcer finished his rounds; Trent took over the microphone, and they all prayed. As the lightly slowly illuminated the arena, Skyler could see Tate in the alleyway. She stood up and got close to the rail.

"Dr. Tate Feldman." Skyler yelled.

He looked up in disbelief.

"What are you doing here?"

"You think the BRA could come to Billings and I wouldn't be here, you have to be kiddin' me."

"Good to see you, Jace showed me the newspaper. You sure are making a name for yourself."

"Have to do somethin' memorable." Tears started to grace her eyes. She couldn't cry in front of Tate. Though, he still held her dream captive. She wanted to ask him why, but her heart told her not to. All the way her brain is in limbo, trying to fight her heart out of the words she wishes to say.

"You're getting there. You still wear that necklace." The lights shined off the silver horseshoe. Skyler had forgotten she had even put it on. It lay in her jewelry box for months after graduation. Until now, she had to wear it; some cosmic force field pulled her to it.

"Sure do, Tate, will there ever be a spot for me on your team?" she could no longer hold the words back.

"I don't know, Sky. I want there to be, but I can only afford to pay so many people right now." He admitted.

"I understand, if you get swamped and need an extra set of hands, you know where I'm sitting. I'll do it for free."

"I will come get you for sure." He said as he smiled.

She sat down, waiting for Kale to ride.

Kale

He prepared himself in the chute as he heard the screaming fans. He knew Matt had ridden Podunk. It was his turn to dazzle the crowd. He knew he had to ride Joker. Not only to avoid harassment from Brayden and Dakota, but also to ensure a steady climb up the standings. He could feel the heat from the lights, sweat accumulated in his helmet. He wasn't going to waste any time. After tightening his rope, he nodded.

Joker flung out of the chute like a hot potato. The Mulley bull spun left hard. Kale felt like a tiny ragdoll on his monstrous back. The centripetal force of Joker's spin, stirred dust around them. Kale found it harder to see as Joker increased his speed. To the crowds amazement, Kale stayed on for the full eight seconds.

He got off and ran towards the clown like always he pretended to box him. He lifted his helmet, and his smile shined across the screen behind the chutes.

Skyler

She was so excited. She screamed for two minutes as he exited the arena.

"You must like him a lot to be that loud." An older woman said.

"He is a real nice guy, is all. About time he gets recognized for it too."

"Yeah, it's true. Been a long time coming, Kale breaking on the big leagues and blowing the mind of the fans." She mentioned.

"Definitely, but all the bull riders have a different riding style that's unique to them. Some can adjust better than others. It took Kale awhile to get into the groove." She felt nerdy talking to this lady about Kale like this. What she really wanted to tell her is that she still fighting the temptation of wanting to be with him.

"You can tell you've been around the sport the way you talk about it like that. You're face looks so familiar. You have the eyes of some bull rider I used to know." The old ladies words sent chills up her spine.

"Ben Pendleton?" Skyler took a wild guess.

"Why yes, that's his name." The old lady chuckled.

"I'm his daughter Skyler, and if I remember right, you're his 12th grade science teacher Mrs. Makowski."

"Sure am, how did you know?"

"A hunch, my Dad said you were the only one to understand him. He said he knew you came from a bull riding family. All the problems you related back to him as bull riding scenarios." Skyler couldn't believe it. Ms. Makowski had been her Dad's favorite teacher other than the rodeo team coach.

"I sure did. You're dad was smart, but brains don't matter when all you see is dollar signs and big league tours."

Skyler had to keep her composure. She remembered Kale is in boxer shorts all of a sudden. "Yeah, most of these guys are smart. They don't see themselves that way, but who needs to when they have million dollar genes running through their bodies."

"You said your name was Skyler, right?"

"Correct."

"Dr. Skyler Pendleton?" She nodded in recognition of her name. "It's an honor to finally meet you."

Skyler was confused, why Mrs. Makowski would be honored to meet her. "Thanks, if you don't mind me askin' I'm a little confused. So, why are you honored to meet me?" She didn't want to be too blunt with her.

"You helped my grandson. He got a concussion when he wrecked his ATV, pretty bad one if you can remember. He is doing great now thanks to you. He is back to playing baseball; he is running around like a normally seventeen year old." Her eyes lit up as she spoke to Skyler. It had been a scary ordeal."

"Well, I'm glad to hear that. My dream was to get people back to lives as close to normal as they can." Skyler couldn't help adding her own little mantra.

The crowd roared as Jace rode his bull.

"Well, Skyler, I sure hope you sit here the rest of the nights. I am going to leave before people start racing down to get autographs."

"I will be seein' you then, Mrs. Makowski."

"Skyler, please call me Deborah." The old woman insisted.

"See you tomorrow, Deborah."

Skyler parted ways with Mrs. Makowski and tried to get as close as she could get from the bars. She wanted to surprise Kale when he looked up from signing an autograph for her.

The guys circled around slowly, Matt smiled as he saw Skyler. She motioned to him not to say her name, so they silently greeted one another. Kale slowly walked around, and when he started signing her sheet she whispered his name "Kale Weston." She hoped he would hear her over the lull of the other fans. He looked up and was astonished.

"Skyler? Skyler, what are you doing here?" He couldn't find any other phrase to say it better.

"I live in Billings. It was part of my Grandpa's agreement."

"It's great to see you, Skyler." Kale stuttered. The look in his eyes told Skyler that it wasn't going to be like it was before. If Kale had been the guy to give her the necklace, he didn't seem to matter seeing it dangle from her neck. If Kale had been the one, then the spark was gone now. She tried to camouflage her disappoint.

"You too. Where's Dakota? I have to give that girl props. Two bulls now; before too long Harley and Donaldson's name will disappear and the entire world is goin' to hear about is North Carolina Cattle."

Even, though she knew Kale didn't care anymore. She couldn't help but still care about him. She wanted to still be close with him.

"They sure are. Look down the alleyway. If she isn't kissin' Brayden, I would yell at her."

"Will do, you take it easy, Kale." She watched him aimless as he rounded the arena. Then she felt a tap on her shoulder. She turned around and saw Dakota.

"Dakota! Oh my gosh, I was tellin' Kale about you. How are you doin'?"

The two girls embraced like long lost friends.

"Great, the bulls are getting better. The money looks nice; Brayden and I spend a lot more time together. Look at you Ms. Hot-Shot-Doctor." Dakota smiled.

"I ain't no hot –shot. I'm doin' my job. You cute your hair, it's cute."

"Thanks, it took a week for Brayden to notice."

Skyler laughed, "Dakota, rule one, guys never notice the little things."

"I finally realized that after two years of marriage. You should come out with us. You look all cute to go dancing anyways. I know the guys would love to hang with you."

"I wouldn't want to be imposing on you guys. I can tell you guys have gotten a lot closer as I left."

"You won't be Sky, I have to go give the little guys some water, so pull your truck around what we call bull alley. It's on the backside of the arena." Dakota wanted Skyler to give in. She wanted to show Tiffany, in hopes that she could snap Kale out of it.

"Will do, Dakota, how's Kale doin'?" She looked at Dakota searching for an explanation to his behavior earlier.

"I don't even have words to describe it. You will have to see for yourself tonight."

Kale

Tiffany ran up to him, as he came near the truck.

"Way to go baby, riding the bull for eight seconds and all. No one can stop you." She leaned in and kissed him.

"Thanks babe, the score wasn't that good though. The score could jeopardize my placement for the championship round. If I ain't careful and I don't make it to the championship round than I won't go home with money."

"Hunnie, you keep riding those bulls. Forget about the other guys." She supportively replied.

"I'm tryin' to. Let's go have some fun. I can't wait to spin you around the dance floor."

They climbed in the truck and sped off towards the bar.

Kale couldn't shake the sight of Skyler, but he wasn't going to let it interfere with Tiffany. He liked Tiffany, but again Skyler floated through his head. They entered the bar and found a table; he knew that Brayden and Dakota would soon be there. Ten minutes later he spotted them walking in; followed closely by the girl who had stolen his heart.

"Hey guys." Brayden said smiling.

"Hey, Brayden." They both said.

Dakota butted in, "Kale you remember Skyler. Don't you? Tiffany this is Skyler."

"It's nice to meet you Skyler." Tiffany scoffed. She could see Kale looking at Skyler like a porcelain doll. She couldn't stand that.

"You too." Skyler politely responded.

She sat across the table from Kale.

"Great ride tonight, if you don't mind me sayin' so myself cowboy." Kale watched as she bit her lip after calling him cowboy. She knew it was intimate to the both of them.

"Thanks, been a long time since I felt this good." He muttered with a smile.

She smiled back, "How's that elbow of yours?" He knew deep down inside that Skyler still had deep concern for him.

"Never felt better. You sure are a miracle worker, Skyler."

He hadn't wanted to be to front with her. He had to think about being with Tiffany. His chance to be with Skyler was gone, and he didn't want to drag her into a complicated web. Though, he couldn't let go of her himself. He believed immensely in her talent as a doctor. Seeing her Hazel eyes glisten slightly underneath the lights resurged an inferno inside his soul.

Tiffany grabbed his arm, "Let's go dance baby."

"We'll be back y'all." His eyes seem to have frozen on Skyler. Tiffany tugged harder and off they went to the dance floor.

Skyler

Skyler couldn't help but laugh as Dakota stuck her fingers in her mouth, promoting a gagging expression.

"Can't believe I thought a man like him could be my Rhett Butler." She scoffed. Watching him dance with Tiffany made her feel empty. When they danced, it was as if two butterflies were dancing against the wind, together as one body. That wasn't her perception of him and Tiffany dancing.

"He was." Brayden exclaimed. Knowing that if he spoke up maybe it wouldn't be late for the two of them.

Sky's face turned pale. She had been dealt with a blow. It felt as if a missile had pierced her heart, leaving nothing alive. How could he have not held on? Why didn't he wait for her to come back on tour? Why did he decide to move on with the fake blonde standing in front of him? Was she really better than Sky? Why hadn't she come forward sooner? All this made her feel sick in the stomach.

"Sky, listen, I know this isn't how you wanted things to go. Tiffany and he won't be together for long. He loves you, he barely likes her."

"Brayden, you listen. You don't have to make me feel better, I'm great. I'm hanging out with the two coolest people on the circuit. Don't tell that to Matt and Walker. I'll get in trouble. Guys, I don't only miss Kale though. I missed this, us all talkin' and jokin' around. I missed the bulls, the pyrotechnics. Sure, when I was getting' ready I begged to differ that she would be here. I put this necklace on determined to find Rhett. I found him, and I may not be his Scarlett O'Hara, but don't justify Kale's actions to me. He is a grown man and you guys don't need to protect me. You guys are great friends. There is no denyin' that." She smiled. For the first time since Loren passed away she felt like she belonged.

"So you miss this tour, Sky?"

"Brayden, what kind of question is that?" Skyler glared at him.

"It was a question. The way your eyes lit up when Tate noticed you, I saw how bad you miss it." Brayden said in his soothing North Carolina accent.

"I do, but I love my job here, ironically. I'm adaptin' to life I didn't think I was goin' to be able to live. This isn't the first time." She took a sip from the coke that Dakota had gotten her.

"Skyler, you have so much more than she does. Any guy around here would be lucky to have you, expect me of course, I have Dakota."

"Way to save yourself, hun." Dakota whispered.

Skyler smiled. She wanted everything that Dakota and Brayden had but she wanted it with Kale. Her dreams started to turn into nightmares right before her eyes.

Jace came up from behind her, and screamed, "Skyler Pendleton. How I missed you."

She knew he was drunk. She wanted nothing more than to play with his mind.

"I missed you too darling, the least you could do is spin me and Dakota around the dance floor."

"Sky, ever buckle bunny this side of Billings knows I have two left feet."

"Well sugar, isn't that a shame."

She stood up and gave Jace hug.

"Skyler, you smell good. Dang girl what did you do? Soak in the field of wildflowers?"

"No, Jace it's called perfume, and if I'm correct cowboy you're wearin' the cologne that pairs this."

"Sure am, when you get it free why not." He held her close as he tried to stabilize himself.

"Cowboy, it was great seenin' you again, but I think I'm gonna go."

"Bye Sky." He said with a slur of his words.

She waved to Dakota and Brayden and walked out of the bar.

Why in the heck did Kale having a girlfriend bug her so much? She hadn't made any solid leaps to tell him see she was interested. Sure there was those letters but were those any indicators to Kale that she adored him. Maybe he saws the notes as a little joke, a game that only would satisfy his interest for a short amount of time. If he was Rhett then why was it he who lied to her; she recalled her lying to him too. Each we're in the wrong that summer, but she hadn't moved on. She had held on to the possibility of him. A possibility that seemed like it would come true.

    She was tossed back into reality when a song on the radio came on. She had sung it many times alongside Loren. Usually, when the guys in high school treated them like crap, or the man they thought was Mr. Right turned out to me Mr. all-wrong. She couldn't help but roll down the windows and scream the lyrics down the quiet country road.

    "Stupid Girl, I should have known, I should have known, I ain't a princess, this ain't a fairytale. I'm not the one you sweep off your feet, lead her up the staircase. This ain't Hollywood, this is a small town, I was a dreamer before you went and let me down, now it's too late for you and your white horse, to come around."

    Arriving home, she immediately put the truck in park. As she fumbled to open the door she could feel the hot tears searing down her cheeks. Once she got the door open, she slammed it. The stairs were a quick right turn. She ran up them like a gazelle. She didn't want to talk to anyone. She sure didn't want to cry in front of anyone. As she fell on her bed, the tears came pouring like a monsoon.

Kale

Billings proved to be a trail for Kale. Here was Tiffany the girl he was dating, and Skyler…the girl who still held his heart. The tug on his heart seemed to spin the whole world into orbit faster.

He was ready for the last night's events. He wanted Billings to be prosperous for him. With his clouded mind he figured it would prove disastrous.

As the round got underway he saw Skyler leaning over the rail talking with Walker and Matt. He could hear her laughter echo in his heart, and the spark in her eyes triggered emotions he had been hiding since the last time he saw her in New Mexico. He saw her smile illuminate the alleyway. Her eyes sparked a new flame in his heart. Since the last time he had been close to her, the sun had kissed her skin, her hair was a bit darker, and the way her button up hugged her was irresistibly attractive to him. He saw Tate toss a shirt at her. What was it he wondered? He walked over to Matt after Sky had run off.

"What's up, Matt." Kale asked trying not to be nosey.

"Nothin' waitin' for my ride, also excited that Sky is back."

"Skyler's back. Yeah. It's great to see her here. I hope she comes to Billings again."

"Yeah, that's cool, but what I meant was Tate hired her." Matt didn't understand why Kale seemed so jumpy about Skyler's return.

"Well, that's great. She deserved the spot all along."

Kale walked away in disbelief. Should he have waited for Sky's return? He felt that he was overanalyzing things. He was with Tiffany. He repeated to himself and he walked back into the locker room.

Skyler

She felt the shirt engulf her. He heart beat faster with each clank of her boots against the alleyway. She was in the zone. A place she had missed. A place she dreamed of returning too. That dream was no Skyler's reality. She saw Dakota as she was walking to the Sport Medicine room.

"Ummm…what are you doing back here, fan." Dakota scoffed.

"I ain't a fan. I'm a staff member." Skyler put a little fire behind her response.

They hugged each other and smiled. It was the dynamic duo back in action. It felt good.

"I need to thank Jace for showin' Tate the article. Never would have happened without his help."

"Yeah, it would have. Tim was getting ready to leave. There you were at the perfect time." Dakota explained.

"Well, glad I could be of service."

They heard the crowd roar, and the name Brayden Carter echoing through the arena.

"Ain't you lucky, your husband owns two Billings buckles now?"

"Dang straight I'm lucky. Way to work this event Skyler."

"Sorry, I was basking in the moment. I will see y'all in Tulsa."

"Later Skyler, see you in Tulsa."

Kale

The plane ride home seemed long. He was glad that Tulsa would be closer. He looked at Tiffany while she was sleeping. She seemed so beautiful, but she wasn't Skyler. He didn't know what had brought him back to Skyler, with such intensity. Was it fate, were things with him and Tiffany ending. He nudged her to wake up.

"Tiff, we are landing in Texas, get up darlin'."

"Kale, don't call me darlin'." Her words were full of spite.

"Alright, well, we are about to land, so you need to get up."

He was confused what had he done to her? He had taken her to Billings, spun her around the dance floor every night, and although he didn't claim money, he couldn't figure what he did wrong. Sure he talked to Skyler, but she was his friend. It wasn't like he snuck around with her. They hadn't physically touched at all.

They exited the plan and Kale tried to take her hand in his. She quickly jerked away.

"Kale, please leave me alone."

"Tiffany, what is wrong?" His voice anxiously asked.

"What's wrong? You don't think I don't know where you heart lies, Kale Weston. She holds every part of you, Kale. The way you look at her, the quant conversations; I ain't as dumb as I look, Kale. You love her and I can't handle that. We're done and over with. I'm gonna go call my mom." She left him standing alone in the baggage claim.

He couldn't believe it. He had been dumped in the airport, at home. Who knew how many people knew him? He walked out as quickly as he could get in his truck to go home.

Skyler

The whole week prior to Tulsa, she had been antsy. Now, sitting on the plane with her Mom, she couldn't help but wonder how it would turn out.

"I'm getting off in Tulsa, and then flying to Dallas. I will be in Abilene for a few days. We can meet back up in Tulsa and fly home. Sound goods?

"Yeah, and mom tell Grandpa I love him, will you?"

"Sure will, hun. I think we are getting ready to land."

They exited the plane, and hugged each other at the baggage claim.

"Don't forget to get my craft box. I have a few things to finish in there." She reminded her mother.

"I won't. I love you. Don't work too hard."

"Me, work hard? You must be jokin'. I can never work too hard."

Skyler smiled at her mom as they parted their separate ways. She headed to rent a truck, while he mom went to board her next plane.

Kale

Driving to Tula seemed to be the only peace he could escape to. Since Tiffany's big blow up, he couldn't keep his thoughts straight. He saw clearly everything Tiffany had told him. He did love Skyler its true. Her presence had sparked possibilities, but he had never acted on them. He couldn't help but wish things could have changed. It's not that he didn't want Skyler to get the job, but why did it have to happen now.

He made a left into Tulsa, hoping that this old fashioned oil town could help him make the pay. He drove to the arena, and pulled beside and black rental truck. He saw Skyler getting out of it.

"Hey Skyler." He smiled. She had been one face that he needed to see.

"Hey cowboy." She returned his smile. The spark in her eyes made him feel a little uneasy. While seeing the necklace around her neck made him feel proud of what he had done for her.

They both parted their own way after greeting each other. Kale entered the locker room and ran into Brayden.

"Hey Kale, you look bad man. What's going on?" Brayden was concerned for his friend. It seemed as if Kale hadn't eaten for a few days, hadn't slept either.

"Nothin' really Brayden, tired is all." He yawned.

"You drew Rapid Revolver again. Thought I'd let you know, should be a round win." Brayden tried to coax a smile from his friends face.

"Nice, he is all I need to conquer." Kale sounded depressed.

"Kale, you sure you okay. You wanna talk? You know I'm here right." Brayden really wanted to shake him out of it. What had happened for Kale to look like this?

"I'm fine; I'm goin' on a jog."

Kale left Brayden standing in the locker room being concerned about his friend.

Skyler

Skyler sat behind the chutes tapping her boots against the platform. The action had gotten underway, and nothing seemed to be happening. She turned to look at Tate.

"I'm goin' to go count supplies. You need me, come get me." She reminded him.

"Alright and count right this time." He joked.

Tate wasn't going to let her live that down. As an intern she had tried to calculate how many rolls of tape were left and she actually multiplied instead of subtracting.

Less than ten minutes into her counting, Kale walked in accompanied by Tate holding his wrist. Kale's face had a painful look frozen on it. Skyler had never seen Kale hurt during an event. Her heart started to beat rapidly as she tried to flight back the tears that started welling up in her eyes.

"Skyler, splint him comfortably, alright, put some ice on it."

'She went to do as she was told. She gently lifted his wrist up. She watched as Kale's eyes fixated on every wrap around his wrist.

'Kale, are you okay?" Her voice rang softly. The concern seemed to float out right along with it.

"What... huh?" She saw that he was in outer space in his eyes."

"I asked if you were okay, you're spacing out. Your head doesn't hurt does it? I can run some test if you need me to." She hoped the worst of his injuries lay in her hand; his wrist.

"Mentally yes, emotionally no, and physically the wrist does hurt a bit."

"Emotionally no, what happened?" She hoped it had nothing to do with the way she had acted in Billings.

"Tiffany broke up with me in the middle of the airport. Can you believe that?" His head hung low. She knew he felt ashamed.

"No. Kale I'm really sorry. I hope I didn't have anything to do with it." Her heart pitter pattered as she waited for Kale to respond.

"No, Skyler, you didn't." he raised his head to stare into her eyes. "Skyler, it was me. It's about time I tell you, I'm Rhett. Well, I was Rhett." Kale confessed with a confused look on his face.

"Yeah Brayden told me in Billings. Though I had a hunch it was you. It sure is nice to hear it from your lips though. You're a great writer, a great bull rider, and a great guy. I have to come clean too.... I'm Scarlett

O'Hara...well, was Scarlett O'Hara." She shrugged not knowing how he would react.

"Yeah, I figured it out, the handwritin' on all the notes matched. I then saw a picture of you, Matt and Walker; you were wearing a yellow and green faded dress."

"Kale listen will ya I'm sorry for lyin' before it's unlike me. I wanted you to know that I'm here for you whenever you need me. As a friend, a fellow country kid, fellow uses to be Texan, whatever you need me to be." She couldn't believe she had poured her heart out to him once again. She felt horrible about Tiffany leaving Kale in shambles. Though, something about coming clean about being Scarlett O'Hara felt like she was renewing hope for them to be together.

"Thanks Sky, the offer is the same." A smile briefly graced his face.

The touch of his hand on top of hers sent Vibrations up her spine and into her brain. She was falling again. Like Kale had fallen off the bull hard, she was falling into the orbit of Kale Weston, harder than before.

A
Year
Later

Billings, Montana

Kale

The seasons seemed to fly by. It was another year in Billings, another opportunity. He was the only one of the three not to have claimed a world championship buckle, and the North Carolina kids had their own little way of harassing him.

"Kale, what state does world champs come from now?" Jace enquired.

"Texas, they will always come from Texas." He defended.

"Kale, are you geographically stupid? The last two have been from North Carolina. So, Texas boy, step down away from the throne, the North Carolina kids are back in town." Jace bragged.

Kale shook his head. He didn't care that he didn't have a buckle claiming he was world champ. He was riding with more precision than he ever had before. He was confident, and this year. He wasn't going to let Skyler off for the prank she pulled on him in Omaha.

He loved having such a playful friendship with her. Though, he was going to show Sky, who the King of pranks really was.

"Hey, Kale." She mentioned as she passed him in the alleyway.

"Hey Sky, where you goin'?" Kale asked with a smile on his face. He knew Sky would be caught off guard.

"To meet Tate behind the chutes? Why?"

"I think you've been misguided, Tate is in here."

Kale pushed her into the locker room where the rest of the guys were changing.

"Kale Weston, I'm seriously going to hurt you." She said with vengeance as her cheeks appeared red.

"You can't hurt me. Your job is to help me. Haha Sky, was that like the first time you ever walked in on me?" Kale asked tauntingly

"Kale, no it wasn't, but they were hotter half naked than you." She stomped down the alleyway. Kale knew; she would cool down.

"Right Skyler, whatever you say." He yelled after her.

"I said that alright, I got to go to work, okay?" She yelled back. "Watch your back cowboy." She shot him back a smile and laughed.

He could tell she was still a little furious. He knew his apology would make her smile. As the round was underway and intermission hit Kale took the microphone from the arena announcer.

"I want everyone to get introduced to the staff that saves our butts every weekend out of the arena the Sports Medicine team." Lights soon shown on Tate, Skyler, and Sam, "The Sports Medicine team, everyone knows, Tate and Sam. Although, we have a cute, 26 year old doctor. She is real sweet. She is smart, and I want y'all to tell her how you like her Billings. She is a hometown girl so let's hear y'all scream of Dr. Skyler Pendleton."

He watched as she left from behind the chutes. He had no clue what had happened. He thought it was cute, but obviously she didn't."

Skyler

She walked out of the arena furious. It was one thing to embarrass her in front of the rest of the guys. It was another to scream her name in a microphone for twenty thousand plus fans.

She entered the Sports Medicine room and sat counting supplies. She didn't want to speak or see Kale Weston right now. Nor did she want anything to do with the thousands of fans who would be staring at her. The room was quiet, its serenity was calming. It took a lot to get her head from spinning but something about the Sports Medicine room mesmerized her. Maybe it was how surreal working for Tate had seemed growing up. Perhaps it was finally getting recognized for all the great things she pushed towards.

She couldn't help but crack a smile. Kale Weston was the kind of guy that drove Skyler nuts. He also drove Skyler crazy mad in love.

She didn't know if it was his Texas charm, his drawl, or the emotional side he possessed. As she heard them crown Jace Montgomery round winner; she slipped out to the truck and drove back home.

The stars show in the sky like many nights before, however, it was something about tonight that made Sky wonder. Could Kale be in a trace like she was? Could this star be a little piece of their already complicated love story? Or was it the fact that it brought a smile to her face. The star seemed to resemble the sparkle in Loren's eyes. It was a sparkle Skyler saw often. A sparkled that caressed her eyes when Skyler and her talked about their future with two of bull riding biggest stars.

"Skyler, so how do you think my name will sound? Loren Nicolette Montgomery." Loren said in the same bubbly tone she always exuded.

"Sounds great Loren, splendid indeed." Skyler joked. "Loren, sometimes I wonder if you're kidding me, or if you are lost in a fairy tale, although Weston would be stupid not to spend the rest of his life with me. Right?"

"Of course he will be with you Sky, he would be dumb not to. Look at you." Loren assured.

"Nah, it doesn't happen like movies Loren. We can dream, but I highly doubt Skyler Kay Weston will ever grace the page of a prescription tablet."

"Skyler, lighten up. You told me all the time dreams are not impossible. What happened to that outlook?" Loren demanded to know.

"I don't know Loren. There are so many men in this world. How can I pinpoint my future with one of the hottest cowboys on the Bra, it seems entirely impossible, entirely fictional, entirely too crazy to fathom." Skyler mentioned. It wasn't uncommon for her to go from believing in the fantasy to disregarding it in reality.

"Skyler, I will hit you if I have too. Dreams are what life's moments feed off of. Sky, feed off the possibility that Kale Weston will fall madly in love with your hazel eyes, your dorky self and mischievous smile." Loren laughed. Skyler's smile always held some mystery behind it.

"Jace Montgomery will be stupid not to fall in love with your baby blues, you're adorable smile, and that crazy dancer stuff you do."

Both girls laughed and fell asleep.

The headlights of the oncoming traffic woke Sky from a blissful memory of her beloved friend.

"So Loren, Kale loves me alright. Loves to embarrass me!! Did you see that? I guess it's like middle school again; he picks on me because he can't tell me his real feelings. He should know that I'm crazy about him. Everythin' about him Loren, I'm plum crazy about him. The dream is never impossible Loren. You listenin' to me Buckle Bunny. I ain't goin' to let Kale Weston leave this time. I promise I won't let him out of my grasps.

She murmured as she turned into the driveway of her parents place.

Kale

The night sky outside the arena seemed different than anything he had seen before. The sky was scatter with bright lights that only could be revealed in Montana. He looked up, and saw a star shining brighter than the rest. His heart beat started racing. Why was this star so special? Why was it pulling him into its cosmic orbit?"

All he knew at that moment was he wanted to apologize to Skyler for what he did. He thought she took jokes better but obviously he was wrong. He climbed into his rental truck and chased the star all the way back to the hotel. It felt haunting to him. A memory of how many times he had let Skyler go. He couldn't let his escapade tonight ruin everything he ever wanted. The star brought him into a glimpse he had never seen before.

Skyler was walking around a big log cabin in his favorite t-shirt. She had her hair all messed up, and a smile holding a mystery, a mystery only Kale could unlock. He walked in from outside covered in mud. It was the first time he heard her voice.

"What happened, Darlin'?" She said with a chuckle in her voice.

"A few of the bulls got away from me." Kale explained.

"Should have woken me up? I could of came out and helped. It ain't like this is my first ranch, cowboy."

"I know, you looked too sweet to wake up. I decided I could do it by myself."

"Obviously not, go get those clothes off and shower up. I'll make you something to eat. Then we can find the rest of those bulls."

He smiled as he walked towards her. He wrapped his muddy arms around her and kissed her.

"I've been waitin' for that."

"I bet you were. Now go get those clothes off ya hear, and shower up." She pointed her finger in the direction of the bathroom.

Kale trailed up the stairs looking back over his shoulder and smiling at her.

His cell phone started to ring and the glimpse was gone. The phone call was from an unknown number. He wondered if it was Skyler. He didn't want to call her back, even if it was her number.

As he picked it up he also noticed a text message. He was never good at reading and driving so he let the phone rest next to him until he pulled into the hotel parking lot.

He picked it up and saw a message: Have a good night, Cowboy. Don't think you're gonna get away with what you did. Sweet Dreams,
Scarlett O'Hara

He quickly saved the message and smiled. He also saved the number while he was at it. If this was any indication of what the star was secretly telling him, he liked it, and hoped that things would continue to go this way.

Skyler

She couldn't believe she had over slept her alarm. She had missed cowboy church.

She had missed the opportunity of getting Trent involved in payback. She could find her button up, and knew that Tate would be looking for her in a matter of minutes. She grabbed her cell phone off the nightstand and called Tate.

"Hey Tate, I'm runnin' a little late. I promise I will be there."

She heard Tate's muffled voice and hung up the phone. She threw on her work shirt, some jeans, and her black cowboy boots. She found a ponytail and threw her hair up in a messy bun.

"Where are you goin' at that speed?" Her father asked as she barreled down the steps.

"Goin' to go to work, Dad; if mom calls and I miss her; tell her I love her. Love you; I will be back later tonight."

"Alright Skyler, be careful flying down the road."

"Thanks Dad, I'll be careful." She was out of breath as she slammed the front door.

She climbed into her truck and sped off towards the arena. The traffic seemed like flashing lights all around her. Her heart was racing, she hated being late, but she was beyond late now. For the first time in her life she was late. She didn't know what Tate would say, or if Kale was making another mockery of her. She turned left into the parking lot and ran for the Sports Medicine room. As she ran through the door she ran smack dab into Kale.

"Hey, you. I didn't think you were showing up. Church sure wasn't the same with you there." Kale smiled.

"Sorry, I couldn't be there. I was tired and overslept."

Kale nodded and walked around her to go back to the locker room.

The event had started and most guys were standing behind the chutes. Matt came to see her at the end of the alleyway; she was nervous as she saw the look on his face.

'Nice to see you finally show up." Matt said.

"Yeah, that's what happens when you over sleep the alarm."

"Maybe you need to make your alarm louder." Matt said like a big brother.

"I guess I do, but I was so tired." She added.

She bid farewell to Matt and started her trek back to the Sports Medicine room to count supplies. She noticed she had left her cell phone on a supply table. It was flashing like she had a missed call. It was from her Mom. She immediately redialed the number. Her mother's voice quivered on the other side of the line.

"Hello Skyler, you need to get to Abilene."

"What Mom? What's goin' on?" Panic rang out in her voice.

"You're Grandpa got hurt Skyler. He is in pretty bad shape, kiddo. Please, hunnie, get here. Your Grandpa needs you." She could hear the tears in her mothers' voice.

"Okay Mom, I'm on my way."

At the exact moment she hung up the phone Tate walked in.

"Tate I have to go. My Grandpa is seriously hurt. I need to be there for him. I'm sorry I was late and that I have to go like this. I'll find away to make it up."

"Go Sky, we will be waiting for you when you get back. Go!"

She was so glad that Tate understood. She rushed out of the Sports medicine room, and again Kale was her wall.

"Skyler, it makes me smile how every time we are apart, we get brought together again." He said sweetly.

"Yeah, Kale, it's really funny, but I gotta go." She tried to go around him but he pulled her back in front of him.

"Skyler, I'm sorry for the joke, and for the announcement, but Billings loves you." He reminded her with a smile.

"I know they do Kale, but I really have to go." Skyler urged him.

"Skyler, slow down, really you shouldn't be embarrassed."

"Geez, Kale it's not about that okay. I have to go." She fought back the tears.

"Skyler, Skyler come on. I'll take you wherever you need to go."

"Kale, I'm fine. I need to do this alone. Alone you hear. Don't follow me out those doors, cowboy. You have two friends in the championship round, and a stock contractor who could use your help. I will see you later Kale." Why was he being like this? She needed to go and here he was with his hands on her shoulder and staring into her eyes.

As she tried to walk away again, he grabbed her arm and spun her back around.

"Skyler let me come with you please, I know you need a friend." He tried to rub his hand up her arm but she pulled away.

"Kale, it's sweet really. I need to go. Like I said cowboy, Alone…A-L-O-N-E."

He looked her in the eyes. She knew he didn't like what she was saying. He wanted to take her into his arms, she could tell by the constant pulling on her limbs. He let go of the arm he had and she smiled.

"Thanks Kale. I will see you later. Go have fun."

Skyler ran down the hallway and out the backside of the arena.

Kale

He wanted to run after her, but she had told him not too. Most of the time whoever pleaded with Kale he would do. This time however, he couldn't hold himself back. He went back behind the chutes to find the event over and Matt Leeton to be the winner. He was happy for Matt, but wanted so bad to go after Skyler. So he turned around, walked down the back alleyway and almost made it out the door before Dakota spotted him.

"What are you doing Kale?" She asked suspicious of the way he was taking off like he was.

"I'm goin' after Skyler." He innocently commented.

"Where is Skyler? Isn't she in the Sports Medicine room?"

"No, she told me to stay and not to follow her. I think she was on her way to the airport. I can't let her go again." His eyes showed the words his heart couldn't unveil.

"Hallelujah, someone knocked some sense into you. Come on, I'll drive you to the airport. Plus, your likely to get into less trouble if I come along."

"Thanks Dakota."

The both ran out the back door to Dakota's truck. The ride to the airport seemed extremely long.

"Kale, you may think you are being foolish right now, but for the first time in three years, I think you are actually thinking clearly."

"Well thanks, Dakota. Somethin' in my heart tells me not to let her go this time."

"Keep using whatever you're listening too. I think it knows when things are right more than you do." She chuckled.

"I wouldn't doubt it. This had been three years in the making. Three painstaking long years that I let pass me by because I didn't have the guts to say anything."

"At least it won't be more than three years." They both laughed.

Brayden

Brayden went in search of Dakota.

"Man have you seen Dakota?" He asked Jace puzzled.

"I saw her and Kale leave a few minutes ago. They sure were flying out of here." Jace mentioned.

"What is with you guys? I can't trust any of you. One minute you're my best friends, the next you're gallivanting off with my wife."

"Brayden....chill dude. No mental break down, please. Let's go. We can catch them at the airport. Maybe cut them off."

"What are you waiting for Montgomery? A Texan is with my wife, and I can't let that happen." Brayden screamed.

"Brayden, did you forget at one point and time Dakota was a Texan." Jace reminded him.

"Yeah, but she has been a North Carolinian for a long time. So I can't let the Texan brain wash her." Brayden tried to explain.

"It's only Kale and more than likely you wife isn't his intentions." Jace rolled his eyes at his spastic friend.

"What do you mean?"

"I think he is chasin' Skyler."

"Goodness gracious. Good think for Kale or I would have had to hurt him." Jace laughed and put his truck into gear.

Skyler

The drive to the airport was nauseating, she couldn't remember the last time her stomach twist and turned liked it did now. Then it hit her like a ton of bricks. It had been five and a half years ago, the night of Loren's accident.

She had planned a weekend full of movies, boys, football, and rodeos. The rain pounded outside and she was scared for Loren's safety so she called.

"I'm lost Sky, by some trailer place." The confusion consumed Skyler.

"Lor…listen to me. Are you listening? Find a big building that's the plant I told you about earlier on the phone. Are you near there?

"I have no clue Skyler, I'm lost." Loren said in utter disbelief.

The rest remained a blur, she was angry at Loren for not listening. All she wanted was for Loren to be there at her place safe. She heard scattered noises and the nothing.

"Loren…Loren," Skyler hung up the phone in fear. She waited and Waited for Loren, until the phone rang, it was her Mom.

"Skyler, I'm so sorry hunnie, Loren is dead. She was in a car accident. Sky… hun I'm so sorry." Her Mom said with a quivering voice, masked by the sound of tears.

Skyler first and only reaction was to scream. She did just that.

The droplets of rain brought her back from the vivid memory that still haunted her. The memory she wished was no true tell this day.

"Hey Loren, I miss you. Loren why did he have to get hurt? Why did you have to die? Loren I can't understand it all. I've been through so much shit. It's like I can't have a happy moment without being brought back to reality. I really care for Kale but it's not workin' out. Loren thank you for watchin' over me I truly owe you everythin'. I love you like pizza love; the kind in the back of my refrigerator about to be all moldy. Yeah you know the kind. Don't worry buckle bunny, I know you're here holdin' my hand." She chocked down some tears.

Until finally she let a stream of tears roll down her cheeks.

Kale

His nerves started collecting in his throat. What would he say? He thought of the possibilities.

"So Skyler, Yo Skyler, Skyler wait?" He didn't know how the phrase would be released from his mouth. He was becoming deathly afraid. What if the feelings she expressed two years ago had changed by now? What if he couldn't speak from his heart? He looked out the window and watched the rain power down. He hoped it would delay her take off. He wanted her to be smiling. He wanted her to run into his arms. He didn't want to let her go.

"Kale seriously...you're drooling." Dakota told him.

"No, I'm not." He said wiping his cheek. "Dakota, what if she doesn't love me anymore?" He could feel sweat accumulating in his fisted hands.

"She would be stupider than you Kale."

"Thanks Dakota." He commented not knowing how to take her compliment, if it was one.

"Kale, be yourself. That's who she fell in love with."

"I will be, or try to be." He glanced back out at the rain dripping down the window.

Dakota

Dakota smirked. She knew his blood was boiling and his mind was running all over the place. She couldn't blame him though. His nerves resembled the exact nerves she had on her wedding day.

Brayden and she had decided to get married in South Dakota, away from the hype of Texas and North Carolina. She remembered how the fall leaves glistened and danced like stars across the ground. The sunlight played peek-a- boo behind the clouds and the birds sand their unique melodies. Her grandfather was dressed to the nines, and ready to walk her down the aisle. Her mother's eyes couldn't stay dry.

"You look stunning, hunnie. More beautiful than any sunrise or sunset."

"Thanks Mom. I love you." They embraced.

"I love you too Dakota. Brayden is the luckiest guy in the world." Her mother had mentioned.

"I'm the luckiest girl in the world." Dakota responded.

All she could hear is Kale's girly scream in her ear. It brought her out of the memory of her wedding day.

"What were you doin' speed demon? Tryin' to kill me?" He muttered as he took a deep breath.

"No, I'm trying to get you to the love of your life." She retorted in a sarcastic tone.

"Well please don't run anymore red lights. I want to get there in one piece."

They both laughed as they saw the runway to the airport.

Skyler

Her knees started to tremble. The airport seemed hot to her. Sweat droplets dripped from her forehead. Her mind was playing tricks with her like it always did. Sometimes she felt over dramatic but what if her Grandfather really was dying? What if the reason he needed her to come to Texas was to hand the ranch over to her? It had been a dream, her and Loren's. They had dreamed of the ranch in Texas often. It was a paradise to them, a paradise that was untouched by human hands. She remembered the first time she took Loren to Texas. It was late July, and the southern heat excited the both of them.

The girls drove all the way from Billings to Abilene. They went through 26 cd's, a 24 pack of soda, and a couple of king sized candy bars. Loren's eyes lit up as they crossed the Texas state line. They were in Cowboy country, although to Loren, North Carolina held the hottest and most athletic cowboy on Earth.

"So what's up with all these cars?" Loren asked a little confused.

"Loren, it's called the interstate for a reason. We are about to enter Abilene, believe me it's the closest thing to the boondocks I have been, but you'll love everything about it." She said smiling.

They pulled into her grandfather's long gravel driveway. The four wheelers were sitting outside the shed, but Grandpa's truck was nowhere to be seen.

"Want to go for a ride? I can't get into the house until Grandpa gets here." Skyler insisted.

"Of course I want to go." The girls left their bags and went to ride four wheelers out to the creek.

Skyler was abruptly brought out of her dream. They had found a seat for her on the flight to Dallas. She had to go. She made her way to the gate, before her heart told her to stop and a voice came from the distance.

Kale

"Skyler wait," rang Kale's nervous voice. He saw her hair say. She was shocked. Her mouth was frozen like she didn't know what to say. She walked back down the walkway.

"Kale, what are you doin' here?" Her voice shook as she spoke.

"I can't let you go. I lost my chance too many times. This is fate Skyler." He put her face in his hands.

"I know Kale. I know that fate is workin' here. I don't know how to let you in. I have to go though." She was afraid she would miss the plane.

Dakota glared at Kale. He could feel the heat of her stare. He heard more boots clanking in the airport. Dakota turned around.

"What are you two doin' here?" Dakota asked.

"Dakota, you don't love Kale do you?" Brayden asked.

Jace laughed as he saw Skyler lean over her mouth inches from Kale's.

"No, I don't love Kale. I love you." Dakota insisted walking over to him. She grabbed Brayden's hand to silence him.

"Skyler, I've been waitin' a long time to say this to you. I'm not sure even how to say it. You would think that I was ready for this, but the truth is Skyler I'm scared. I don't want my heartbroken again, and somethin' is tellin' me to shut up." He looked at her move closer; their bodies almost touching one another.

"Yeah Kale, I won't… I wouldn't dream of breaking you heart. Ever since I met you the first time, I knew I couldn't dare be without you. Kale…I…I…I love you." She managed to stutter out.

Kale wrapped his arms around Skyler and picked her up, pressing his lips to hers, it felt like a movie to Kale. It felt like a dream. Here he was holding the woman of his dreams, in his arms, for all to see.

"Skyler, please don't go, please Skyler, and let me come with you." He muttered, breaking their kiss and pressing his forehead to hers.

"Kale, you can't come. There is only one seat left on this place. I promise I will be back. I promise this isn't a dream." She said as Kale let her feet touch the ground once more.

"Will you pinch me to show me I'm awake?" Kale asked her. Feeling as if he was some sort of fantasy world.

Skyler kissed him once more. "Wake up Kale, you're not sleepin' this is real." She smiled.

"Geez, Skyler. I can't believe you are standin' right here in my arms."

"Me neither, since I told you to stay. Although, I guess the event is over."

She looked at Dakota, Jace, and Brayden. Kale kissed Skyler to catch her off guard.

"Kale, how did you learn to steal girls hearts like this?" She wondered.

"Like what?" He leaned in and gave her a quick peck.

"Like that, I can't glance into your eyes without my stomach fluttering full of butterflies, my heart racing, and my lips cracking a smile." She admitted as she ran her hand across his cheek.

He turned to look and Brayden and Dakota. "I guess I learned from the best."

"You sure did." She said winking at Dakota.

The loud speaker announced the rows that were boarding.

"How much longer do we have in this bliss?" Kale asked, wanting the moment to last forever.

"A few more minutes, before the last seat on the plane are filled. If I could I would freeze this moment forever, I truly would." She glanced deeply into Kale's eyes.

"Skyler, this moment will forever be frozen in my heart. I don't even know what to do?" He said a little embarrassed.

"Well, you could say I love you too." She mentioned.

"Oh Crap Skyler. I do. I love you Skyler Pendleton."

The words never sounded sweeter in her ears. "Don't worry about it. I love you too Kale Weston. Kale Joseph Weston, you're the one person I want love to last with."

The time seemed to speed up, after every line they spoke to each other. Each intercom sent chill up their spines. She didn't want the moment to end, and by looking into Kale's eyes, he didn't either.

'Sky, what are we?" He asked with a sparkle in his eyes.

She couldn't help but chuckle, "Well, Weston I though we were together, unless I'm the practice dummy for the girl about to walk in here." She tried to keep a straight face.

He didn't find her comment funny, but he knew it could possibly be the truth, even though it wasn't.

"Skyler, I can't believe after three long years, you're standing in front of me. Our arms tightly wrapped around each other." He pulled her closer allowing her to rest her head on his shoulder.

"I can't believe it either. I kind of can't believe the rest of them are here. I guess it wouldn't have worked out any other way." She gently kissed his neck.

"Sure wouldn't. They say you fall in love with someone, you also fall in love with their friends." He tilted his head and rubbed his nose against hers.

"I would have to call you lucky than cowboy, because I adore your friends." She lifted her head and saw as all three of them were in a trance. Waiting what would happen next between Kale and Skyler.

"Don't run off with Jace, and I will be fine. If you do, we will be in trouble." Kale joked wrapping his arms even tighter around her body.

"Kale, I would never run off with him. Have you seen his ears?" She said laughing.

"They are big ain't they?" He lifted her chin up so he could stare into her eyes. It was something about the combination of green and brown that drew him in. It was also the mystery behind them. What was Skyler going to reveal to him.

"Huge, definitely not as cute as your ears are." She said as she tugged softly on his ears.

"So, is that why you are in love with me?" He got all debonair.

"You know it. That is the only reason I feel in love with you. That and the wranglers you're wearing." She softly patted his butt and winked at him.

"I have to confess then, I feel in love with you because of those eyes. Mmm." Kale kissed her on her forehead.

"Thanks, at least we are being honest with each other, but Kale I fell in love with you for everything you have."

Kale didn't have a response, but he knew that it was time for Skyler to board the plane. She heard her number called. Though, they stood frozen.

"Goodbye Kale, I'm so sorry, but I have to go now." She said not wanting to leave the comfort of his arms.

"Good bye Skyler, I love you." It felt so natural to him.

"Have a safe trip home Kale. Please be safe cowboy." She pleaded with him.

"Be careful on your flight. If you get scared you know you can call me." He reminded her.

"Will do, I totally will. Kale I have to go." She was being pushed with the stream of travelers.

"Good bye Skyler." A ping in his heart made saying goodbye the most difficult part of the night.

"Bye Kale. I love you." She said trying to tighten her grip on his hand that was being tested by the stream of passengers brushing by. She didn't want to let him go. She didn't want to leave. Her heart was telling her to stay, but her mind was focused on getting to her grandfather.

He leaned in one last time to kiss her. She smiled and couldn't help but fall in love with Kale even more.

'Kale, I really wish I could stay. If I don't go I could regret somethin' I don't want to regret. Believe me there is no other place I would rather be than right here. I don't even know what else to say except for I love you." She bite her lip hoping she wasn't being to forward as the rush of the other passengers got stronger.

"Skyler, I love you too." More pressure from other passengers strained Kale's grip on Skyler. She was being pushed into the sea of other people. The tension on both of them seemed greater than before. Skyler tried to break free, but she couldn't. She was being swept away at a faster pace then she could push forward.

"I LOVE YOU SKYLER. I Love everything about you cowgirl. Be safe. Good bye Sky."

"Bye Kale, I love everythin' about you too cowboy. Stay safe y'all have fun."

He couldn't help but want to chase after her but something made him stand there. Something made him look into her eyes. It brought him away into a possibility of the future.

They were both sitting in Kale's F-150 singing along to the radio, on there way to Vegas. It was his first time to be there with the love of his life. He had fallen in love and Vegas seemed like the perfect place. It would be such a surprise. On the strip with all the lights flashing, would be the perfect place to pop the question. He had chosen a day, and he thought that it would be the perfect time. She turned and kissed his cheek.

"How do you steal my heart like this every time?"

"It's easy actually, I can't tell you my secret or else it would be ruined. Plus, the excitement we have would be gone."

"I don't believe the excitement will ever leave us." He mentioned.

"Sky, your eyes aprk excitement, your smile is a mystery. I'm still tryin' to solve, and your humor. I now know why Loren and you got along so well."

"Yeah, we were two peas in a pod, but we are pretty close ourselves. I wouldn't say we are two peas quite yet, I haven't gotten the boxing thing down."

"You will in time." He said leaning over to kiss her.

"Kale, keep your eyes on the road."

"Will do...I love you Skyler."

"Love you too dear."

He was brought out of his dream by Skyler. "Good bye handsome. I love you Kale. Love you." She yelled.

"Goodbye Skyler. I love you hun. See you next weekend."

"Next weekend, cowboy. She turned to walk into the plane. Kale watched as she disappeared. He couldn't believe he had chased after her. He didn't even realize until she had gone in that he was drooling.

"Geez Kale, you have to be so romantic." Brayden teased.

"Yeah, I am Rhett, you know I can't let an average man show me up." He retorted back.

"Yeah, well you're using my lines. Saying goodbye four times." Brayden looked at him with one eyebrow cocked.

"Brayden, that's what you do when you're in love." Kale laughed.

Thank You's!
- First off I would like to thank my Heavenly father, for giving me the gift of writing to share with the world.
- I would also love to thank My Mom and Dad for always supporting me and believing in my dreams.
- I would like to thank the rest of my family, for always standing by my side.
- Thank you to the Nelson's who allowed me to become a part of there family and for letting their daughter Linsey become a part of my life.
- Thank you to the PBR, PBRO, Resistol Relief Fund, and the rest of the affiliates of PBR Inc. For bringing the excitement of bull riding to fans around the world.
- Thanks for my friends. Who encouraged me to chase my dream of writing a novel, this is for you.

Acknowledgements

Taylor Swift for song lyrics from white horse and I'd lie on Fearless, produced by Big Machine Records, November 11th 2008. A big thanks to Taylor for writing songs that speaks to the heart. That tells stories, and adds emotion in all the right places of The Western Dreamer. Thanks again, Taylor.

Tracy Byrd, Keeper of the stars, on No ordinary man, produced by MCA Nashville, 1995. Thanks Tracy Byrd and the writers of Keeper of the stars. This song is an iconic love song and found a solid place in The Western Dreamer. Thanks, all those involved in the creation of this song!

Mitchell, Margaret, Gone with the Wind, 1936, publishing company, Simon & Schuster. I would like to thank the great Margaret Mitchell for in part inspiring The Western Dreamer. Also, for the code names that Skyler and Kale use. Gone with the Winds intense romance, is what I hope will continue on through Skyler's and Kale saga in finding everlasting love! Thank you Margaret writing a book that shows that love conquers all.

Also, thanks to Clipart.com for the bull image as the divider for the Western Dreamer.

Made in the USA
Lexington, KY
25 February 2010